La trattoria di amore series

Dominated

but not *Subdued*

JP Sayle

Book Cover Design by Tina Lowen
People in images are models and should not be connected to the characters in the book. Any resemblance is incidental
Editing by Lucas Cornelius
Proofreading by Tanja Ongkiehong
Book Formatting by Champagne Book Design

References to real people, events, organisations, locations, or establishments are only intended to give a sense of authenticity and have been used fictitiously.

The author acknowledges the copyrighted or trademarked status and trademark on Apple, Audi, Pepsi, BMW, Levi, Superdry, Calvin Klein, Mercedes, Timberland, Caithness Glass, Dalton, Jimmy Choo, and Hugo Boss.

Films, music, and lyrics mentions are the property of the copyright holders.

Warning
Some of the content of this book is sexually graphic, with the use of explicit language and adult situations involving two males. It is only intended for mature adults.

Why does he want to be a "boy" to a man twenty years his senior? A man who is so much more than big and burly. Is he a Daddy or a Dom?

Adam Grainger learnt the hard way that coming from an affluent family does not guarantee love or affection. It makes him doubt anyone could ever love him.

That is until Carl.

Carl showing him the darker pleasures in life leaves Adam revelling in the true meaning of letting go.

Carl standing up for him allows Adam's need for a "Daddy" to surface.

But too many secrets and a driving force to not submit might prevent Adam from gaining what he never knew he craved: a Dom Daddy.

Dominated but not Subdued is the second book in the La Trattoria Di Amore series and can be read as a standalone. It is M/M romance with Daddy kink, aspects of BDSM play, an age gap, and a Dom Daddy who needs a strong boy to keep him on his toes.

Dedication

We are what are parents create, but what we remain is up to us.

In loving memory of my parents, John, Wendy, and Nicola, you may no longer be here, but you live on inside my heart.

Prologue

CARL GLANCED AROUND HIS RESTAURANT. THE BEAUTIFUL ROOM filled him with a sense of pride. The tableware gleamed under the lighting. The vibrant, bold Italian prints used for the tablecloths, chairs, and curtains stood out against the stark white walls and dark wooden tables. Subdued tiny pink lights embedded in the ceiling took away from the harsh white and gave the room a dreamy quality.

It was perfection…if only he didn't have interviews today. He sighed. Why did he do this to himself?

Interviewing for staff was one of his least favourite things to do.

He fidgeted in his seat next to Sebastian, who sat sipping his espresso, giving him a hard stare.

"I hear your mind whirring all the way over here. That guy was a total loser. Who turns up dressed like that? He burnt the lenses right out of my eyes with that bloody day-glow top." Carl shivered and rubbed at his eyes for effect. "Whoever told him orange was back in fashion needs shooting."

He glanced at the next application form, doing his best to keep the laughter inside. Ever since they'd become partners in the restaurant, Carl had worked hard to loosen Seb up a little.

His gaze skimmed down the CV and the accompanying letter Adam Grainger had submitted. It was well written, and on paper, the guy looked like he was worth an interview. But still, he was a baby.

Knowing he could use this to get a rise out of Seb, Carl schooled his features.

"Dear God, why have you printed this one off? He's a fucking baby, for Christ's sake. How does a nineteen-year-old know how to manage shit all? I bet he woke up one morning, saw the advert, and thought, 'oh I can do that.' Every applicant we've had has been clueless."

"Carl, everyone is too young as far as you're concerned. Since you hit forty, it's like you think you're over the hill and everyone else is an infant. What were you like when we interviewed for the wait staff? I'll tell you. You acted like you were older than God," Seb huffed.

Carl looked up, pointing at Seb. "You wait till you hit forty. Then tell me you aren't looking at all these young whippersnappers and feeling every one of your years."

Carl bowed his head, finished reading, and then placed the application down. He glanced at the wall clock. "He's late, so that's a strike…"

"Hello. Is there anyone back there?"

A head popped around the partition separating the main restaurant from the reception. The man stepped forward, continuing, "There's no one manning the desk, and I've been waiting for ten minutes."

His enquiry was directed at Carl, who slouched in the booth, well aware the man was letting them know he'd heard their conversation.

Adam Grainger—because who else could it be—walked towards the booth, without waiting for an invitation, and stood looking down at Carl and Seb.

Seb stood. Carl paid him no mind, feeling a little flustered at having been caught unawares.

Seb held out his hand. "Hello, I'm Sebastian Smythe, owner of La Trattoria Di Amore, and this is part owner and head chef Carl Bentley."

Carl, who remained sitting, ignored the raised brow Seb aimed in his direction, and the "get up off your backside" glare.

Seb's clenched jaw, Carl's surmised, was because of his lack of acknowledgement and apparent display of rudeness. But Adam Grainger had poleaxed him, and Carl wasn't convinced his legs would hold him up, so he remained sitting.

"Sorry, I should have sent someone to check you'd arrived. We're running a little behind because we are prepping for the evening dinner service."

Seb offered Adam a seat. Doing his best not to show how ruffled he was, Carl shuffled the papers with the interview questions laid out in front of him. He tried to get his mouth to work, but fuck, he'd all but swallowed his tongue. Adam Grainger was a total wet dream. The fitted dove-grey suit and pale pink shirt open at the collar highlighted a lean body. Cropped dark hair streaked with blond highlights framed his stunning \golden face. Pale green, luminescent eyes reminded him of the sea in the Caribbean, whereas his full pouty lips made him consider if Adam would be as sweet and juicy as a ripe peach. Those full lips hid a perfect set of pearl-white teeth. Were they veneers?

The thought fled under the full impact of the flirty smile, which showed two little indents in Adam's cheeks. Carl all but groaned out loud at how his body reacted to the idea of licking those two little dimples.

I'm far too old, so forget it. Besides, my likes would scare this little boy.
Would it, really?

Carl ignored his internal questioning and sat forward, offering his hand. "Hey. Shall we get on with this?"

Adam's soft hand took hold of his in a firm grip, squeezing. His pale eyes challenged as they held Carl captive before releasing his hand. Carl sat back, distancing himself when his common sense flew out the window. His dominant side surfaced, wanting to show this man *who* exactly was in charge. His hands twitched. He almost felt the weight of his beloved paddle in his palm with the thought of bringing Adam to heel and making his arse glow red from the swats.

Seb, unaware of Carl's battle, picked up his pen and asked, "Shall we start?"

Adam nodded, and Seb launched into the pre-prepared questions.

Seb made several notes on his pad. Pulling himself together, Carl finally managed to find his tongue and join in, asking the questions he'd been given.

Adam liked to talk, and Carl liked the flirty tone a little too much. His fears Adam's young age meant he wouldn't know jack shit faded after about ten minutes. The guy seemed to have his act together. The list of questions he'd compiled for them, wanting to know about their business model, showed insight and understanding about managing a restaurant. He'd even pointed out a gap in their service when they were full. His question about whether they directed their patrons to their sister restaurants had Seb scribbling on his pad.

Carl fiddled with the papers in front of him, though his brooding gaze never left Adam.

An hour later, Carl was desperate for a moment alone. Adam's herby-scented aftershave was doing a number on him, and he was finding it harder and harder to concentrate as the minutes ticked by. He willed Seb to wrap things up.

"I think that answers all our questions," Seb stated, flicking a glance at Carl for confirmation.

Carl nodded.

Seb carried on, "Once we've reviewed all the applicants, we'll give you a ring. It should be later today, and if not, it will be tomorrow. Unless you have anything else you want to add, you're free to go."

Adam shook his head. "No, I think you answered all my questions." He stood, giving a toothy smile. "Thank you for your time and your consideration for this post."

Carl felt the weight of his sea-green eyes.

"I'd just like to say I know I'm young, but you won't find anyone more dedicated or committed. When I put my mind to something, I always make it work." He paused, looking at both men. "I'd work my backside off to make sure your business runs smoothly and efficiently."

Carl imagined said backside doing more than running the

restaurant. Instead he'd be bent over Carl's spanking bench, which would be a more apt place for the gorgeous man. The vivid thoughts ran wild in Carl's head, and he was reluctant to touch the offered hand as Adam leant over the table towards him and Seb.

He let out a relieved breath when Adam thanked them again for their time. He felt Adam's final flirty grin all the way down to his toes. Adam spun around, hips swaying, as he walked with confidence across the room and out of sight, not once looking back.

The moment his pert backside disappeared around the partition wall, Carl slumped against the booth and rubbed his sweaty palms down his baggy black chef's trousers.

Then Seb spoke. "I liked him, but I think you were right. He might be just a tad young for our clientele, though I'm not sure how much longer I can carry on doing the manager's job and my own. Maybe I should ask Ellie if he'd be willing to step in while we advertise again. What do you think?" Seb asked.

Carl almost saw Seb's mind working overtime, already trying to figure out the logistics of whether their office assistant could take on the additional role.

At the very idea of giving the job to someone else, Carl's pulse skipped a beat. "Oh, come on, he's perfect, and you know it. Those were some great ideas he offered. Streamlining our processes and generating business. The reward scheme for valued patrons was a stroke of genius," Carl said before he could stop himself.

A voice in his head told him that being in close contact with Adam would be like putting kryptonite around Superman's neck, but he couldn't seem to stop. A part of him was desperate to have Adam in his vicinity, even if it was only to be able to see him daily, and nothing more.

Who am I kidding?

Seb stopped what he was doing, eyeing Carl. "Are you serious? You were dead set against the idea before you met him."

"Yeah, maybe. But he is the only one who seemed to have what we need." He shrugged, doing his best not to fidget under Seb's appraising stare. "His age seemed irrelevant once he got talking. You kinda forgot he was a kid."

Seb held his hands up as Carl continued to heap on the praise. "Okay. Okay. If you're sure. There was no one else close to him anyway. We'll offer him the job. But mark my words. I bet he won't last longer than five minutes. And on that note, we'll start him off on a temporary, six-month contract. If he fails miserably, we have an out."

With the pile of papers clenched in his hands, Seb stood, and Carl ignored the considering look he was giving him.

"You can ring him to tell him. Oh, and make sure you tell him it's on a temporary basis till he's proved himself," Seb said.

Seb strolled through the door leading to the kitchen. Carl's gut clenched. *Have I just made a big mistake?*

He stood and ambled around the tables, his mind fixed on how Adam might look sitting at his feet in submission.

Stop, so not going there. Seb's written rule, remember?

In every restaurant contract—no exceptions—was a strict rule: no staff fraternisation. It was a big no-no, and he needed to remember that. Never mind that Adam was far too young for him.

Carl went into the kitchen. He needed some busy work to take his mind off a certain little cheeky imp and give him time to figure out why Adam's show of dominance towards him had rubbed him the wrong way.

Carl was a Dom through and through. *That might be why.*

He huffed and rolled his eyes. *Yeah, like I don't know.*

Chapter One

Adam

ADAM OPENED HIS WARDROBE AND PERUSED HIS CHOICES. HIS HANDS trembled as he pulled out the Hugo Boss lightweight dark brown linen suit. He laid it on the bed before choosing a cream fitted shirt. He dithered over the choice of tie before going with the sedate pale pink and brown stripe. No point in showing off his more flamboyant side just yet.

He grinned and eyed the half of the wardrobe that contained his more colourful array of non-conservative choices. *Not for your first day.*

With a hip bump to shut the door, he turned back to the bed, and dressed. He took his time, not due at the restaurant till ten am to meet Sebastian and Carl.

Carl. The guy had been on his mind far more than he should have been. Even his name conjured fantasies. Fantasies Adam's cock was more than happy to have. The fact that they left him hornier than a bitch in heat couldn't be helped. A delicious shiver raced up his body. *Come on, not going there. I need this job.*

Adam glanced down his body, to his now waking cock. "You don't get a say."

When his cock bucked against his trousers, he heaved a sigh. "Get over it. It's not happening." He hunched at the lack of conviction in his voice and that he was talking to his cock. Readjusting himself, he ignored its defiance.

His pulse skipped and danced. The fact that he'd got his dream job under his own steam, with no help from his family, was a big thing for him. All his life, his family's name had meant he'd been treated differently. At the interview, he'd purposely avoided talking about his family and who they were. No one needed to know as far as he was concerned.

He sat on the bed and slipped on his shoes, doing his best to concentrate on the list of questions that showed he was serious about his new job. A sense of insecurity crept up on him. Doubts that he could normally push away slipped past his defences. Would he be able to do all the things he'd said he could? He chewed his fingernail and stared at himself in the mirror. Worried eyes stared back at him. *Stop it. I mean it. Pull it together.*

He got up off the bed and gave himself a pep talk all the way to the kitchen and through breakfast. When he walked up to the restaurant door an hour later, he had himself well and truly under control.

He knocked on the locked door and waited for someone to answer. The ornate glass door shone in the brightness of the sun. Not a smear tainted the glass, and Adam sensed that Sebastian would be the type of person to check it daily to ensure it stayed that way.

When instead of Sebastian, Carl sauntered towards the door, Adam's heart sank. A bright red bandana kept his dark hair swept back off his stunning face. The aura of a bad boy rolled off him, his non-traditional black chef's outfit only adding to the image. Adam's cock took notice, and all the hard work he'd done that morning fled. His body hummed in appreciation. *Oh, this will not do.*

Adam's hands balled at his sides. A spark of attraction shot in Carl's dark eyes, and Adam struggled to remove his tongue from the roof of his mouth. The door opening pulled him from his stupor. When Carl beckoned him in wordlessly, he offered a sunny smile he wasn't feeling and stepped through the door.

"Morning, Carl, it's good to see you again. I'm so happy to have been given the chance to work for both you and Sebastian." He licked his dry lips. "Is Sebastian about?" A hint of desperation edged his question, and he stood straighter. Was it obvious he didn't want Carl showing him the ropes?

Humour danced in Carl's eyes, killing any hope he hadn't noticed. Adam refrained from sighing.

"Morning… Sugar Lips. Seb is on the phone. So you've got me for the time being."

Too busy trying not to react to the underlying suggestiveness in Carl's tone, Adam didn't initially notice what Carl had called him. He squirmed. "Sugar Lips, what the heck is that all about?" he asked in a breathy voice that would have been embarrassing had he not been working on controlling himself.

Carl stepped into his space and lowered his head until his mouth was next to Adam's ear. He tensed. The fragrant aroma of Italian food and fresh citrus surrounded him. Warm breath touched his ear, and a shiver coursed through him.

"Those plump, ripe lips of yours suggest they would be as sweet as sugar. For a man with a sweet tooth, you'd be a tempting morsel. A man could feast on them for hours and never get enough of a sugary hit," Carl whispered into his ear.

Carl's lips brushed the rim of his ear before he raised his head. The dark intensity in Carl's expression set off Adam's body. With effort, Adam stopped the shudder, knowing damn well he'd have looked like he was having a seizure the way his body was responding to Carl. *He wants to play, does he?*

Never one to let a challenge go, Adam gave his best sexy grin and flashed his teeth at Carl. "I've never had any complaints in that department. The men who've felt my lips against their body were more than happy, if the noises they were making were anything to go by," he said suggestively, giving a saucy wink.

Carl inhaled loudly and widened his eyes. Adam was sure he'd scored in that round. Whatever Carl was about to say was cut off when Sebastian walked around the partition. The gleam in Carl's eyes said it wasn't over, and Adam's stomach clenched in anticipation.

"Good morning, Adam," Sebastian said and offered his hand.

Adam took it. He got distracted from all thoughts of Carl as Sebastian led him towards his office. Carl strolled off, saying nothing more. A little disappointed Carl wasn't going to join them, Adam convinced himself it was a good thing as Sebastian handed him a file and encouraged him to take a seat.

Once Adam was settled and had pulled the papers out of the file, Sebastian explained how the restaurant worked.

"Right, I've compiled a file of all the information on what is required to run the restaurant. We'll work through the information, and I'll answer any of your questions as we go," Sebastian said.

Adam listened, writing down comments and questions in the margins of the sheets. The organised information was easy to follow, and Adam relaxed. He was going to be able to manage the job easily.

The days flew by, and by the end of the first week, Adam had a true sense of how the restaurant worked and who all the employees were. The staff were all male and, from what Adam could tell, were mostly gay. Not unusual, Adam sensed that Seb, as he liked to be called, possibly hadn't even noticed his tendency to employ gay men. He wasn't complaining, not by a long shot. The men were all friendly, and he'd already formed friendships. He couldn't see himself dating any of them, though, with Seb's contractual non-dating clause, was probably a good thing. *What about Carl?*

Adam rolled his eyes heavenward while he sat at the front desk. The first day had only been the beginning of Carl's antics. He took great pleasure in trying to wind Adam up on an hourly basis. The more time he spent in the kitchen, the worse it got. Why did he look to find any excuse to go into the kitchen, then?

The answer was more than obvious and not something he wanted to think about. He needed the job, and no attraction was worth losing it over. *Yeah, right.*

The following week, he hid in the toilet. He clutched at his aching cock, denying why he was aroused to the point of pain. He stroked his hard length before it dawned he was at work. "Fucksake," he muttered as he dropped his hand and prayed his body would behave. Sometime this week would be good.

Why had he thought poking the beast would be fun?

Half an hour later, Adam entered the kitchen and explained one of the customers wanted to speak to Carl because he was unhappy with his dessert. The chef stomped into the dining room, only to return five minutes later with steam coming out of his ears. Adam didn't know what a can of worms he'd opened. It seemed that Carl was not one to take any form of criticism when it came to his food.

The dark stain of colour riding his cheekbones and spark in his dark eyes should have warned Adam to back off. Never one to let common sense prevail, he ignored the warning signs.

"Oh, dear. Sweetcakes, did you make a booboo with your tiramisu?" The new nickname was something Adam had dreamed up the night before, after Scott his friend, and colleague had insisted Adam try one of Carl's desserts. The rich chocolate pudding was as light as a feather and melted in the mouth. The sweet cakey goodness gave Adam the perfect nickname and the chance to one up Carl for calling him Sugar Lips.

"There was fuck all wrong with my dessert. The guy wouldn't know what tasted good if it hit him in the bloody face," Carl said while he pinned Adam in place with a simmering stare.

The panicked racing of Adam's heart left him breathless, and he stood stock-still for a moment, which gave Carl the opportunity to step into Adam and tower over him.

"And who are you calling Sweetcakes?" Carl asked.

The low timbre and sexy growl caressed every nerve ending in Adam's body. His cock hardened painfully and left him dizzy. He lost the ability to speak. The urge to grab hold of Carl and hump on his thigh unfurled, much like a snake ready to strike. His fists balled when the urge increased as Carl brushed his body against Adam as he moved past him.

"You've been thinking about me and… my desserts?"

Adam's body shuddered at the sexual undertone in Carl's voice. The fact that he'd kept his voice down so Billy his assistant head chef, who was standing a few feet away, couldn't hear, added to Adam's torture. He licked his lips and tried to work on a witty comeback, but all the blood pooling in his groin made it difficult to pull a coherent thought together.

"At a loss for words, Sugar Lips?" Carl's hot perusal of his body got Adam moving. His dick fighting a losing battle with his tight-fitting trousers was not something he wanted Carl to notice. Adam swung around on his heel and pretended Carl's laughter wasn't aimed at his trouser predicament as he left the kitchen.

He sagged against the closed door of the toilet and questioned his own sanity about constantly ribbing Carl. The aching throb reminded him how much his body enjoyed it. "I've told you before, you don't get a say in all of this," he ground out through clenched teeth. Then he rolled his eyes at the stupidity of talking to his cock, yet again.

How can you survive years of verbal sparring and yet be ready to throw in the towel with Carl?

Not finding an easy answer, he hid for several more minutes until he had his body under control. In that time he came to a decision. *No more messing around. Ha, ha, like I've ever listened before.*

Chapter Two

Carl

STEAM ROSE, OFFERING A HINT OF THE FLAVOURS THAT WERE BEING infused into the sauce Carl was making. He glanced about for his testing spoon, but not seeing it, he shouted to Lenny their kitchen hand, "Lenny can you bring me a spoon, please." Carl didn't glance up from the pot but continued to stir the simmering sauce.

"Here you go, Chef," Lenny said, offering Carl a teaspoon.

"Thanks," Carl said, absently taking the spoon without taking his eyes off the pan.

Carl dipped the spoon into the pot and took a taste. The sauce spread over his tongue as he savoured the flavours. The slight bit of chilli blended beautifully and offset the sweetness of the ripe tomatoes, but it needed more basil.

The door opened from the dining room, catching Carl's attention. His pulse betrayed his excitement at seeing the man now walking with confidence through the kitchen. Today's suit was dove grey and, like most of Adam's clothes, fitted like it had been made for him. The cut of his jacket highlighted his trim figure and obstructed the view of Adam's arse disappointingly. Not that he'd been looking. Well, not right then.

How many months would it take for the feeling to wear off?

Too many it would seem, if he counted the last five months. He still couldn't get to grips with the ridiculous fluttering inside his chest every time he saw Adam.

His jaw bunched at the sassy smile gracing Adam's face when he looked back over his shoulder. Carl's cheeks warmed at being caught staring. He worked hard on not giving Adam any more ammunition. Checking Adam out clearly had to fall into that category, *right?*

Adam walked towards Sawyer one of the waiters, who was leaning against the counter, having a drink. They stood together, and Adam turned his back fully on Carl. He strained to hear what they were talking about, his head tilted toward them. Catching himself as he stepped closer, he ground his teeth together.

This is getting beyond a joke.

The meeting he'd had the previous week with Seb and Adam played over in his mind.

Carl sat on Adam's left in the vacant chair, feigning disinterest. It was Adam's day off, but he'd agreed to come in. Carl had seen him come in through the back door several minutes earlier.

Never having seen Adam in anything but his business suits, Carl was struck by how different he looked in casual clothes. The cheery red fitted trousers were paired with a strikingly bold print top. The colourful shirt should have been garish with the vibrant reds, blues, and greens, yet it wasn't. Adam looked like he'd just stepped out of some high-class magazine. The rolled-up sleeves revealed tanned forearms and several leather bands tied around his wrists. The leather gave Carl far too many ideas about Adam, bound and tied down, for his own good.

He had avoided talking to Adam so he could get his thoughts out of the gutter. Now, as he watched Adam out of the corner of his eye, he fidgeted in his seat and knew it was a lost cause. The attraction he felt towards the younger man was becoming a real nuisance. It was getting harder and harder, literally, to control, the longer he spent in Adam's company. His quick wit, positive attitude, and diligence made it impossible not to like him. What about his stunning face and sexy arse?

Carl shut out the voice, not wanting to even contemplate how many times he'd imagined Adam naked and writhing under him. Nope, not gonna happen any time this century.

Only when Seb shuffled the papers on his desk did Carl move his attention to his business partner. The nervous movement of his hands was the only indication of how Seb was feeling about offering Adam the permanent job. They'd discussed at length Adam's suitability long term, and Carl saw no problem with it. Bar the obvious one, that Seb had no clue about.

When Seb spoke, Carl let out a relieved sigh at having something else to focus on.

"Adam, thank you for coming in on your day off. But I'm hoping you'll be pleased with what we're here to discuss. Carl and I have given this a lot of thought..."

"Oh for God's sake, just get on with it, will you?" Carl said impatiently when it looked like Seb was going to continue to waffle nervously.

Seb threw a hard glare in his direction, and Carl shut his mouth with a snap.

"As I was saying, Adam, the reason we've asked you to come in is that we'd like to offer you a permanent contract. I know it's a little earlier than we'd initially discussed when you started on your trial contract, but we realise what an asset you are"—Seb shrugged, a blush coating his face—"to us and the business."

Carl's brow furrowed. A look of utter astonishment crossed Adam's face and left Carl wondering why he was so shocked by the offer. Didn't he know how good he was?

"Wow... seriously?" Adam asked, his voice trembling.

The vulnerability did strange things to Carl's chest. His heart leapt uncomfortably against his ribs and made swallowing difficult. The need to give Adam a cuddle welled up to the point that he had to tuck his hands under his legs to stop him from reaching out to Adam.

What the ever-loving fuck is this about?

Voices carried past Carl's thoughts and, along with an arid smell, brought him back to the present. Then Adam leant around Carl and peered at the once bright red sauce. At Adam's loud laugher, Carl curled his lips in disgust. The brown tinge and scent wafting on the steam indicating that his sauce had been left to burn while he'd been busy thinking about things he shouldn't.

"What's up, Sweetcakes, you getting 'too old' to remember you need to stir the sauce so it won't stick to the pan and burn?" Adam said with glee as he bounced out of Carl's reach.

Heat crept up Carl's neck and infused his face at the dig about their age difference. Adam had upped the ante since he'd signed on the dotted line and knew he was reasonably safe. Carl was equal measures frustrated and turned on by the way Adam challenged him.

He forgot himself for a moment and stepped towards Adam, intent on teaching him a lesson. "Come back here, Sugar Lips, and say that." At the low growled demand several people turned their heads in his direction, and the spell was broken.

He sucked his lower lip between his teeth and took a step back from the devilment on Adam's face. The risk he would do something stupid increased when Adam sashayed closer, a sexy sneer on his face.

"What, Sweetcakes? You think I'm scared of you?" Adam asked, his eyes brimming with laughter. "Dream on, big guy."

With that parting shot, Carl watched Adam head into Seb's office. Over the months, Carl had grown accustomed to how his palm twitched to hold a paddle and spank the sassy fucker. No amount of telling himself he didn't want to made a blind bit of difference.

Resignedly he went to grab more ingredients to start the sauce again.

As Carl walked past Billy, who raised his brow, he offered him a shrug of indifference. Billy had more than once asked him why he let Adam wind him up. Not having a suitable answer, Carl fobbed him off and avoided thinking too hard about it. *Is that so? Then why spend hours going over the contract and clause?* A clause that was clear as day: no staff fraternisation, regardless of the fact that he was part owner. Seb was clear it applied to them all, no exceptions.

There were plenty of fish in the sea, so why didn't they appeal to him?

No fucking clue.

Seeing where he was headed and not liking it one bit, Carl plonked the ingredients on the counter. He went to retrieve a clean pot after dumping the burnt sauce down the waste disposal unit. Placing the pot down, he busied himself with remaking the sauce.

At the end of the day, too tired to do more than head home, he stretched out on his sofa. He closed his eyes and willed all thoughts of Adam to bugger off. They were becoming an obsession and he wasn't at all happy with how often he thought about the other man. He needed to find a distraction and fast. Someone to take his mind off what he clearly couldn't have, no matter how much his body craved Adam.

Knowing the pattern of thoughts that were about to start, he heaved himself up and reached into his pocket for his phone. He searched his contacts and hit dial before he could overthink it.

"Hello, Ferron, I know it's a little late," he said as an afterthought when he caught sight of the clock. "You up for a play date?"

"Yes," came the soft, timid answer from the sub he'd occasionally played with at the club. Carl wasn't sure if he was making a mistake as he gave Ferron his address before hanging up.

"Shit," he cursed, even as he walked out of the lounge and up the stairs to check his playroom was clean and ready for a guest. And that right there was the problem. Carl didn't think of Ferron as anything more than a guest, rather than the sub Ferron so desperately wanted to be for him.

On reaching the playroom, Carl shoved his worry aside and checked out the room. He smiled at only having to pull out what he needed for the night.

He wandered around the room, his hands trailing over the pieces of furniture he'd bought over the years to fill it. The need to have a space to play with his subs had been a dream up until he'd bought the land and been able to design his own home. His architect had been a little perplexed by his demands and specifications for this room, but Carl had never elaborated on what its purpose was. It was no one's business but his, and whoever he chose to use the room with him. Not that there had been many; he usually kept any causal relationships to the club.

The sound of the doorbell got him moving. His hand dropped from the St Andrew's cross as his boots thudded on the hardwood floor. He sighed at the lack of excitement he felt. *This has to be enough, it has to be. Let this be enough.*

With the almost desperate internal plea going on inside his head, he walked down the stairs. On reaching the bottom, he sucked in a deep breath and made a promise to himself. Adam was to stay firmly in the friend column. The movie, *Friends with Benefits*, jumped into his mind, and he cringed at his own silliness.

Enough now. There is a list of reasons why Adam is off limits. Don't forget them.

Not quite convinced he wasn't fighting a losing battle, he opened the door and, offering a smile he didn't feel, invited Ferron into the hall. Shutting the door, he closed his mind on all the wayward thoughts of Adam before turning back to Ferron.

All he needed to do now was make himself believe it was that easy. *Piece of cake!*

Chapter Three

Adam

DAM PARKED OUTSIDE HIS BEST FRIEND'S HOUSE AND LET OUT AN exhale that would have rivalled a foghorn. He blinked back the tears wanting to fall and stared up at the house with a sense of dread filling his stomach. How could one's life change so much in a year?

He wanted desperately to go back to when his biggest problem was sparring with Carl or wondering why Carl had suddenly distanced himself and left him bewildered by the change. The timing coincided with devastating news that had taken the wind right out of his sail's and left him dead in the water. Carl had no longer been his every waking thought when Richie, his best friend, had uttered a word no one ever wanted to hear. One single word: cancer. And boom, life had never been the same again.

That fated day felt like it was yesterday and not months ago. His mind seemed to think he'd not been punished enough and replayed the moment in all its glory.

His dark brows rose when he saw no sign of Richie's mum's red Audi TT. Adam released his seat belt, lifting the bag of goodies he'd brought, and tried to recall if Richie had said his mum would be home or not. He was aware today was D-day on getting the results back from the tests they'd carried out a few weeks back and the reason he'd asked for the day off from work. He wanted to be here to support his friend and his surrogate mother.

Adam exited the car and immediately regretted the thick linen shorts and heavy polo shirt. The blazing sun and sticky, humid heat made him melt faster than a bar of chocolate in a child's hot little hand.

He grumbled. The oppressive layer of warmth blanketing the whole of London seemed endless. And as much as he enjoyed lounging in the sun in foreign climes, the heat of London wasn't the same when there was no lovely sea breeze to take the edge off the roasting temperatures.

He increased his pace, wanting to get inside the gorgeous old Victorian house that for years had been more of a home to him than his own parents' house.

He'd met Richie in primary school. Being a tiny thing, Adam had suffered at the hands of the bullies. When Adam had been knocked down by one of the boys in the playground, Richie Bellinger had come to his rescue. This friendship had sustained him through some tough times and self-discovery. He often said to Richie's mum, Marian, he and Richie were kismet brothers.

Marian might not have given birth to him, but she was more of a mother than his own ever was. And Adam loved her unconditionally, just as she did him, which was more than he could say about his real parents.

His mood took a dip as he thought about his lacking parents. Adam knocked on the bright red front door. As soon as it opened, Adam sighed and shoved past Richie into the cold hall, not giving him time to say a word.

"Christ, it's hotter than hell out there. I know they said it would reach the top thirties today, but I swear you could fry an egg on the bonnet of my car."

"Hello, to you too," Richie said at his back.

Adam felt Richie's gaze on him. He knew Richie was too used to his behaviour to be affronted by his lack of acknowledgement. Richie shut the door and followed him.

Adam flicked a glance over his shoulder. "I need a drink and a nice shady seat in your back garden. It's been a hell of a week. The restaurants have all been heaving, and the air con unit broke in the main restaurant. So you can only imagine how hot it got, and that seemed to set off everyone's temper."

With trembling hands, Adam continued to chat nervously, pulling out the makings of their favourite cocktails. He worked hard not to look at Richie's face. He hated seeing the pain in his tight, pinched features when he'd opened the door.

His stomach pitched at what was coming. He lost the smidgen of hope he'd held on to that everything would be fine.

Richie appeared to be preoccupied, and Adam figured it was because he was attempting to find the best way to explain what the doctors had told him and his mum at the appointment they'd had that morning.

He placed their drinks and nibbles on a tray and glanced at his silent friend hovering in the doorway. He sucked in a breath for courage. "Come on, let's go and sit outside, and then you can tell me what happened."

Adam sat on the striped, padded swing nestled in a shady corner of the garden, and listened to his best friend. Adam did his best to keep his emotions in check.

"They said my mum has breast cancer, Adam. How the fuck did that happen to my mum? She looks after herself, doesn't smoke, and hardly has a drink. Yet here she is with cancer," he cried, getting up off the swing.

The devastation on Richie's face tore at Adam's heart, his own pain mimicking that of his best friend.

"The doctors said she needs to have a double mastectomy. Like, immediately, because of the biopsy results. They're planning the surgery for next week. My dad is a total dick about it for some reason. It might just be the shock, and maybe it just hasn't sunk in yet," Richie's eyes sparked with temper, and his face flushed with colour as he continued, his voice rising several octaves, "The bastard is away and refuses to come back early. I have no fucking clue why! He part-owns the bloody company, so it's not like he has to ask for permission to come home." Richie tugged his scruffy hair, glaring at Adam.

Focusing on the first bit of information, Adam ignored Richie's rant about his dad. "So it's definite? They haven't made a mistake or something, like mixed up your mum's reports with someone else's?" Adam clung to the hope for all of a millisecond before he saw Richie shake his head.

"No, Pip, they showed us the scan and let us read the report from the biopsy. Not that we understood it." Richie shrugged and stopped pacing. "They did their best to explain it. But you know when you're there, listening, it doesn't seem to sink past the layer of shock. So when we got home and mum went out, I went and googled it."

Adam stared at Richie as he sucked in a muggy breath, his eyes welling.

"Fuck, man, it's some scary shit," Richie whispered sadly.

Richie's teary voice set Adam off.

"Oh, bloody hell, what are we gonna do?"

Tears spilt down his cheeks as he got up and clung to his friend. Adam laid his head on Richie's shoulder, and his heart broke for them all.

How will I survive without Marian?

The question rocked Adam back to reality and left him reeling, much as he had done all those months ago. He was such a selfish bastard. All he could think about was the effect it had on him. Though he tried, he couldn't seem to stop himself. Marian had been his protector from the personal purgatory he'd had with his parents. He'd survived for two reasons: Richie and his mum.

Their love and acceptance didn't make up for the loss at home, but it sure as hell helped get him through his teenage years. When his parents noticed his gay *tendencies*, they'd put two and two together and come up with a number they didn't like. From the age of eleven, Adam learnt a hard lesson. Love was not a given, even from your parents.

So he'd sought refuge with Marian and Richie, and that in turn became his one real, stable foundation. Adam wasn't sure how he was going to cope when he lost that vital part of his life. And as sure as day was light and night was dark, the reality grew with every new treatment that didn't seem to do more than give Marian crap symptoms and little else.

He laid his forehead on the steering wheel, gearing himself up to step out of the car and face Richie and Marian.

A realisation he needed to stop being a selfish arsehole, had Adam pull himself together. He recited, "I've got this. I've got this." He ignored the wobble in his voice and opened the car door. The freezing November air sliced at his lungs as he sucked in an icy breath. He lifted his bag off the passenger seat and hurried to Richie's front door. He pressed the bell and waited for Richie to answer.

The door opened, and he only needed one look at Richie's drawn face to know that no words were needed. Adam stepped into the house and shut the door. He dropped his bag and pulled Richie into his chest, hugging him tightly. Adam inhaled the familiar scent of fabric softener and let the childhood memories it evoked rise to the surface. He held on to all the good times he'd had in this very house, needing them to sustain him.

Several minutes later, when he'd gathered his strength, Adam released Richie. Adam gave his brightest smile, praying Richie wouldn't notice it was forced. "Is your mum here, or is she still at the chemo suite?"

"I dropped her off about two hours ago. She didn't want me to stay." Richie shuddered. "I can't cope with the needles. I fainted the first time, causing a massive stir when I hit my head on the hard floor. So as you can imagine, she prefers me not to linger." He sighed.

Adam took his hand and squeezed it. "I don't think I'd be much better. At least you tried. What about asking Milly to go instead?" Adam spat out the last part as if he'd swallowed something unpleasant.

Richie's bossy girlfriend was the only thing they ever argued about. Adam didn't get why Richie let her walk all over him. Why she insisted Richie do a business management Masters instead of the art course he'd set his heart on was beyond Adam. He just couldn't understand what her appeal was, and okay, he was gay, so he was never going to be interested in her. And yes, he wasn't blind, so he could see she was attractive on the outside. Her figure would have rivalled any supermodel. But it was only the outer shell that was gorgeous; inside, she was mean and nasty to the core. Her eyes betrayed her, and that was what confused him. How someone as lovely as Richie couldn't see it.

"No way. Mum would have a fit."

Adam refrained from pointing out that he would too. He jumped as his phone vibrated in his pocket. He dug it out of his trouser pocket and scanned the screen, flicking it open. He rolled his eyes at Richie and answered. "Hey, Sweetcakes."

"Seriously, Adam, how many times do I have to tell you not to call me that?" Carl asked.

Adam chuckled. "Too many to count, it would seem, Sweetcakes. I told you it suits you, given you make such delicious cakes," he said, knowing it would drive Carl up the wall. He grinned, hearing the put-upon sigh coming down the speaker loud and clear. "What do you want, Carl? You do know this is my day off, right?"

"I can't find the order book, and I know you had it last."

Where had he last seen it?

"I think Seb took it yesterday to order the new linens. Why couldn't you ask him, hey? He is probably only a few feet away from you."

The answering warm laugh had him shift, the sound caressing him as it always did. Adam refused to think about the last sixteen months and how he'd worked at pretending indifference to the giant, who only had to smile at him to get his pulse fluttering.

After the interview, he'd been certain Seb wouldn't give him a chance, so he'd been a little shocked to get a call that evening telling him he was in, even if only on a temporary basis. He'd grabbed the opportunity and worked his butt off to prove they'd made the right decision and get the permanent contract. He'd achieved that in a matter of months, but working on overlooking his growing feelings for the chef, who liked to rib him mercilessly, was a lot harder to accomplish.

"He's out."

"And you couldn't ring him and ask him?" Adam fired back.

"Why would I do that and bother him?"

"Seriously," Adam hissed at the phone, then took it away from his ear and purposefully swiped the screen. He tucked it back into his pocket, paying no attention to Richie's gaping mouth. His pocket buzzed, but he resisted the urge to see if Carl was ringing him back.

Instead, he picked up his discarded bag and walked down the hall to the kitchen.

This game of cat and mouse the two of them had established never failed to make his blood heat. Carl was a contradiction in terms. He gave off a dominant vibe, but not all the time. Mostly he showed his gentle giant side. A side so laid-back, you could almost believe he was horizontal most of the time. It left Adam unable to figure out which was the real Carl and if one side was meant to mask the other.

"Are you gonna answer your phone? That's the third time in two minutes it's vibrated in your pocket," Richie said, his brow arched.

Without wanting to explain to Richie his need to always push at boundaries. He was well aware that Richie worried he was skating on thin ice.

Dimples flashing, he gave Richie a cheeky grin. "Nah. Stop stressing. It's my day off, and if Carl wants to wind me up, he can wait till I'm back at work tomorrow."

Adam distracted Richie with questions about him giving up his uni course, then changed the topic to Christmas. They sat for a few hours, writing lists of the things they were going to need to make Christmas extra special for Marian after all she'd been through. It wasn't till he got home later that night that he thought about how angry Carl was going to be at his lack of response to his six missed calls and four text messages.

As he stripped off his clothes, Adam wondered if he should have answered the last call after which the texts started. Carl's failure to find the order book meant his text messages had become a little testy, to say the least. It was also the first time Carl had ever threatened to spank his backside.

A rosy bloom covered his body, and his cock stiffened alarmingly fast when he read the message. A little disturbed by the images that continued to flutter through his mind, of being tied down and paddled by Carl, Adam flopped onto his bed naked.

He glared up at the mirrored ceiling and at his all too obvious arousal. His hairless cock twitched, the slit gleaming with wetness. He rolled towards the bedside cabinet sitting next to his queen-sized, four-poster bed, giving in to the urge to call his boyfriend, Simon.

Adam's hand hesitated over the phone as he chewed his lip. He and Simon had been dating for a couple of months now. They'd met on one of Adam's work nights out. And even though Adam had been insistent he wasn't interested in a boyfriend because of his confused feelings for Carl, Simon wouldn't give up. Deciding there was no future with Carl, Adam had experienced a moment of weakness and given in.

He gave his cock another glance and huffed, blaming Carl for his quandary. It was wrong to use the arousal another man caused on his boyfriend. Yet Adam still picked up the phone he'd placed on the bedside cabinet when he'd finished undressing.

He scrolled to his number and hit dial. Adam offered up a silent prayer that the universe didn't kick his butt for this. Then Simon answered.

"Hey, lover, you busy?"

Chapter Four

Carl

CARL CHECKED THE HANDWRITTEN INSTRUCTIONS HE'D BEEN WORKING on that evening, after clear down. He normally gave himself some time to relax, tinkering with new recipes if he didn't have any plans to go to his club and let off steam.

His groin tightened when he thought about how long it had been since he'd allowed himself to unwind at the club. The ever-growing challenge to keep the menus fresh and keep on top of what was happening in the food industry was time-consuming. His tripled workload would be a test for anyone to find some personal downtime. Not that he didn't love it, because he did, but it was hard on his personal life. *What personal life?*

Feeling out of sorts, Carl went and got changed, then headed to the one place that would allow him to gain back his centre: The Playroom. The BDSM club was a home away from home for him.

When his best friend and fellow Dom, Nathan, had approached him with an idea to open their own club in an abandoned warehouse in Notting Hill, he'd jumped at the chance. Ten years later, they had a thriving business. And though they were fifty-fifty partners, Carl had always been the silent one.

Nathan had recently been discussing expanding and renovating the top floor of the warehouse. It now looked more like a reality, and it was something Nathan was hassling him over. The problem was that Carl couldn't make up his mind whether he wanted to invest more in the club or take on a new restaurant. Carl had mentioned several times to Seb about finding another failing restaurant and adding to their business portfolio, but Seb had been distracted lately, and Carl couldn't figure out why.

Carl pulled his thoughts away from his worries about Seb and parked in his designated parking space at the back of the club. He stared out the windscreen, thinking about why he was here.

He stared down at his now silent phone in bewilderment. There was no way Adam had just put the phone down on him, surely not?

He hit dial again and listened to it ring and ring. Six unanswered phone calls later and he trembled with rage. He was wasting his time, Carl sent a text and then followed it up with three more.

His eyes narrowed on his twitching hands. The pounding in his temples made it hard to focus. His gut danced a merry tune at the thought of getting a grip on Adam and showing him exactly what happened to naughty boys.

Had anyone ever been able to make him feel like this before? The question sat there at the forefront of his mind, nagging like an old fisherman's wife. Not liking where his thoughts were headed, Carl closed his eyes, and he used the familiar scents of Italian cooking to calm his racing pulse. He inhaled deeply and opened his eyes.

The thought of contacting Seb never crossed his mind as the anger continued to burn through him. Carl shoved the mobile phone back into his pocket. He should have known the moment Lenny had said "Chef, I can't get this bloody mixer to work again" that it was going to be up to him to deal with the problem. He picked up the phone on Seb's desk, scrolled through the pre-programmed numbers, and dialled the wholesaler.

After three additional phone calls to different distributors, Carl was finally able to get back into the kitchen. He shut out the chaos around him, eying the food he'd laid out on the counter. He tried to get his head back into the mindset needed to be creative.

That right there was why he was feeling off. He'd not been able to let go. Hoping that would change, he jumped out of his truck. He stretched his long legs and headed to the private entrance and keyed in the code.

When he stepped inside, familiar scents of leather and musk assailed him. He checked the door locked behind him and gave a wave to the security camera positioned above the door leading into the backroom of the club.

Carl eyed the black vest and fitted distressed jeans he'd chosen in lieu of his leather. The heat inside of the club had directed his choice of clothing—not that he cared what anyone thought of his attire. He wore what he felt comfortable in. And after sweating his bollocks off all day in a kitchen, he really didn't want to be doing it tonight as well.

The air con system they'd spent a fortune on for the club worked to some degree. But they'd quickly learnt that with a full club and bodies generating lots of heat from the activities, it never offered the benefits they'd expected.

Carl pushed open the solid, black metal door leading into the club. The sudden shift in volume took a moment to acclimatise to. His eyes widened in the darkened room and adjusted to the dimness while he was hit by the anticipated wall of heat.

The slide of sweat dripping down his back had him shift uncomfortably. The scents he'd smelt in the hall increased tenfold, but now he could also detect the distinct fragrance of cum.

The large open-plan room gave him a sense of satisfaction. The deep red walls harboured numerous large black leather booths that could seat thirty people comfortably. Each was situated around a large dais so everyone could see the action. Throbbing music poured from the speakers, though not loud enough to drown out the beautiful moans and groans coming from those playing. The sounds mixed with that of flesh being caressed and teased by whatever instrument the Doms chose.

His gaze swept over several of the booths, lingering on one where two subs were tied to a St Andrew's cross back to back, while two Doms used floggers on their naked bodies. Their faces and body language spoke of their enjoyment. Serenity emanated from both men, and their erections, standing proud, sought their Master's touch. The sight evoked his own Dom persona to slip into place as he shed the laid-back chef he wore daily. The ease with which it happened gave him a secret thrill.

Out of the corner of his eye, he caught sight of Nathan as he moved from behind the curved bar housed on the far wall. The full-length mirrors cast reflections back to the other occupants, allowing those sitting at the bar to watch the action behind them while enjoying their drinks. It also gave a perfect view of the empty stage positioned in the middle of the room. It was sunk into the ground so that wherever a person was in the club, they were eye level and able to watch with an unfettered view.

They had worked hard on designing the vast space so it gave everyone the best possible experience. Nathan's hate of fighting to see what was going on when they'd been in other clubs went in their favour. The design he'd come up with was a big hit and created a membership waiting list that Carl left Nathan to deal with.

A grin spread across his face when Carl gave Nathan his full attention. Nathan towered over everyone at six foot six, and his dark blond good looks never failed to make a statement. The plain black T-shirt and loose linen trousers didn't hide his true nature. Stealthy movements belied Nathan's enormous size. The way he moved often made the club's unattached subs weak at the knees.

Carl had seen it time and time again. The problem was that Nathan liked to play, and he rarely kept a submissive for more than a few weeks. More often than not, he left them broken-hearted when they didn't capture his heart.

While Carl accepted Nathan's warm hug, the following back slap nearly felled him. "Hey, come on. I know you're bigger and heavier than me. You don't need to prove it."

Carl eyed his friend's massive chest and bulging biceps. Carl was convinced Nathan had grown since he'd last seen him, several weeks ago. He could have rivalled any of the linebackers of the American football teams.

"Shit, man, have you been doing extra training? Christ, if you get any bigger, you could compete for the world's strongest man."

"Fuck off, Carl," Nathan groused good-naturedly. "It's good to see you. Is it a formal visit, or are you here to play?"

Nathan flicked his tiger eyes to the bar, drawing Carl's gaze to the sub sitting alone sipping at a pink cocktail.

Carl gave Ferron a passing glance before looking back at Nathan. "Nah, he is too needy, and he wants more than I have to offer." His gaze moved to the opposite end of the bar where a man caught his attention. His close resemblance to Adam had him considering. "Who's that at the other end of the bar? The cutie in the tiny leather shorts and green tank top."

His gaze remained on Nathan as he answered.

"He's new. He's been coming about five weeks."

Carl waited, knowing Nathan would use his eidetic memory to give him the information he was after.

"His name is Saul. And if I remember correctly, he's unattached. He's played some with a couple of the regulars. I think he could handle what you like to dish out." Nathan smirked.

Taking Nathan at his word, Carl gave him an absent wave and headed to the bar, shoving away any lingering ideas that he'd prefer to be working over a particular work colleague. He knew full well Seb would have his guts for garters if he breached his contract, regardless of their work partnership. So instead, Carl let his mind imagine the sounds the sub, Saul, would make at the feel of his whip teasing his golden flesh, and insisted he'd have to be satisfied with that.

The fifteen-minute conversation they had before Saul agreed to be his sub for the evening revealed Nathan had spoken the truth. Saul did indeed enjoy the feel of a whip caressing his skin.

Carl didn't question why Saul wasn't looking for anything more than one night, not wanting to open himself to any personal questions he wouldn't be happy to answer.

He carefully tethered Saul to the St Andrew's cross on the main stage. Saul's naked limbs glowed in the soft lights situated in the ceiling.

Carl's gaze swept the room as he stepped back. He was already drawing attention from some of the other Doms and subs milling about. He ignored the crowd and checked in Saul was ready.

"Saul, do the straps feel okay, not too tight?"

"No, Master, they are fine."

Carl nodded, his lips lifting in a smile at the air of impatience he could sense coming off Saul. "Remember, boy, if at any time it becomes too much, use your safe word."

"I will, Master."

The conviction in Saul's voice was clear, and Carl relaxed his shoulder muscles.

Nathan stood a few feet away, holding his whip. Chuckling, Carl strolled across the stage to where Nathan stood. His friend knew him all too well and had picked his bullwhip.

Carl took several deep inhales to centre his thoughts. His pulse beat steadily.

Carl kept his focus on Saul. "Ten lashes, Saul. I want you to count them for me."

"Yes, Master," Saul said.

Carl lifted the whip and landed the first lash. He revelled in Saul's loud mewl, full-body shudder, and a breathy count of "one."

Saul's body undulated beautifully with each lash of the whip, his submission sublime.

The connection with a sub was so ingrained in Carl's play it took him a second to register that it wasn't there. His arm faulted mid-air before he continued.

Carl's brow furrowed. His eyes narrowed on Saul as he completed the ten lashes.

Carl masked his face as he finished.

Why aren't I feeling it?

Fuck, what has Adam done to me?

In what felt like endless minutes, Carl released Saul's arms and legs and aided him to the small room where Doms could deliver aftercare. They had spared no expense to ensure subs had a space to come back to their senses in privacy, if that was their wish.

Two hours later, Carl walked into his home. He flicked on the lights in the hall and headed upstairs to have a shower, his shoulders hunched. The satisfaction he'd initially felt with having Saul agree to sub for him had faded quickly, leaving him with a heavy heart and a sense of disquiet that had remained on the drive home.

His hope that the club would fix his headspace had been misplaced, and in truth, the whole thing had been a complete mindfuck. Why hadn't the club fixed his woes? *Shit.* He'd never felt this way after leaving the club, and he could think of only one reason why he would feel like this now: Adam.

In his bedroom, he stripped, then walked into his bathroom. He hoped a shower and several hours of sleep would make things look better in the morning.

Yep, like that's gonna happen.

Chapter Five

Adam

Keeping his head down, Adam skirted around the centre aisle in the kitchen. He made sure not to make eye contact with anyone and draw attention to himself. Well, not *anyone*, but a certain giant oaf, who growled at anyone who went anywhere near him. The same oaf, who'd also threatened to tan his backside with his favourite paddle.

Who knew Carl had a favourite paddle? Maybe he was messing with me? Whatever it was, it had planted a seed inside his head that had taken root. And since then, he hadn't been able to dig the fucker out.

How could he, when his arse was making buttons to find out exactly what that would feel like? It was also the reason he was single, yet again. It would seem asking for a spanking was a step too far for his vanilla and now ex-boyfriend, Simon. He was convinced he'd have hearing loss for months after the yelling match they'd had.

Adam sighed. *Another one bites the dust.*

When Lenny motioned for him to follow him out into the dishwashing room, Adam let the depressing thought go. His forehead creased. *What's this about?*

"What, Lenny?" he asked impatiently.

Lenny eyed the open doorway, motioning Adam closer to him. "Keep your voice down. Carl is still on the rampage after yesterday. I just wanted to warn you. Your name is mud. Carl kept threatening all sorts. I've never seen him so mad. Shit, I nearly cacked my pants, man. Seriously, his eyes were red and bulging." Lenny shuddered.

Adam didn't fail to notice Lenny's alertness. "Really? All over the fact that he couldn't find the order book?" Adam kept the part where he'd hung up and refused to answer any of the following calls or texts to himself. He was entitled to a day off, wasn't he?

Lenny filled him in on the previous day's full fiasco, and Adam's brow rose.

He felt a little bad now for putting the phone down on Carl, but if the chef hadn't been his usual dickish self, then he'd have helped. So really Carl had no one to blame but himself. That didn't mean that Adam didn't feel shit for the rest of the staff, who had to field all the flak thrown at them by a raging chef. He was aware Carl very rarely lost his temper, but when he did, by Christ, everyone knew about it.

He thanked Lenny for telling him.

Building up his own head of steam, Adam stomped back into the kitchen. He went into Seb's office and rooted through the files, looking for the receipts he needed to pay. It was why he'd come into the kitchen in the first place.

His gaze flickered to Carl tucked in the corner of the kitchen, his back to the room. Adam was aware that this was his week for working on the new menus.

When he'd started working for Seb, Adam made it his business to spend the first couple of months learning what everyone did and their schedules, so he could work to fit in with them. It made good sense and allowed him to keep ahead of the game when it came to making sure they all had what they needed.

He never admitted it out loud, but he might have spent a little more time on Carl than anyone else. Carl was a fascinating mixture of contradictions. So much so Adam spent hours thinking about the chef and how he gave off a laid-back vibe that didn't always fit him. Adam felt a dark undercurrent coming from him, not evil but something more. Like there was an intensity he kept hidden.

If he was truthful with himself, which he rarely was when it came to Carl because he knew he'd be sunk, he'd have to admit that his fascination had morphed into something more, months ago. Something he didn't want to name. The slither Carl kept hidden spoke to something inside him. The only problem was he hadn't been able to figure out what it was. It was an enigma, much like the man.

It wasn't that alone that kept him away from Carl. The clause in his contract couldn't be disregarded, not if he wanted to keep his lucrative job. He just needed to remember the job was his way out of the horrible hole his parents put him in, so it really should be no contest.

Why am I even thinking about this? He let out a self-deprecating laugh, knowing full well why.

Lost in thought, Adam didn't see Carl step into the office.

"Are you going to stand there all day, or are you actually going to do some work today?"

Adam started. His eyes darted up to Carl's hard, unsmiling face. He didn't fail to miss the emphasis on the word "today." He scoffed back, "Of course, Sweetcakes, as soon as you move your lardy arse out of my way."

Holding the receipts, Adam stepped away from the desk. He stopped a couple of inches from Carl, who was blocking the doorway. He tilted his head back, looking Carl directly in the eye, and gave a shooing motion with his hands.

Carl's flared nostrils and lip curl pleased him immensely. Adam stood his ground, not giving an inch. The tension mounted, so much so a bead of sweat slid down his back. Carl's eyes darkened to coal, but Adam refused to back down. The intensity increased, and it felt like a tsunami was building out at sea, getting ready to sweep them both up with its ferocity.

Carl's gaze demanded Adam submit.

Adam fisted the receipts, crumpling them as his will ebbed under the weight of the stare. His jaw thrust forward. It took every ounce of his willpower to hold still and not lower his eyes.

"You'll pay for that."

Stunned, Adam blinked in a daze as he was released from their stare-off. Carl strolled back to the counter, whistling as if nothing had happened. Adam's pulse skipped a beat. He all but ran out of the kitchen and back to the reception desk.

Silently seething, Adam ground his teeth together. *How fucking dare he make a threat towards me?* It was probably just Carl sounding off, and it meant nothing. *Then why do I feel like it meant something?*

The buzz of anticipation he felt said that he clearly wanted it to be something. Perplexed, he sat on his high stool behind the reception desk and pulled the chequebook towards him with his empty, shaky hand. He laid down the crumpled receipts and smoothed them out. He pretended his hands weren't trembling and got to work, keeping his mind occupied and firmly away from thinking about the threat.

As the last customer left, he heaved a sigh of relief, and he locked the door behind them. He eyeballed his feet with some trepidation. Now everyone was gone, he wasn't sure he could take another step in his brand new Hugo Boss Derby shoes. Though they were gorgeous, it would seem they were not for the faint-hearted when you wore them for eight hours straight.

The throbbing had escalated to epic portions in the last hour. He eyed the carpet. Sighing, hoping his white linen trousers wouldn't end up with smeg from someone's shoes, he lowered himself to the floor and undid the laces.

He yanked off both shoes and dropped them to the floor, barely resisting the urge to throw them into the bin next to the counter. He peeled his socks off next. Several small, raw, blistered areas had formed around his big toes and the heels. He moaned loudly, rubbing at his aching toes.

His brow furrowed. He tried to remember what spare clothes and shoes he had stored in his personal locker in the changing room, for emergencies. He'd been running late, so he'd come ready for work in his white linen suit and blasted new shoes.

After giving himself a moment, Adam heaved himself up. He picked up his shoes and socks and hobbled through the empty dining room. No one was there, though that wasn't unusual. He was usually one of the last to leave, and recently, even Seb left before him.

Distracted, Adam paused.

Chewing his lower lip between his teeth, he wondered if it had something to do with Ellie no longer coming into work in the office here. Adam had long ago suspected there was something going on between the two men, though they kept pretty much to themselves. There was something in the way Ellie had behaved towards Seb, and he was sure he'd heard him call Seb "Daddy" once.

Not that Adam was judging. He thought it was hot. Hell, he'd gone home and done a little Daddy porn surfing, and what he'd found had definitely got his engines revving. He hadn't mentioned it to Richie. His straight friend had a few taboos where Adam was concerned, and talking about kinky sex was definitely one of them.

The kitchen door opened, and Adam refocused and turned to see who was still in the building. He wanted to grumble about his bad luck at being caught by Carl, and yet he couldn't bring himself to do so. A light danced to life in Carl's eyes as they travelled down to his bare feet, though Adam couldn't work out what kind.

"Is this a new fashion statement? Buy new shoes, get blisters for free?"

Going on the offensive, Adam poked out his chin. "Ha bloody ha, you're too funny. My sides are splitting with laughter. Now if you've quite finished trying to be a joker, I need to find something to put on my feet." With as much dignity as he could muster, Adam hobbled towards the kitchen.

"Erm, where do you think you're going? You're not walking in my kitchen with bare feet. That, matey boy, would breach about a dozen health regulations," Carl snarled, his meaty fists going to his hips.

After a night tossing and turning, the heat and exhaustion of the day left Adam spoiling for a fight. Common sense deserted him. He shook with rage, and his mouth engaged before his brain. "Then how am I supposed to get my other shoes, you dumb nitwit, when they're in the locker room off the kitchen?"

Eyes widening, Adam squealed when he was dangling upside down. Carl threw him over his massive shoulder as if he weighed nothing. The scent of delicious food wafted around him as Adam gulped in fright.

Feeling a little breathless, Adam dropped what he was holding and pounded on Carl's rippling back. "Put me down and stop manhandling me, you big…"

His rant died. His body jerked at the sudden burning heat that came after the large palm connected with his backside.

Thoughts from the previous night flew to the forefront of his mind and awakened the arousal he'd wanted to deny.

Adam panted through each smack. He ground his needy cock into Carl's solid chest, unable to stop, even if he'd had the desire to. The heat spread from his backside and tingled up his spine before lodging in his tight sac.

His body thrummed, and he canted his hips up to meet each blow. He sagged against Carl's body, the fight leaving him. His world narrowed down to each swat to his now burning cheeks. He moaned and writhed. His ears buzzed from the rush of blood from being upside down, but Adam didn't care, so lost in the desire that his body took over. His orgasm built to the point of no return. His cock bucked violently, only to be left straining as the spanking stopped as fast as it had started.

Adam found his feet back on the ground before he could take in a shaky breath. His lungs sawed in and out, desperate to take in some oxygen and clear out the fog clouding his mind. He blinked up at Carl in a daze. The world seemed to have shrunk, and all Adam could focus on was Carl's coal-black eyes glowing with something akin to feral need. A need he'd witnessed on safari in the eyes of a lion when it immobilised its prey, ready to devour it.

Adam shuddered at his thoughts and how his body really wanted to be devoured by this man, one greedy bite at a time. His hands moved without conscious thought towards his hard, dripping length, needing to alleviate the ache.

"No touching, not unless you want more than a spanking. You'll be a good boy and leave your dick alone until such time I tell you can come."

Adam opened his mouth, but he couldn't find anything to say. Speechless, Adam watched Carl saunter to the kitchen door, open it, and holler to Lenny to get him a pair of the Crocs they used in the kitchen in the summer.

Even when his mind screamed at him to tell the big fucker to go to hell, Adam obeyed.

When Lenny came out of the kitchen and offered him the shoes, Adam took them without complaint. Adam avoided meeting Lenny's furrowed brow. He was probably redder than the carpets they used for VIP events. He convinced himself it was being upside down and refused to admit it had anything to do with his smarting backside or the hard-on that wouldn't quit.

He was grateful for his loose-fitting linen trousers and tight underwear. Otherwise, Adam was sure Lenny would have got a show he probably didn't want or need.

He slipped on the Crocs and hesitantly walked back to get his shoes and socks. Picking them up, he mustered his courage and flicked a quick glance under his lowered eyelashes at Carl. He hadn't moved an inch and was watching Adam's every move. He wanted to sigh but refused to let himself do so.

Clutching his stuff to his stomach, Adam willed his body to behave. He stuck his nose in the air and, putting his acting skills to the test, walked past Carl like he didn't have a care in the world. He didn't stop once until he'd grabbed his car keys and sat in his car. Only then did he let out a mournful sigh.

The pressure of the leather against his arse reminded him all too well of what had just happened, as if his aching dick wasn't enough of a recap. His hands itched with the need to find a release, yet something held him back.

He pushed the ignition button and started the engine. He put the car in gear and drove out into the quiet road, concentrating on getting home. His head was doing its level best to keep what had just happened right at the front of his mind. His stomach fluttered. It was tiredness, nothing more. That was all that was wrong with him. *It had to be, right?* Then why did he feel the need to do as he was told? All the way home, Adam assured himself it was tiredness.

Yeah, dream on.

"Oh, shut up!"

Chapter Six

Carl

CARL SAT OPPOSITE SEB, NOT SURE WHAT WAS WRONG, BUT THERE WAS something decidedly off with his friend. Something he couldn't put his finger on. Though Seb was driven for whatever reason to keep his distance from everyone, Carl made sure he didn't let those barriers interfere with their working relationship. *Why wasn't Seb choosing to confide in me? They were friends, weren't they?*

Carl got straight to the point. "What's up? You've been skipping out early and coming in late. And you're distracted, which isn't like you, Seb."

"It's nothing you need to worry about. I've got..." Seb paused, glancing up from his paperwork.

When Seb hesitated, clearly undecided, Carl's hope rose, and he willed Seb to talk to him. When all Seb did was heave a sigh and go with his usual fallback about work, Carl swallowed the urge to say something.

"I'm snowed under with the amount of work, that's all, and with Adam having both Christmas and New Year week off, it's left me a little behind," Seb stated.

The mention of Adam had Carl getting up out of his chair. The use of Adam as a topic of conversation derailed Carl's thoughts. Seb had already lowered his gaze back to the papers on his desk, shutting him out. Carl stomped around the small office, his body vibrating.

The problem Carl had with Adam having two weeks off was something Seb didn't get. *Am I just being a miserable git?* Maybe. But since the little spanking incident, their natural bantering relationship had disappeared, leaving Carl edgy and disconcerted. And somehow not seeing Adam for days on end exacerbated the issue. Carl wanted to get back what they had before.

Six weeks. Six whole weeks since I've laid hands on Adam. He huffed in exasperation. *What the fuck is wrong with me?*

Like, I don't know.

Fuck!

Adam's determinedly avoiding him and making sure they were never alone together before he went on holiday grated on Carl's last nerve. He acknowledged, if only to himself, that he wasn't being much better, having also exerted time and energy to keep out of Adam's way. Carl had spent a month cursing himself six ways to Sunday for giving in to his temper and letting the little spitfire get the better of him. The sass Adam had given him that day only added fuel to the fire already burning inside Carl. His failure the night before to find pleasure in taking his whip to Saul had been the driving force behind his need to teach Adam a lesson.

The only problem was that that lesson had backfired on him big time. The way Adam had reacted had left Carl wanting far more than he should. The list he'd compiled of reasons why Adam was off-limits was endless: their contractual obligations, his age, inexperience, his big mouth, his lack of ability to submit, Adam's light to his own darkness. The list went on and on.

Yet here he was, six weeks later, avoiding going to the club and facing reality. A reality Carl had to face every day at work. No matter how much Carl's head said no and created lists, his heart wanted Adam, regardless of no-nos.

The blasted thing fluttered like a zillion ruddy butterflies had taken up residence in his chest. It fucked with his head, and for the first time in his life he wanted, no, needed a deeper connection.

He balled his hands at his sides. *Could I put myself out there like that?* Two years earlier, his one long-time sub had wanted a commitment, and he'd run a mile. The seven years he'd spent with Daniel had been good, but not once had Daniel set his pulse racing or left him with the urge to throttle him. And as perverse as that was, those aspects of Adam's personality made his blood pump with anticipation and excitement.

Carl swung back round, stomped the length of the tiny room, and stopped in front of the window, staring out. His teeth ground together as he looked back at Seb. "Why was Adam insistent on having the two weeks off? You never said."

Seb took his gaze off the computer, shrugging his shoulders. "He wouldn't say, only that he'd work both holidays this coming year to make up for it. He seemed sad. The normal sparkle when he asks for holidays wasn't there. He did mention something about spending time with close friends."

Since Adam was always eluding him, Carl was finding it harder and harder to ferret out information from the staff about his personal life without being too obvious. *I've turned into a bloody stalker.*

The thought was pushed away when Carl turned back to the window. Keeping it casual, he asked, "When is he back from his holiday anyway?"

"He's back. Haven't you seen him? He's manning the restaurant. Who did you think was doing it while I was here?" Seb asked. "Is there something wrong? Something I've missed by any chance?"

Carl tensed. He worked at dropping his shoulder blades back to where they belonged. He glanced back and aimed for a natural shrug.

"No, no... nothing at all," Carl stuttered, his face flushing.

He twisted his head to the side to avoid eye contact with Seb. At a loss as to what to say, Carl stomped to the door. "I've got stuff to do. I'll catch you later."

The feeble excuse and throat clearing coming from behind him were enough to make him want to hunch. He stood tall instead and went back into the kitchen, heading over to his workbench.

He pretended not to notice how excited his heart rate got at the thought of seeing Adam. *Not that I've missed him. Not at all.*

To distract himself, Carl asked where everyone was up to. The entire time he kept his eye on the door leading to the dining room.

The time flew, and before Carl knew it, he was on his own, cleaning down the tops. When he'd opened the door to get rid of the rubbish, he'd seen the snowfall was heavy. He'd offered to do the close-down so the staff wouldn't get trapped. His truck was more than capable of getting him home. It was only a short drive from the restaurant.

He hummed to himself, enjoying the quiet. Finishing off, he went back into the small locker room and stripped off his chef's outfit. The heat from the kitchen made the room pleasant enough to warm his naked body. He threw the soiled clothing into the linen basket ready for collection the next day, then stilled at a noise behind him.

The hairs on the back of his neck rose, and a shiver racked his body. He spun round, not questioning how he knew it was Adam who'd gasped out loud. Carl's eyes bored into Adam's startled gaze.

Carl's boxer briefs weren't hiding his body's reaction to Adam's assessing appraisal of his nearly naked body. Carl was aware the long hours spent in the kitchen kept his body in shape, and his workouts, both in and out of the gym, did the rest. His stomach held not an ounce of fat. He stood perfectly still, his arms relaxed at his sides, letting Adam look his fill.

It was only when the tip of Adam's tongue poked out and swiped over his lower lip that Carl closed the gap between them. He strode across the chilly tile floor, his attention entirely focused on Adam. His alarmed expression and sudden backpedalling got Carl speeding up.

"Where do you think you're going, Sugar Lips?" Carl growled, lifting Adam up under his arms as if he weighed nothing at all. "Wrap your arms and legs around me."

When Adam obeyed without hesitation, Carl almost purred in satisfaction. However, the skinny-legged trousers Adam wore hampered his ability to do as requested. Carl didn't have time to voice his disappointment when Adam whined.

"How is anyone supposed to do anything in these trousers? I mean, it's not exactly a selling point, is it, when they won't let you spread your legs?"

Adam's feet connected with Carl's shins, even as his lean arms clung around his neck. Carl rocked them both with his laughter as Adam huffed in his face.

"What are you laughing at? You were the one getting all growly and demanding I wrap my legs around you."

When Adam continued to rant, Carl couldn't hold him up any longer for laughing. The ridiculousness of the situation was not lost on him, even if it was lost on Adam. The humour that had been missing from their relationship returned full throttle. After putting Adam down, Carl held on to his sides, while the boy continued to prance in front of him, spouting nonsense about the selling points of fashion.

"Seriously, can you hear yourself?" Carl choked out. He wiped at his eyes, finally calming down as Adam frowned up at him.

"What do you mean? I'm not the one who spanked my arse a few weeks ago and then avoided me." His chin thrust and sparkling eyes advised of the next tirade.

Uncertain why Adam had segued into what had happened weeks earlier, Carl held up his hands, attempting to ward him off. "It was six weeks ago, and two of those weeks you were on holiday. And you know fine well why you got that spanking. You were all but asking for it, and I don't know what you're complaining about, since you enjoyed it. If I hadn't stopped, you'd have come all over my chest." He wagged his finger in Adam's face.

Adam's curling lip was enough of a warning that he was about to deny it.

"If you lie, I will do it again. Only this time, I will use a paddle. And if you're a good boy, I might even let you come." Adam froze.

Carl wanted to take back the threat and was about to apologise and lie, claiming it was a joke, but Adam beat him to it.

"Can you do that with a paddle?"

Carl couldn't quite believe his ears. His lips flapped shut, and his pulse skipped a beat. His body hummed to life, just from the awe in Adam's voice. He kept his eyes on Adam, willing him not to look down at his growing problem. Carl answered honestly. "Yes, if it's something the person enjoys."

The question on the tip of his tongue wanted out, and before he could stop it, he asked, "Adam, do you think you'd like it, to be paddled to orgasm?"

He held his breath. Had he taken things a step too far? Adam's cheeks pinked, and he lowered his long dark lashes to conceal his eyes as he sucked his lower lip between his teeth. Carl's stomach dropped.

"Do you have a paddle?"

At a loss for words, all Carl could do was nod.

Adam raised his lashes and stared at Carl, revealing the flush of excitement lighting his eyes, and asked, "Do you have one here?"

It was like a punch to the gut. Carl felt the effects from front to back. It nearly knocked him off his feet. He clenched his fists at his sides to stop himself from grabbing hold and ravaging.

Carl inhaled. The scent of disinfectant and Adam's expensive aftershave filled his nose. He let his chef persona drop and his Dom take charge. He straightened his shoulders and narrowed his eyes.

"Go into my locker and open my sports bag. Bring me what's zipped in the back compartment." He waited to see how Adam would react. When he all but skipped eagerly to his closed locker, Carl—with difficulty—kept the smile off his face. The thought he got away without Adam asking twenty questions, as was his way, faded when Adam talked with his head buried in the locker.

"Why do you have a paddle in your bag? What would one need one for at work? I mean, it's a little odd, right?"

"Adam, I'd shut up now if I were you and just bring me the paddle.

That is unless you want me to increase the number of swats you're going to get."

The loud harrumph and muttering was too much. Carl raised his hands and covered his face, struggling not to let the laughter out. Never had he ever had a scene with someone where he'd ended up laughing.

It's not a scene, though, is it? The voice inside his head unnerved him, and the laughter died. The urge to question what it was warred with his need to continue and pretend this was more than Adam being curious.

Adam returned, all flushed and clutching Carl's favourite leather paddle in his small hand, and it was enough to derail all Carl's good intentions of stopping this before it went too far. He walked to the small bench tucked in the corner of the room, pulling Adam with him. Carl sat and asked without preamble, "Have you ever heard the term 'safe word' before?"

Carl barely held the chuckle in at Adam's eager nod, "Adam, in this kind of play, it's essential that a person has a safe word. I need you to know that if at any point, it gets too much for you, that you can use a chosen word to make me stop."

"I can just say stop. Come on," Adam interrupted, giving him an eye roll.

"No, Adam, that won't work." Carl's chest heaved. "People tend to use 'stop' when they don't mean it. So it needs to be something you wouldn't automatically throw out there when you didn't mean to." The chuckle Carl had held on to escaped at Adam's furrowed brow and his fingers clicking.

"T-shirt. It's not like anyone would scream that in the height of pleasure, right?" Adam said with a huge grin on his face.

Unable to argue with Adam's logic, Carl shook his head.

The excitement in Adam's expression gave Carl a secret thrill. Clearly, the conversation hadn't scared him off.

Pushing aside the desperate need to ask Adam to strip, Carl

took a breath. The paddle could be a little intense on bare flesh, and he didn't want to scare Adam into refusing to try other things. There would be a next time, he'd make sure of it, and then he'd get to see Adam's backside glow as he worked him over.

Jumping the gun, much?

While taking hold of Adam's wrist, Carl gave himself a mental slap. He tugged Adam closer and then lifted him off the ground to lay him over his lap, face down.

"Hey, you could have warned me," Adam panted and wriggled on his thighs, looking like he was trying to get comfortable.

Chuckling, Carl took the paddle out of Adam's hand. "What fun would there be in that? You're lucky I'm letting you keep your trousers and underwear on."

Carl locked his leg over Adam's and cupped the back of his neck, pinning him down. "Remember to use your safe word if it becomes too much." He didn't give Adam any further warning and raised the paddle and landed the first swat.

"Owwwww… shitttt."

Pleased with the shout and the increased wiggling, Carl clamped his leg tighter and squeezed Adam's neck in warning. "Do not move, Sugar Lips. We're only just starting."

"That hurttttttttt."

Adam's howl was music to Carl's ears, and though he was shouting, his backside was straining back into each swat. Adam's erection hardened and dug into Carl's inner thigh with every stroke of his paddle.

When the shouting turned to mewling and moaning, Carl decreased the speed but upped the strength, wanting the intensity to increase with each hit.

Adam's chanting and sweaty hairline as he undulated in pleasure ramped up Carl's desire for more. Adams's reactions were so beautiful. Carl gazed, riveted, at his face. There was pain, but Adam felt the intense burn and shortly would struggle to remember his own name.

Carl changed the position and angle to ensure his boy felt the paddle on every inch of his bottom, wanting Adam to fly.

He was unsure how long he'd been going, but his arm ached, which indicated it had been a while. This was Adam's first time, and he might not find his release. He was about to stop when Adam's loud mewls turned to tiny panting gasps. Then Adam's whole body went rigid and spasmed. His juddering hips and wide-open mouth releasing a wailing scream made Carl's own cock throb painfully.

He clenched his thighs, and Adam collapsed against him. After what felt like endless minutes, his leg became slick with cum as his Sugar Lips soaked through the trousers he wore.

The wetness spread over his naked thigh. Carl shifted and dropped the paddle on the bench. He lifted Adam and gently sat him in his lap. Cradling him into his chest, he tucked his head under his chin. Then he swiped at his leg as best he could, not wishing to disturb his boy.

His mind played back to the night he'd spanked Adam and he'd demanded Adam didn't come without his permission. Carl eyed the soaked trousers. *Had Adam done as I asked?*

A shiver rippled over his body at the thought that Adam might have.

Dark lashes shielded Adam's eyes from Carl's gaze. The peaceful, almost angelic contentedness made him wonder if his sweet boy was floating in subspace. Each sub was different. Very few were able to obtain it so fast and with minimal work. He slid his hands down Adam's arm, rubbing in gentle motions, letting him know he wasn't alone.

Please let this not be a one-off. Carl saw now they'd been moving towards this moment for months. He just wasn't a hundred per cent sure if he was ready for the changes it would bring between them. Carl's brow furrowed. A pressure sat within his chest. The weight of his choice tonight sat with a profoundness his heart might never recover from.

Soft puffs of air came from Adam's lips against his bare skin, and

Carl's cock pulsed. Carl gave a frustrated sigh. His eyes rolled heavenward at the effort it took not to rub against Adam.

Behave, for fuck sake!

Carl grumbled and held Adam a little closer and prayed he'd be able to keep his libido under control long enough to let Adam come back to his senses.

Chapter Seven

Adam

THE BLIZZARD CONDITIONS THAT HAD STARTED A FORTNIGHT AGO were holding the country in their grip. Adam used to think that snow was pretty, especially when he went skiing in the winter, but this...not so much. He stepped outside his toasty flat, cursing the thick, dense clouds, laden with yet more snow. Shivering into his duck down puffer jacket, Adam gave his bare hands a passing thought as he slammed the door behind him.

With trepidation, he eyed the path leading to the road. The gritted walkway hardly looked as if the salt was making an impact on the grey, sludgy, snow-trodden ground. The ice liked to lurk under the snow, trying to fool a man into thinking it was safe to walk on, then bam, said man was on his arse, his legs akimbo.

He snorted. For a second he considered whether using his skis would get him to work safer than driving.

He cautiously stepped towards the railing. His once warm fingers lost their feeling as he clung to the icy-cold metal. He traversed down the side of the path, using the tortuous metal to hold on to, till he reached the pavement.

The leather soles of his shoes skidded the moment he stepped past the gate. The unmanly screech "shitting hell" was enough to have his cheeks heating with mortification. With a thud, he slid into the side of his silver Mercedes, and the air expelled from his lungs in a frosty haze.

He gave a sweeping glance up and down the road.

Before he could think better of it, he sagged in relief against the snow-covered metal. Adam let out another string of curses, his brow scrunching at the odds of getting to the other side of the car and remaining on his feet. He stepped hesitantly away from the car, inhaling the icy air, and brushed at the wet mess covering the left side of his coat.

He muttered under his breath, "Why, oh why, did the weather Gods have to be so vengeful? In summer, we roast like bloody turkeys, and in winter, we freeze our bollocks off." Adam did his best impression of a terrible ice skater, barely staying upright getting around the front of the bonnet to the driver's door. Anxiously looking at the solidly iced windows and doors, Adam hit the car fob to release the locks, but the door didn't budge.

Swallowing the urge to holler in frustration, he rolled his eyes heavenward. He took a deep breath, searching for the path he'd just made in the snow, and gingerly headed back to his front door. He turned the key and stepped back into the warmth of his home, releasing a foggy breath.

Hair clung to his sweaty forehead while he dragged his coat off, throwing the wet jacket over the bannister. How could it be that his hands were numb, yet he felt like he'd spent two hours at the gym sweating his arse off? His pristine, pinstriped suit jacket was now wilted and creased. The trousers and shoes were splattered with grey sludge and dripping all over the floor.

He huffed, "Why did I even bother?"

Same reason you bother every day.

"Yeah, yeah, yeah." He knew he was ridiculous talking to himself, but he was at a loss as to what to do. He'd never been in this situation before, having always been able to get to work. He knew public transport was out. The radio announcement he'd listened to while getting dressed had stated the police's advice was "only travel if it was necessary". He was so up shit creek without a paddle. They were fully booked, and he had no choice about going to work.

How he was going to get to work when his car was out of action he had no idea.

His brow puckered. Carl has a big shiny truck.

He nibbled on his chilled thumb, sucking it between his lips. *Would Carl come and collect me?*

His pulse spiked at the thought of ringing Carl to ask. Adam wasn't sure if it was fright or excitement. With things between them being a little awkward since the paddling two weeks earlier, neither of them appeared to know how to act around the other. The fine balance they had maintained for over eighteen months was now gone, and in its place was an undefinable situation they'd yet to work out how to navigate.

The trigger was the very first spanking incident, where Carl had used his hand to redden his arse. Shocked initially, Adam had wondered how Carl would dare. That quickly turned to fury at the cavalier way Carl had behaved afterwards, leaving Adam hanging with a hard-on that wouldn't quit for days. His misbehaving cock seemed to think Carl had it on speed dial. It was embarrassing how many times Adam had sprung wood just from standing near him.

Unable to figure out what the hell was wrong with his cock, Adam had avoided Carl. *Don't forget the lack of activity in said pants.* Adam rolled his eyes at the weeks of refusing to have a wank after Carl left him hanging. His mind seemingly took Carl literally. No matter how many times Adam had attempted to have a wank, Carl would pop into his head with a stern look on his face and put Adam right off his stride.

He'd wanted to talk about it with Richie, but with Marian going through another round of chemo and his dad fucking off with his secretary, he had enough on his plate. The problem was that Richie knew Adam better than anyone, and it wouldn't be long before he asked questions. They'd always shared the personal aspects of their lives, so Richie was aware of how odd it would be that Adam didn't share anything.

How to explain Carl's mindfuck extended to dating? Or should that be, not dating. Adam released a pent-up sigh. Twice he'd tried, but both times were dismal failures. Carl had wormed into his subconscious and took up residence like an unwanted squatter. It was nigh on impossible to get naked with someone when Adam's head was full of thoughts of large hands caressing his arse. Yeah, happy naked time flew right out the bloody window if he started the comparison game. It would seem no one, could match Carl.

The weeks that passed made the situation no better. The sensible plan had been to stay away from Carl. Something he'd planned on continuing for the unforeseeable future. Carl had well and truly scuppered those plans. Adam finding a nearly naked Carl in the locker room had stopped all brain activity. All the worries and doubts had been quashed by a broad expanse of naked skin.

A shiver raced up Adam's back. Adam glanced down. Icy water seeped through his shoe. Grey sludge dripped from Adam's trousers down his shoes and all over the parquet floor. For a moment, Adam dithered. Then he went to the small hall table at the bottom of the mahogany staircase.

He paid no attention to the exotic, colourful birds and plants on the wallpaper in front of him. He struggled with himself for another minute before he lifted the old-fashioned seventies red Bakelite phone, dialling the number he'd learnt by heart.

Was this the emergency Carl said his number was for? *I mean, really, what did one constitute as an emergency?*

The moment Adam heard Carl's voice, the nerves took over.

"Hey, Carl, it's Adam. I'm in a bit of a pickle, and I need some help. The thing is… the snow… and I can't get into my car. And well, if I want to get to work, then I need some form of transport, and clearly mine isn't going anywhere. Well, not in its present condition. It's frozen solid, worse than the freezer we had to defrost before Christmas."

Carl shouted over the top of Adam, stopping him in his tracks.

"Adam, shut up. Shit, why you can't just get to the point, I have no fucking clue," Carl said none too kindly.

The slice of hurt cut deep. "There's no need to be like that. I was trying to explain that I need a lift."

"Then say that, for shit sake, and stop going around the houses." He snorted. "I'll be there as soon as I can."

Adam glared at the phone, hearing nothing but a dialling tone. "Well, thanks. I appreciate that, Carl. No, Adam, it's all my pleasure, I'm sure." Adam sighed. He shut up and placed the phone down.

Adam swung round, then halted, his foot hitting the bottom stair.

How does Carl know where I live?

Trying to recall if he'd ever mentioned it, Adam rubbed at the back of his neck. Coming up blank, he swung back to the phone and was about to dial when a smile lit his face.

Carl wouldn't say he was coming if he didn't know where he was going. That just wasn't Carl. He was the kinda guy who liked to be prepared, and his kitchen demonstrated that.

What about the paddle in his bag? Didn't that show he liked to be prepared?

Adam squirmed, doing his best not to think about why Carl had a paddle in his bag in the first place and who it was meant for.

He skipped up the stairs to change, forgetting about his dirty shoes.

Carl knows where I live.

His heart did a little somersault. Carl had taken the time to find out personal information. Adam unlaced his sodden leather shoes. His gaze glanced back over the carpet, and his shoulders sagged. He tossed the shoes through the open door of the dressing room. Then he stripped down to his undies and shirt. Adam flung his trousers and jacket onto the pile for dry cleaning and put his wet socks into the clothes hamper.

Adam's feet sank into the carpet as he made his way to the en suite in search of a towel to mop at the rug. He flicked on the overhead lights and blinked away the blinding white spots. With the clever use of lights and mirrors, the all-black, windowless room didn't feel small or closed in.

For him, the jewel of the room was the large Jacuzzi bath that sat in the centre, on a high plinth. It was easily big enough for two people. He glanced up at the ceiling, chuckling. When he'd first viewed the flat, he'd been a little shocked. The previous owner's fixation with mirrors was evident here as well as in the bedrooms. He couldn't deny it had taken a bit of getting used to when he glanced up and stared at his own reflection.

He snatched a towel off the heated rail and went to clean up the mess. He paused on entering his bedroom and tried to view it as he had the first time.

The patterned wall coverings weren't as bold as in the hallway downstairs, but they were still eye-catching. The colours were more subtle, with an earthy palette to complement the vegetation and trees. Often, Adam imagined he was in a forest when he shut the curtains and switched on his brass lamps, letting the soft glow illuminate the walls. The green carpet blanketing the floor added to the overall effect. The room was dominated by his large, mahogany, queen-sized, four-poster bed. The soft natural calico bedspread and large, fluffy mountain of pillows, in forest greens, enticed him to burrow into the bed and forget about going out into the freezing temperatures.

He imagined doing just that, but with one added extra: Carl.

Stop that right now.

Adam's mind didn't listen and drifted to places he didn't want it to go. He clutched at the forgotten towel. A vivid picture of him sprawled across the bed on his stomach, limbs tied to the four posts, and his backside raised to the perfect height had his chest heaving. He had to check the mirrors above the bed. Adam was focused on whether he would be able to see Carl paddle him in that position.

When his knee hit the crisp cotton, Adam jumped back like a scalded cat. *Get a grip, for Christ sake! How many times do I have to say it? It's not happening. Again, evidently.*

Giving himself a stern talking to, Adam purposefully turned his back on the bed and ignored the growing problem in his underwear.

He marched to the now dark stain on his carpet and got down on his knees to pat at the wetness.

His teeth ground together, and a growl rumbled low in his chest when he realised his head had turned back to the bed. The computer sitting on the side table caught his attention, and warmth spread up his neck. If anyone went through his browser history from the last few months and particularly the last couple of weeks, they'd discover his dark secret.

He sat back on his heels, his shoulders dropping in defeat. How could it be so hard not to think about the change to his preferences and who had caused it? In fact, how could a spanking, a paddling, and talk of safe words make him crave things he'd never considered before?

With the first spanking, though it had stung, it had been the simple shock factor, rather than anything else. Yes, he could easily have come all over Carl, but the paddle had taken it to a whole new exciting level. A level that for two weeks had kept him on his computer, trying to figure out what it was about seeing the purplish bruising on his arse and feeling the accompanying pain that got him so worked up.

The pain, and there'd been plenty, left him confused by how his body had desired it. When Carl had used the paddle, Adam had felt each swat sing through his backside and right up through his whole body. The pain was so sweet it left him dazed and floating on endorphins. The confusing thing was that the sexual encounters of his past had never done that to him, ever.

He froze at the sound of the doorbell peeling loudly. "Fuck." His eyes darted to the door. Carl can't be here already, surely? Unthinking, Adam dropped the towel and bolted for the stairs in his pink shirt and bare legs.

Breathless, he yanked open the door and shivered violently at the blast of cold air hitting his naked skin. He looked down, realising too late his state of undress. He quickly glanced up, then wished he hadn't when he was met with a formidable scowl.

He huffed. "What is your problem?" He didn't give Carl time to answer as he clutched his snow-covered coat sleeve, encouraging him inside.

The shivers increased when Carl stepped right into Adam's space. The thick layer of sleet covering his dark wool jacket pressed against Adam's shirt front. He quivered. His nipples pebbled under the wet material. He exhaled, his eyes transfixed on Carl. Adam didn't register the door closing, though, as a moment later, large hands were gripping him under his armpits.

"Wrap your legs around me."

Carl's voice was barely recognisable, but the husky command was clear. The need to obey was too much to resist. Adam's legs wrapped themselves around Carl. Adam winced when his thighs tightened around the sodden coat and the icy water touched his bare skin. His shirt stuck to his chest. The trembles had him wrap his arms tightly around Carl's neck.

The tension sparked between them, and the tiny hairs covering Adam's body lifted in anticipation of what was to come.

Chapter Eight

Carl

THE MOMENT CARL STEPPED INTO ADAM'S HALL, THE SIGHT OF HIS enticing bare legs and citrus cologne clouded his mind. He inhaled, wanting to drown in Adam's scent, which evoked memories of their last encounter. Carl's body vibrated, and his Dom wanted out to play.

He moved his hands under Adam's armpits. Carl didn't care he was covered in snow. He lifted him up easily and ordered Adam to wrap his legs around him.

Carl's chest puffed out when Adam obeyed without hesitation, and his erection pulsed to life. Slender thighs gripped his waist, and his groin pushed against Adam's arousal.

"We can't be late for work," Carl said as an afterthought, even as he was moving towards the stairs. "Where is your bedroom? We need to get you dry."

Tiny shivers racked Adam's small frame, and with them came an urge to take care of him. Carl ground his teeth together.

"It's the second door on the left at the top of the stairs," Adam said as he burrowed into his neck.

Carl tightened his arms around Adam. *Come on, keep it together.* He mounted the stairs. His eyes widened at the sight of the garish wallpaper and his feet faltered. His desire was forgotten for a moment under the attack of bright colours. "Holy shit, please tell me you didn't decorate this place."

Adam raised his head from his neck, his eyes sparkling with mirth. "Why? You don't like my exotic birds and flowers." He giggled.

The girlie sound should have been off-putting, but Carl found it endearing. He gave an internal sigh at his own sappiness, knowing Nathan would laugh his arse off at him. His thoughts were interrupted when Adam continued talking.

"Nah, I never decorated. Though I have to say, I love it. It's wacky, but it fits the rest of the house."

The mischievous grin got Carl wondering what other sights he was in for. "This has to be the worst of it, right?"

"Erm, no."

Carl grumbled when Adam stayed close-lipped and didn't elaborate. He carried on up the remaining stairs, walking into the bedroom Adam indicated was his. The laughter escaped before Carl could stop it. His gaze swept the room, missing nothing. His eyes lingered on the large bed and then the mirrored ceiling.

His mind racing with possibilities, Carl slowly lowered Adam to the floor. His fingers twitched with the urge to rip off the layer of clothing preventing him from touching Adam's naked skin. The scent of Bold detergent wafted from Adam's wet shirt, and though it shouldn't have been a turn-on, it left Carl hard and aching.

Work, you have work. He kept up the litany as he stepped back from the tasty wet morsel, who was eyeing him like he was a meal to be devoured.

Work colleague, remember? You can't go there! He almost laughed at his own ridiculousness. *What happened when Adam was paddled to orgasm?*

All thoughts fled the moment Adam's nimble fingers unbuttoned his shirt and revealed the pale, golden flesh beneath. Pebbled rosy nipples, begging for some adornment, were exposed, along with a solid erection that was playing peekaboo with Adam's Calvin Kleins.

Carl struggled to swallow.

Adam's lack of submissiveness was having an effect on him that was both startling and surprising. All his adult life, a person's submissiveness was the one thing that got him revving. Yet the sight of Adam boldly taking charge took his breath away. His perceived desires melded into something new as he watched Adam stand proud and continue to brazenly stare him down, daring him to take what he wanted.

The dark side of his needs hungered for more. Carl's jaw ached. He eyed the bed behind "his" sexy boy. He didn't question why he knew Adam was his. Carl figured now was not the time when he had better things to occupy himself with.

The bed called to him, but he knew that if he did what he wanted, they'd not leave the room for hours. He narrowed his eyes and rubbed his chin.

A grin spread across his face. "Do you have a silk ribbon, preferably a long piece?"

Adam arched his brow and shrugged slightly, but Carl didn't explain. *Will Adam do as I ask?*

About to break the stalemate, Carl swallowed a chuckle when Adam huffed and puffed before stomping out of the room.

Carl quickly removed his soaking jacket and placed it on the old-fashioned rocking chair sitting in the corner of the room. He walked back to the large bed. He tilted his head. Was Adam an exhibitionist?

The mirror above the bed said yes. A smile spread across Carl's face, and he rubbed his hands together at the possibilities. It definitely cast a different light on him divulging his true nature without Adam running a mile.

Maybe, maybe not?

Distracted by the sounds of drawers opening and closing somewhere down the hall, Carl's lips twitched. A petulant-faced Adam returned holding a piece of purple ribbon about a metre long. "Perfect." Saying nothing more, he sauntered over to Adam. Carl kept his eyes on Adam's, watching for any hesitation.

The excitement sparkling in the depth of Adam's eyes was enough for Carl to continue. Towering over Adam, Carl took the silk from his hand. He ran the soft material through his fingers, his mind working on the pattern he'd like to create up Adam's shaft.

He stood before him, his arms twitching. Carl bit his lower lip between his teeth. Adam's nervousness was endearing and forced Carl to rein in his own desires. His fingers clasped the satin.

"Take off your underwear and lie down on your back, on the bed." The stern Dom voice worked a treat. Adam skipped to the bed and dropped his pants as if they were on fire. He climbed onto all fours, wagging his pert backside at Carl, before stretching out before him, like an all-you-can-eat buffet. He groaned under the onslaught of wild need to do just that.

Inhaling and exhaling twice, Carl walked to the bed. An ache built in his jaw. Glorious glowing skin rippled against the pale cover. With trembling legs, Carl lifted his knee onto the bed. He straddled Adam's lean, naked hips but kept his weight off the boy.

Carl eyed the cream cover with trepidation and left his booted feet hanging over the end of the bed. Balanced on his haunches, Carl swept his gaze over the flat hairless stomach to the turgid cock bobbing eagerly for attention. His mouth watered when it reached the glistening tip.

His eyes crinkling, Carl chuckled. "Eager, much. Remember you can use your safe word if you need to, Sugar Lips."

Adam's quick nod was all he needed. Carl took hold of his erect shaft, firmly. He bent forward and licked over the head. After a few swipes, he drew back and let the first taste of Adam linger on his tongue.

Carl hummed in appreciation. "You taste as good as any of my desserts." He ignored Adam's whine and hip punch. "You need to know something about me, Sugar Lips. I like to be in control."

"No shit, Sherlock, as if I couldn't have figured that out by now," Adam interrupted.

Carl tutted. "Now, that has earned you a punishment. Yes?" His brow rose when Adam's mouth opened. The huff and lip pursing were more than Carl could take, and he sniggered. "You are too distracting, by far. Now, where was I? Ah, yes, I was about to bind this lovely cock of yours."

His cock bucked in response to Adam's in-drawn breath and full-blown pupils.

"Have you ever had someone bind your balls and cock?" Though the question was simple, Carl felt the weight of it. He held and released his breath quickly at the shake of Adam's head. Relieved for reasons Carl didn't want to examine, he took hold of the silk, dragging it through his fingers. His hands shook under Adam's fixated stare.

Carl stroked up Adam's hard length. His mouth watered for another taste. Resisting, barely, he lifted Adams hairless sac with his other hand and slowly pulled the end of the silk around one ball, then the second, making a figure-eight pattern. He tugged the silk snug against Adam's skin and then checked the circulation. Whimpers and moans floated out of Adam's mouth, and Carl growled in satisfaction.

Weaving the silk up Adam's cock, Carl created a crisscross pattern until he reached the head. His hands caressed the silk-encased cock while he calculated the amount of time Adam could be bound for. Carl's gaze narrowed on the meaty head. Should Adam remove the silk binding to pee?

He shook his head and tried to block out the sexy sounds tumbling past Adam's lips. Deciding to leave it bare, Carl tied a bow under the leaking head. Sitting back, he eyed his handiwork critically. Though not as neat as some, Carl was happy with the way Adam's balls were bound and the way his cock was pushed forward. There would be no way Adam could come or, at least, not without great effort.

Carl bent forward again. Only this time, he sucked the slippery head into his mouth. His body thrummed with pleasure at Adam's low, elongated moan and full-body tremble. Carl teased the head with little flicks of his tongue and then nibbled on his slit. The temptation to delve into Adam's slit was too much, and Carl pushed the tip of his tongue in and moaned at the burst of flavour.

Carl shifted to get comfortable when Adam shouted, "Nooooo... don't stop. Suck my cock."

"What did I say?" Carl pulled back, even though it pained him to do it. "I'm in charge here. For trying to take control, you are now going to have to wait to get more."

Carl climbed off Adam and the bed, his cock throbbing painfully against the zip of his trousers. His jaw thrust forward. The groan of complaint sat in his throat at the sight Adam made with a pout on his lips and a mutinous scowl marring his brow. For some perverse reason, Carl relished the idea of a worked-up Adam.

"You're not leaving me like this? Seriously?" Adam asked, his eyes the size of saucers.

"I'm not leaving you. We're due in work"—Carl checked his wristwatch—"in about half an hour. What I'm doing is punishing you and leaving you like that. All you need to do to make it stop, Sugar Lips, is say your safe word." He pointed at Adam's decorated cock. "Otherwise that stays like that for the whole of your shift. And if I feel lenient, I might let you come when I unwrap you later."

Carl gave an evil chuckle. "That should give you plenty of time to reconsider your actions." Satisfied by Adam's wide-open mouth, Carl sauntered to the door. On reaching it, he looked back over his shoulder. "Oh, and by the way, I'd maybe suggest picking a loose pair of trousers and a long shirt or jacket to wear." He roared with laughter at the loud curses following him down the stairs.

Yeah, he really couldn't remember a time where he'd had this much fun. His day had just got a whole lot better after Adam's call had caused his initial meltdown at home.

When Carl had answered the phone and heard Adam, his stomach had all but danced its way up his throat as he readily agreed to come and collect Adam. After putting the phone down, he'd recalled that he had never asked Adam for his address. That had resulted in him cursing every mile he had driven in the shitty weather. Shitty weather, that would have been the perfect excuse to say no. Had he done that? *No.*

He knew better than anyone how the weather in London at this time of year left a lot to be desired. After living in Italy, he'd forgotten how bad it could get at times. His first winter back in the UK had taught him a hard lesson. Be prepared, or get stuck for hours, freezing and stranded. He preferred option one, so he had invested in a truck, adding in all the extras he could think off to survive a winter. He'd gone with overkill, and that right there was why he hadn't used that as an excuse. Adam was well aware his truck could just about cope with any weather condition after he'd bragged about it.

He sighed at the way his stomach sank under the reality he would have moved heaven and earth to get to Adam after the phone call. *So there is no point kidding myself differently.* Carl rolled his eyes and went to wait for Adam.

Chapter Nine

Adam

ADAM WALKED INTO SEB'S OFFICE, HOLDING THE FILE HE'D REQUESTED. He kept his expression masked when Seb glanced at him, brows rising. Adam slowed his step, hoping it would keep his face from screwing up. He thought he'd achieved it till Seb spoke and dashed his hopes.

"Adam, you all right? Have you hurt yourself?"

Muttering under his breath, Adam aimed for nonchalance. He ground out through gritted teeth, doing his best to shrug off the genuine concern he could see in Seb's expression. "No, boss, just a little chafing situation going on."

Adam wanted to snort at his own understatement. *Chafing*, he fucking wished. He ignored the secret thrill he got every time he took a step. Or how his body lit up every time Carl took him aside to check his balls and cock hadn't dropped off. Five hours. Five hours of the sweetest torture, if you didn't count the hourly inspections Carl took pleasure in inflicting on him.

When he arrived at work, Adam had been part grateful and partly gutted at how busy they were. One, it kept him busy, and two, that meant he never forgot his predicament. He'd also given up trying to figure out why he hadn't told Carl to take a long hike off a short pier and unwrap his throbbing cock after hour three.

Braced to take the final steps towards Seb's desk, Adam shook off the worry. Then the fabric rubbed against his sensitive cock. With lips clamped together, Adam placed the file on Seb's desk, sweat sliding down his back at thoughts of Seb wanting to talk about the figures.

"Adam, can you sit for a minute. I need to talk about Matt."

Seb's eyes narrowed on him as Adam gingerly lowered himself into the seat in front of his desk, praying he could keep it together. Seb's gaze never wavered, and Adam didn't miss his head shake or raised brow.

He rolled his eyes heavenward and inwardly cursed before taking a minute to compose himself. Adam was grateful Seb chose not to call him out.

"What about Matt? I thought he'd fitted in rather well at La Trattoria, mark two." Adam chuckled. Seb's scowl at his use of the term "mark two" was as predictable as Big Ben. "Come on. You know I have to keep them all separate in my head. It's not my fault you called them all the same name!" Adam groused.

"Oh, shut up. Where was I? Yes. Matt." Seb scratched at his bearded jaw. "He is fitting in. It's just that there seems to be an issue with him filling in the spreadsheets we use for keeping track of the restaurant's income and expenditure. He's not doing it. I know he's only been in the job for six weeks, but I'd have thought by now he'd be up and running. I want you to spend some time with him, check out what the issues are. I trust your judgement."

It always surprised him when Seb complimented him, having had none as a child. Flushing under the praise, Adam lowered his eyelashes to shield his welling eyes. The ball of tears lodged in his throat made it difficult to speak. With a curt nod, Adam glanced down at the desk.

"Adam, look at me," Seb asked.

Meeting Seb's gaze, Adam blinked back the tears. He sucked in a breath at seeing empathy reflected back at him.

"You are an excellent manager, Adam. I know I had my doubts in the beginning because of your age, but you've more than proven your-self to be efficient, hardworking, and an asset to my business."

Adam held up his hand, fanning his face for effect, hoping to detract from how overwhelmed he was. "Stop. At this rate, I won't be able to get my head out the door." He giggled.

"All right, but it's the truth. You know I wouldn't blow smoke up your arse."

"Who's blowing smoke up whose arse? And why wasn't I invited?" Carl asked as he stepped into Seb's office.

Adam did his best not to squirm when Seb glanced from Carl to him and then gave them both a considered look. Adam had the distinct impression Seb was assessing the tension that suddenly filled the room. They were like two dogs circling each other, each trying their best to figure out a way to take a bite out of the other. Only Adam hoped Seb hadn't picked up on that.

"No one. And what do you want, Carl? I'm busy here with Adam. Oh, on that note. I'm gonna have to take Scott from waiting tables so he can take over from Adam for a few d—"

Carl blustered over the top of Seb. "What! Why? Where is Adam going?"

Adam's eyes widened. "I'm right here, you big lug. If you have questions, you can ask me. And where I'm going is none of your business." Forgetting his dilemma, Adam fired out of the chair.

He froze. The silk restraint pulled tight, and his cock jerked. Adam released a loud moan. Heat spread like wildfire up his neck. Avoiding looking at either man, Adam walked gingerly towards the door, head held high. He shoved past Carl without saying a word.

He made up his mind that he was no longer playing this game and headed for the locker room. The door had barely closed behind him before it was flung open. His hands froze on his zipper. A guilty flush turned his already pink cheeks to crimson. The rapid beat of his heart left him breathless when Carl's stormy gaze landed on his hands.

"You do not get to decide whether you remove the ribbon. I do unless you use your safe word," Carl growled.

Carl's stern voice slid over Adam's cock like an actual caress. Adam didn't know what it said about him that he wanted to beg. Beg for what he had no clue. He just knew there was something about Carl when he became all growly and stern that got him off in a big way. Yet there was another part of him that wanted to fight and show Carl that no one got to boss him around.

Conflicted, Adam hesitated but chose not to use his safe word. Then he moved backwards, and he raised his hands as if to ward Carl off. "Stop right there, buddy. No more. You aren't torturing me anymore. I'm going into the bathroom, and I'm stopping this nonsense right now." Adam hated the lack of conviction in his voice. He took another step backwards.

"Take another step, and I'll have to punish you," Carl threatened.

Adam shivered, and his balls tightened at the genuine threat Carl's face conveyed. A thrill raced up his spine as he took another step back, daring him.

The air whooshed out of his lungs. Adam found himself dangling midair, pinned to the bathroom door, as his mouth was devoured in a brutal kiss.

He clung on to Carl's powerful shoulders, unable to do more than hold on under the cruel assault. His mouth opened under the attack, his moans mixing with Carl's. Carl dominated his mouth. Tongues clashed boldly against each other. Teeth clacked noisily but were drowned out by the wild beating of Adam's heart as Carl feasted on his mouth for the first time.

Adam lost track of why he'd come into the locker room. The fire raging through his body left a powerful ache between his legs. The painful throb caused his hips to jerk, needing something, anything, to help alleviate the unbearable pressure building in his sac.

Dragging his head back, Adam panted, "Please, I can't take anymore. Let me come. I'll be a good boy. Pleaseeee." Unaware of what he'd said to cause Carl to freeze, Adam whined close to tears. "Don't torture me anymore. I need you." He choked back a sob at Carl's snarling face.

Adam released a heartfelt sigh when Carl held him tightly against his broad chest while he opened the door into the toilet. It closed, and Adam heard the click of the lock before he was lowered to the floor. His heart rate kicked up a fuss, but Adam was past caring. The raging desire was like an unwieldy beast, and it was not going to be controlled now.

Carl's meaty fingers worked on undoing his loose-fitting slacks. Adam released a breathy groan when the warm air hit the tip of his swollen cock, the purple head nearly matching the colour of the ribbon.

"This will feel intense when I remove the ribbon. Brace your back against the wall."

Adam didn't hesitate. He pressed back against the smooth, cool surface. His legs trembled as he inched them apart in the confines of his partially lowered trousers.

His eyes widened as Carl lowered to his knees. He barely had time to suck in a breath before his cock was bathed in warm, wet heat.

He shoved his fist into his mouth to stop the howl that wanted to escape. His senses overwhelmed, his hips jerked forward, desperate for more. Adam let out a deep moan around his fist, squirming under Carl's hands as they pinned his hips in place. A wave of defencelessness washed over him and added to the sensations bombarding him.

The warm lips clasping and sucking the head of his cock drove him to distraction. Unaware Carl had released the ribbon, he felt a sudden powerful surge of blood firing along his cock. He chewed on his fist. His legs wobbled. His thighs clenched along with his channel as the blazing licks of pleasure lit up his whole body.

His eyes screwed tightly shut while his head landed hard against the door. His whole body went rigid as cum poured from his painfully hard cock. Burst after burst exploded from him. He mewled in agony, his throbbing cock not letting up for what felt like long minutes. All the while Carl drank him down, like it was his most favourite libation.

Adam wheezed and pulled his hips back, trying to escape Carl. His sensitive cock wanted a break from the laving tongue prolonging his pleasure. Adam cried out around his fist. "Enough. Please I can't take anymore."

He wanted to scream as Carl leisurely sat back, a devilish satisfied smile gracing his gorgeous face. Adam's cock twitched. Carl licked across his puffy lips, giving him ideas. His mind already ten steps ahead, Adam launched himself at Carl and latched on to his mouth, much like a greedy child would run into a sweetie shop, clutching their pocket money desperate to part with it.

Adam felt Carl's surprise when he opened his mouth after a moment of hesitation.

The taste of his own essence was delicious, so Adam feasted. As his tongue swept Carl's mouth, he released a growl. His hands cupped Carl's head, fingers delving into the dark silky strands, holding him in place. Carl's familiar scent of food and sweat engulfed Adam.

He released Carl's lips and cursed his partially open trousers, which were intent on hampering him from straddling Carl's lap.

The tap at the door had Adam's eyes widen. His gaze locked on Carl's. Adam swore he saw resignation and something that resembled regret.

"Come on. It looks like playtime is over," Carl whispered.

Resigned, Adam shouted out, "Give me a sec. Can't a man piss in peace?" Who the hell was outside the door? How on earth were they going to manage to escape without raising suspicion?

He leant closer to Carl. "How are we going to do this?" he asked quietly.

"Get dressed. Then give it a minute. Maybe they'll disappear or use the other loo." Carl shrugged, looking unconcerned.

The reality of getting caught formed a ball of panic in his stomach. Adam did as he was told, fretting. How could he have forgotten about his contract?

He eyed Carl's hulking figure as he straightened his black chef's outfit. Adam shook his head, mentally slapping himself. *Like I don't know how.*

"I can hear you overthinking all the way over here. Stop. It'll be fine."

When Carl's face went all stern on him, Adam wanted to argue the toss but instead shut his mouth. With a resigned sigh, Adam eyed his now clothed cock as it twitched.

Traitorous bastard.

Ignoring Carl, Adam opened the door and poked his head out. With no one about, he scurried out, not looking back. All but running through the kitchen, Adam prayed no one would stop him. He was convinced what they'd just done was clearly written all over him. Breathing a sigh of relief when he hit the reception area unhindered, Adam went and sat on his high stool. Burying his head in his hands, Adam took stock.

He'd just had the best blow job of his life. Yet it might as well have been his worst because of who had given it to him. His lips puffed out.

What am I going to do now?

Adam sat in his leather wingback chair, staring out of his lounge window at the dull, grey sky. His brow furrowed, he counted the number of weeks it had been since he'd allowed Carl to wrap his cock in ribbon. Four weeks. Four weeks that had him no closer to understanding why he liked it so much or what that said about him. Then there was their relationship.

He shuddered.

Relationship? Was that what they had?

He wasn't sure that quite described what they'd agreed to. They had somehow slipped into a weekly torture session. Once a week, Carl would come and collect Adam to take him to work. But before they got out the door, Carl would truss him up in some contraption aimed to torture him.

Carl's ability to torment an orgasm out of Adam left him with a head full of questions. He'd never considered himself to be a pain slut. Yet there he was each week, breathless with anticipation to see what Carl would come up with. The week had narrowed down to that one day. The rest blurred into nothingness, and that is what scared him the most. The time away from Carl and his tormenting ways was endless and boring.

A shiver worked its way through Adam's body at the feel of soft cotton brushing against his growing erection. A flush spread up at the memory of yesterday's play session. The nipple clamps and a small vibrating butt plug had almost been his undoing. *Fuck*, if it hadn't been for Scott's timely interruption while he was sitting at the reception daydreaming about what it would feel like when Carl removed the tiny nipple clamps, he was sure he'd have come right then and there. The demands that he refrain from orgasming without permission were getting more difficult with each test.

All Adam's alone time was spent searching the kind of play they were engaging in. How far would Carl take things?

The fluttering inside Adam's chest matched the thoughts running willy nilly through his head. Did Carl play seriously at BDSM? His familiarity suggested he was well versed in all aspects of the lifestyle. Especially if Adam considered how easy Carl could get all growly and demanding, using what Adam now referred to as his Dom's voice.

Adam shifted in his chair. His cock wilted. He was well aware his misery today was all to do with the research into submissives and their behaviour. Would Carl want him to kneel at his feet? With his stomach revolting, Adam closed his eyes and willed his head to stop thinking.

Chapter Ten

Carl

CARL BLITHELY BUTCHERED THE VEGETABLE HE WAS CUTTING. HIS mind whirred. Every time he recalled the conversation he'd had with Seb the previous month, the remnants of anger would twist Carl's guts into a million knots.

He'd sat listening to Seb explain how he had flouted his own rule about dating employees with Ellie. The one part of the contract that ensured Carl could not publically claim Adam was now void. And instead of jumping for joy, he now had an eerie itch at the base of his neck and a strange unwillingness to change the current status quo.

Carl's gaze went to Seb's office.

This was all Seb's fault.

Seb was suffering because Ellie had left him. Carl got that, yet the anger inside that had burrowed past his defences the moment Seb had spoken about his secret relationship wasn't shifting. Carl couldn't figure out who he was mad at most, Seb or himself. No closer to the answer, he ground his teeth and hacked at the vegetables.

The last four months with Adam had been electrifying. It was as if Carl was an addict. He jonesed for his next hit. Adam was in his bloodstream, and it was a powerful feeling. The deep-rooted connection he'd never found with any other sub was there with Adam.

Adam, however, was not a sub. And as much as Carl wanted to pretend that wasn't an issue, he couldn't ignore it, no matter how hard he tried. The struggle was figuring out if it bothered him. The shift in dynamic from what he loved about BDSM was eye-opening. He'd honestly thought that after twenty-odd years he had himself sussed out. Yet here he was at forty–two, trying to redefine who and what he liked. At the same time, he acted like nothing had changed when, in fact, everything had shifted. *Do I even know which way is up?*

Carl shook off the worry and went back to the issue of Seb breaking the rules. Carl couldn't help how pissed off he still was, though he kept his thoughts to himself. Instead he had generously offered his support and a shoulder for Seb to cry on.

Fuck, Carl had even set Seb up with someone who looked like Ellie, hoping to get him out of his funk. The double dating thing was so not Carl's thing, but he'd done it anyway. Seb just didn't need to know that Saul wasn't his real date, but a sub from Carl's club who'd agreed to help him out. It wasn't like he could have asked Adam. Not that he'd wanted to.

Liar.

That isn't part of their agreement.

He silently cursed up a storm, the words ringing in his ears.

He eyed the butchered red pepper and shoved it into the growing pile of other mangled vegetables on his left side.

"Chef, you all right?" Lenny asked tentatively.

His gaze was on the pile of wrecked vegetables. Carl spun towards him, knife in hand, then promptly burst into helpless laughter as Lenny nearly jumped into the large steaming pots behind him. His dark grey eyes were the size of saucers in his pale, freckled face as he eyed the knife.

"I'm fine. Just got a lot on my mind, is all." Waving Lenny off, Carl ignored the speculation on the other man's pretty face. He was well aware that Lenny liked to gossip. Lenny was like an eager ginger puppy, which was why Carl kept his temper to himself. He wasn't in the habit of kicking puppies, even the human kind.

He flicked a glance at Lenny's retreating back.

Carl released a chuckle when Lenny hiked up a massive pot as if it weighed nothing. His small biceps bulged under the strain. The strain Lenny seemed oblivious to as he strolled back to the washroom, humming as if he didn't have a care in the world.

When Seb had put out an advert for a kitchen hand and Lenny had applied, Carl had had his doubts Lenny would cope with the manual labour required for the role. Lenny, though tall at six feet, resembled a string bean. His skinny frame looked as if a strong puff of wind would break him in two. But there had been something appealing about his eagerness, so they'd taken a chance on him. He subsequently surprised Carl on a daily basis. His wiry body hid a wealth of strength, which often made Carl wonder what Lenny did in his spare time to gain that kind of power.

Turning back to the decreasing pile of usable vegetables required for julienning, Carl groaned under his breath. Using the noises around him, Carl blocked his thoughts and finished his prep. His hands worked effortlessly, chopping and cutting with precision.

Lost in his own world, he didn't immediately register the commotion over the sounds of the busy kitchen. His gaze lifted from the task at hand to the door, where Scott stood fussing. "What is it, Scott?" he asked. His pulse skipped a beat when he met Scott's watery, red-rimmed eyes.

"There's a fight in the foyer. A man has Adam pinned to the reception desk," he hiccupped in fright.

Carl roared and rushed around the counter. He ran to the door. His rule of never going into the dining room during service fell by the wayside in his need to get to Adam. Carl disregarded the spectacle he was making when the dining patrons all seemed to pause at once at the sight of him. He barrelled through the quietly reserved room and shoved past Seb, who was heading in the same direction.

Before he reached the partition separating the reception from the dining room, Carl heard the raised voices. He rounded the corner, stopping for a second to take in the situation. The woman fretting behind the man pinning Adam to the desk seemed to be having no effect on the guy.

Adam's puce face and tiny hands scrabbling to get the man's large hands off his crumpled beige linen suit jacket had Carl seeing red. Not giving it any thought, he yanked the guy back and shoved him with force towards the door. "Get your fucking hands off him," he seethed through gritted teeth.

He towered over the man, using his bulk to intimidate him.

His jaw dropped open when Adam stepped around him and got in the man's face. "I told you. You have it all wrong. You are booked in for next week. If you'd just taken the time to listen to me," Adam ground out.

"What on earth is going on here?" Seb asked in a placating voice.

Fury blinded him to everything, and Carl paid no heed to Seb. "Ask that moron. He was manhandling my… Adam," Carl blustered, flushing scarlet and hoping Seb didn't catch his slip-up. "We don't put up with that shit in here," Carl said.

Seb placed a hand on his arm and squeezed with authority. Carl didn't mistake the steel behind Seb's glare. The warning was clear. The heat surging through Carl was hot enough to peel the paint off the wood. Carl stood to his full height, offering an intimidating scowl. Seb continued to use his silence to demand he back down. The message in his eyes warned Carl not to put on a show.

Carl worked to get himself under control and not do anything stupid, like punch the man in the face.

He edged closer to Adam, and his fingers itched to pull him closer to him.

Seb turned to Adam and the gent. "What seems to be the problem?"

"This dick thinks he's booked into the restaurant. I've tried to reason with him and explain it's booked for next week, but he decided he didn't like what I was sayin'," Adam hissed out.

"Adam, please cease from using derogatory comments." Seb didn't give Adam time to respond and turned to the man. "In future, if you have an issue, please ask to speak to me and refrain from touching my staff. Adam has every right to press charges for assault. Now, let's have a look at the booking."

Twenty minutes later, Carl stomped back into the kitchen. His knuckles ached from how tight his hands were clenched. He needed an outlet for his anger and now.

He made his way towards the locker room. Pausing halfway, he shouted to his second in command, "Billy, take over service. I need to leave. I'll be back for dinner service, and I'll make it up to you." With Billy's acknowledgement, Carl went into the locker room and stripped, dressing quickly in his sweats and T-shirt.

He grabbed his gym bag and went straight out the back door, ignoring the voices shouting at his back. He was aware Seb would be furious with him for leaving in the middle of service, but being forced to be helpful to the dickwad, after it turned out the electronic system had sent the wrong email, left a nasty taste in Carl's mouth.

His body vibrated with rage at the images dancing through his mind. Adam's pale face and frightened eyes as he had struggled to escape prodded at Carl's temper like a Taser. He loathed violence, and yeah, that was fucked up, given he was a Dom, but for him, there was a distinct difference. Every person he had ever touched had given their implicit permission. They knew beforehand what they were getting into, and what he'd seen today was the exact opposite.

He slammed into his truck, sweat dripping down his back as he shifted against the hot leather. He threw his gym bag into the footwell of the passenger seat. When he started the engine, he hit the air con and let the cool air smother the balmy heat inside the truck. It was only the beginning of June, and already the weather was becoming unbearable.

He dragged off his bandana and mopped at his face. Carl raked his fingers through his hair before fastening his seat belt. Then he connected his iPhone to the Bluetooth and dialled Nathan's number, hoping he was at the club.

"Hey, big man, what's up?" Nathan's warm, honey-toned voice floated through the car speakers.

"I'm in need of a sparring partner. Are you at the club? I'm on my way and thought that if you're free, I could spar with you."

Nathan laughed, "Shit, man, it must be bad if you want to fight with me. You usually avoid that at all costs. And yeah, I'm here. Where else would I be?"

"Yeah, yeah. I'll be there as soon as I'm done battling the traffic." Saying goodbye, Carl sped off.

Three hours later, sore and bruised, yet feeling decidedly more relaxed, Carl strolled back into the busy kitchen. He went to the locker room, changed into his chef's outfit, stored his bag, and then went in search of Seb.

Time to face the music.

Carl inhaled the warm, rich scents of the kitchen before he glanced at Seb's office. Giving a resigned sigh, he checked in with the kitchen staff before heading in that direction.

Seb didn't acknowledge Carl's presence. Instead Seb kept on tapping on the keyboard. Carl huffed and lowered his large frame into the small chair. Deciding he could play that game as well, he waited Seb out.

They'd played this game before, and Carl knew his part well. Slouching in the chair, he pulled out a clean, bright red bandana he'd shoved into the pocket of his top. He rolled it a couple of times before tying it around his forehead. Not one to wear a chef's hat, Carl found that a bandana worked to keep his hair under control, with a side benefit of stopping sweat from dripping into his eyes.

It took ten minutes before Seb raised his head and looked at him. Carl almost laughed at Seb's wide-eyed expression. He'd seen the damage Nathan had inflicted on his face. The large area of discolouration covering the left side of his jaw was pretty spectacular.

"What the fuck have you been doing?" Seb demanded, pointing to his jaw. "You look like you've had a fight with David Haye."

Carl sniggered. "It feels like it, only it was my best mate, Nathan, and he could rival Haye for his boxing prowess. Which, in my temper, I forgot when I got in the ring with him."

He shrugged at Seb's alarmed face. "That fucking arsehole got my goat all right, and I needed some space, is all. Before you start, Billy is more than capable of covering the lunch service. And I would have said something, but you were too busy licking that guy's backside." Carl held up his hands, seeing the fire in Seb's blue eyes. "Okay, I get it. It's business, but sometimes you have just to say fuck it."

Carl got up and pointed at Seb. "That might be something you need to think about, now you're single. Being so controlling doesn't allow those close to you to feel supported."

Seeing the shock on Seb's face, Carl paused. "You need to loosen up, okay. I get it, but you were so busy trying to appease that guy because of the business that you never considered that he manhandled a member of your staff." Carl stopped Seb by holding up his hand. "Yes, you told him Adam could call the police. What you should have done is call the police and kick his arse out." Carl's stomach twisted back into knots, undoing all the hard work he'd achieved in the boxing ring.

He waved off Seb's apology and strolled back into the noisy kitchen. After checking they were ready for the dinner service, he headed to his work station. He kept busy and out of Adam's way every time he came into the kitchen with requests for several different things.

Once the last meal had been served, Carl gave Billy the nod to let him know he could go. He started the clean down and sent the remaining staff home. Taking his time, Carl finished tidying.

He waved Seb off a few minutes later. Hanging around the kitchen, he waited for Adam to come through, as was his routine. When he did five minutes later, Carl's brow pinched. His hands twitched at his sides when Adam headed to the locker room, blatantly ignoring him.

Carl followed behind and hesitated in the doorway. Dread curled into a ball in his stomach. Adam made no effort to talk or look at him.

What the fuck was this all about?

He narrowed his eyes. He was at a complete loss with Adam's behaviour. "Is everything all right Adam?"

Adam shot his head round, and Carl was met with a molten angry glare that would have melted metal. Carl's own anger simmered, and the urge to step back was strong. "What? If you don't talk to me, I don't know what the issue is."

Carl fidgeted, watching Adam with fascination.

Adam stalked to him, his chin tilted up, glaring. "Oh, you want to talk now, do you? What about earlier when I came looking for you after that knob left, hey? Where were you then?" Adam stabbed at his chest.

Carl stepped, back rubbing at the spot Adam had drilled his finger into. "I was too angry to stay and not do something I might regret," Carl explained through gritted teeth.

"What about me? Did you think about how I might have felt? You didn't even stay to find out. Months we've been messing around. Don't I warrant your concern?" Adam shouted. "Evidently not!"

Carl stood still, unsure how to respond to the angry tirade. As Adam headed for the door, he opened his mouth, but he had charged out before Carl had a chance to speak. A second later, the back door slammed shut.

"Well, fuck!" he hollered.

Chapter Eleven

Adam

ADAM SHUFFLED THE PAPERS ON HIS DESK, DELAYING THE INEVITABLE as long as possible.

Eyeing his neat and organised desk, Adam sighed, knowing he couldn't put it off any longer. He rooted in his trouser pocket and pulled out his iPhone. He pulled up the thread of conversation with Richie and groaned at how many weeks he'd put off responding to Richie's last text, saying they needed to talk.

Adam had known it was coming. The inescapable moment things went to shit after Richie and Marian's planned visit to the oncologist. It was a reality Adam had been avoiding like the plague. The moment they talked shit was going to get real. *It's already real, dickhead.*

The last visit with Marian left Adam in no doubt the appointment was to spell out what he could already see. Her skeletal frame, sunken eyes, and sallow skin were enough of a clue that the treatments weren't working anymore. And it made Adam a coward. He didn't want to face a life without Marian in it. She'd been his person, along with Richie. The one who got Adam, didn't judge, and loved him regardless of his flaws.

How do I survive without that?

His lips trembled. He swept a quick glance around, swiping at his damp eyes. He cursed his own cowardice. He picked up the main restaurant phone and dialled. No amount of pretending he was too busy was going to help, so he may as well face it. He just hoped that what he had to share with Richie would make up for him being a shitty friend.

At the lack of response, Adam sagged. He placed the phone down, only for it to ring. Composing himself, Adam lifted it back up and answered in his classy work voice.

"Hello, the La Trattoria Di Amore. How can I help you?"

"Err, sorry. I had a missed call from this number. It must have been a mistake. Sorry to bother you."

Adam screeched at hearing Richie. "Noooo. Richie, don't you dare hang up on me."

Richie chuckled and mumbled, "Hold on, Pipsqueak." Adam tapped his fingers on his desk.

"Pipsqueak, is that really you? I thought you'd dropped off the face of the planet. It's been so long. I texted you weeks ago about mum, and you never bothered to text back, you dick," Richie grouched.

Even if Richie did it good-naturedly, Adam wanted to sigh at being called out. He waited for Richie to carry on. When he was met with silence, Adam pulled the phone from his ear to check it was still working. He put it back to his ear and asked, "Are you still there? I can hear you breathing. Are you ignoring me? You know I hate that."

"No, I'm not ignoring you. You didn't answer my question. I was waiting for a reply, you whalley." Richie chuckled.

"I did," he lied. "You just weren't listening. Anyway, I'm ringing to find out if you're still looking for a job? The boss here needs an office assistant."

"Aw', come on, man, you know I need something flexible so that I can look after mum."

Adam interrupted loudly, "Will you let me finish? I don't know how we are still friends. Seriously, listen up and keep your lips from flapping."

"Adam, are you free for a minute?" Scott shouted.

Adam covered the phone mouthpiece and hollered, "Give me a sec."

After Scott agreed, he turned his attention back to the phone. "Now, where was I?" He explained the requirements. "This is your dream. Say you'll apply. I'll send you the stuff right now. Come on, this has to be perfect timing. This is the solution. I know it is." Knowing, Richie's difficult financial situation, Adam offered to help, but his stubborn friend refused to take blood money from Adam's parents. Not that he could blame him. He hadn't touched it since he'd got his first pay packet. It sat in his secondary bank account, mounting up.

Distracted by thoughts of his parents, it took him a second to register Richie's pained question.

"Are you going to come and visit before, well, you know."

The words tumbled out of his mouth with a sob. "Are you sure? I'm frightened, Richie."

"Me too," Richie said in a choked voice.

"Okay, stop. I can't cry at work. I'll save that for the weekend. I'm off, so I'll pack a bag and stay over." Adam used over-the-top enthusiasm in the hopes it would stop them both from blubbering. After saying goodbye, Adam opened the computer file with all the information and sent the links to Richie. Once he'd finished, he went in search of Scott.

Adam walked into work on Tuesday, his feet dragging. He walked through the kitchen unseeing. His mood left little to be desired. It swung from hysterical crying to over-the-top, fake cheerfulness. The last two days replayed in his mind. Marian's quiet acceptance that this was the end left him feeling unnerved and devastated in equal measure.

He went and hung up his lightweight summer jacket, checking his appearance as an afterthought. He huffed at the dark shadows and deep lines etched around his eyes. Knowing there was nothing he could do about them, Adam walked back through the kitchen and into the dining room.

The weekend occupied his thoughts. Adam considered if he could have done anything different over the last two days. The time he'd spent at Richie's, with Marian, was an emotional rollercoaster of ups and downs, dips and turns. He had gone from having a breakdown when he'd arrived, seeing Marian sitting in a hospital bed in the lounge, to organising her wake while getting steaming drunk. Drunkenness that resulted in him trying to ring Carl. He huffed out a moan of despair, rubbing at his face. He thanked his lucky stars Carl hadn't answered. Adam shuddered at the thought of facing him after going all soppy on him.

In need of a distraction, he strolled to the reception and pulled out his diary, checking what was on his list of things to do today. He sighed resignedly at how crammed it was. The remnants of his weekend binging made themselves known. And though he wanted to blame Richie for encouraging Adam to let go, it was the private conversation he'd had with Marian while Richie was busy making dinner that had pushed Adam over the edge of sensible straight into destructive mode.

He chewed his thumbnail, wondering if Richie was going to see what Adam had agreed to as a good thing. He recalled Marian's pleading hazel eyes and their conversation the day before.

"Adam, please. While Richie's busy, come and sit here." Marian patted the bed.

Adam's stomach dropped, a sense of dread filling him at the adamant expression Marian wore.

"What's wrong? Why are you looking at me like that," Adam asked. His heart skipped a beat, and the air in his lungs refused to leave.

Marian's drawn face become as serious as he'd ever seen it. He sat and clutched her icy-cold hand with his trembling one.

"I need you to do something for me. I know this is going to be hard for you because I need you to keep this from Richie for the time being. It's import- ant you promise me you won't say anything until the right time."

Adam's free hand fluttered on the bedspread, plucking at the embroidered pattern. His gaze met Marian's unwavering, pleading eyes. "Okay, but you

better make it worth my while," Adam joked. His gut twisted at the girlie gig-
gle and lips that brushed a soft kiss over his cheek.

He sucked in a breath, giving a watery chuckle of his own. "All right."
He bobbed his head. "That covers it."

She explained what she needed, and he narrowed his eyes when she finished. "You really think he'd go after your life insurance and the house?" Adam
hated what Richie's dad had done to both Marian and Richie, and the timing
was no coincidence. But Adam understood that sometimes feelings changed,
and no amount of trying to make it work altered it. He'd just never considered
that Mr Bellinger would do something to hurt his son.

"Yes, I do. All the stuff he pulled after he left, emptying our joint bank
account and cashing in all our policies. He is capable of anything."

Adam gawped. "Richie never told me that," he exclaimed loudly.

"Shush." Marian glanced to the open door before looking back at Adam.
"He doesn't know. I was trying to keep some of the shit he pulled from Richie.
He was hurt enough when his dad deserted us. I didn't want to add to his
woes. Promise me you won't say anything, Adam."

Her stern mum face had Adam hunch in defeat. "Okay, I'll do as you
ask. I'll sort a day off in the week to come when your lawyer, Mr Carter, is
here. But how are you going to get Richie out of the house?" Adam asked.

"Oh, don't you worry about that. I have a list of jobs," Marian said with
a mischievous glint in her hazel eyes.

Adam blinked back the tears. He stared at the polished desk in
front of him, where his fingers had been absently tracing the grain of
the wood. He did his best not to worry about things he had no control
over, but fuck, how could he not worry about meeting the lawyer and
signing the paperwork to be the executor of Marian's will?

Rapidly swallowing, Adam did his best to dislodge the ball of
emotions choking him. He switched on the computer with trembling
fingers and worked through his list of jobs.

As weary as he'd felt that morning, Adam felt ten times worse as
he pulled his car up outside his flat ten hours later. The day had gone
from bad to worse, with one crisis after another. He rested his head

on the steering wheel, too tired to drag his backside out of the car. He prayed that Seb sorted a date for the interviews for the office assistance post and soon.

Doing both roles was wearing Adam down. Add in the emotional baggage and an overdose of too much alcohol, and boom, he felt as if someone had sucked the life right out of him. He groaned, rubbing at his aching neck as he lifted his head. He glanced out the window at the shadowed path, huffing.

He opened the door with no enthusiasm, inhaling the muggy, sweet-scented air, coming from the little flower bed. He walked up the path, pressing the car fob to lock the car. A smile lit his face at how the flowers were laid out in the earth under his large bay window.

He'd toyed initially with the idea of buying a house of his own, but the moment he'd walked into the flat on the edge of Notting Hill, he'd fallen in love with the feel of the place. The bright, quirky ambience made him feel right at home.

The four-storey house had been split into two and converted some forty years earlier by the original owner. The building now contained two flats, each with two floors and their own front doors. Reluctant to buy somewhere and then be landed with someone he couldn't get along with, Adam had taken the time to go and meet the one other occupant of the upstairs apartment and found Rupert. The meeting had cemented the idea of buying the flat. As Adam stared down at the pansies that spelt out his name, his mouth twitched.

Rupert was a tiny sprite of a man, with a wealth of stories that could keep Adam entertained for hours. His pewter eyes matched his hair. His creased face, though, showed his age. It also gave Adam insight into how attractive Rupert had been in his youth. The mischievous smile that often sparkled in the depth of his eyes made Adam think of naughty elves. And looking at the flower beds, he didn't think he was far off. For some reason, Rupert loved to poke fun at him.

Adam climbed the steps, his feet dragging as he put his key in the lock.

"Where the hell have you been?" Carl snarled.

The keys clattered to the concrete as Adam spun around, clutching his chest in fright. His heart raced as he stared at his unexpected visitor, and he tried to make sense of why Carl wanted to know where Adam had been. Carl knew fine well Adam had been at work.

How should he respond to such a stupid question?

Adam's brow rose as he eyed Carl. Two days of not seeing him and Adam felt the need tug low in his belly. He lowered his eyelashes, masking the want. Adam's lips wanted to smack together at how tasty Carl looked in low-slung combat shorts and a plain white T-shirt. His dark hair was swept back, and his usual bandana was tied around his forehead. He couldn't fail to notice his sun-kissed skin and the rather prominent bulge in Carl's shorts.

Mad at him, remember?

Adam did his best to hold on to the anger at Carl for fucking off the week before and leaving Adam to deal with the fallout by himself. He'd been gutted to go into the kitchen and be told Carl had left for the afternoon. For some reason, Adam thought Carl would want to console Adam, take care of him. What he'd read up about Doms and Daddies alike was that they took care of their sub or boy. It was a little shocking Carl didn't want to do that.

Resigned and unhappy, Adam had kept out of Carl's way, cancelling their play date. He'd been unable to work up any enthusiasm, given that what Adam thought was happening between them was completely different for Carl.

Adam jerked, as Carl's fingers gripped his hand, making him focus.

"Are you going to answer me?"

His body quivered in reaction to Carl's sexy undertone. Adam yanked his hand out of Carl's grip. "I was at work, you moron," Adam said, bending and snatching up his keys. Doing his best to ignore the murderous scowl on Carl's face, he attempted to unlock his front door with trembling fingers. His keys rattled in the ominous silence.

He let out a breath as he pushed the door open, hoping to make a quick getaway. He spun and took hold of the door to shut it. Carl's massive size-twelve feet blocked the way.

Adam scowled. "What? Seriously, I'm tired. I've had a hectic weekend and a busy day. I'm not in the mood for your kinky ga—"

He didn't get the chance to finish as Carl pushed Adam into the hall. Adam narrowed his eyes on the now closed front door and the man leaning against it. "Can't you take a hint? I said I wasn't interested," Adam snarled. He jutted out his chin and pouted his lips.

Chapter Twelve

Carl

CARL'S LIPS CURLED UP AS HE SNARLED, "WHERE THE HELL HAVE YOU been?"

Adam's eventual response and name-calling had him seeing red. He predicted Adam's next move. When the door was unlocked, he shoved a foot through to make sure it couldn't be slammed in his face.

There was no way he was leaving without answers. Carl stepped inside and shut the door at his back. Leaning against it, he contemplated his behaviour and the frustrations of the last few days, which had led to this moment.

He had been sitting in his truck outside Adam's flat tonight, for the third night in a row. His mind was a rampaging mess, with one question swirling around on repeat. Where the fuck was Adam?

He'd come over Sunday, hoping to talk, but there hadn't been any sign of Adam. So he'd sat and waited, and waited, and waited some more. He'd given up after more hours than he cared to count. He'd barely resisted texting Adam, demanding to know where he was.

He'd returned after work Monday, only to find himself in the same situation. Adam's flat sat in darkness, with no sign of life. His mind whirring with possibilities, he'd picked up his phone, but it was dead. He'd left his charger at work. Carl sat with no means to contact Adam and ask where he was. He'd left at stupid o'clock and had come back early this morning, after very little sleep, in the hopes of catching Adam before he went to work. The need to see Adam made Carl's insides jump all over the place. It only worsened when, again, there was no sign of Adam.

Carl had no memory of the drive back to his house. His head was full of why he'd never bothered to talk about what was going on in Adam's personal life. He was at a loss as to what Adam would do or where he'd go on his days off, and he'd wasted the day, driving himself around the bend with thoughts of what Adam could be getting up to. All Carl had achieved was a banging head and a driving need to set Adam straight about what was going on between them. Carl had planned to apologise for the thoughtlessness and hoped that would appease Adam.

He had used the separation to go over their run-in and what he'd done or not done in Adam's eyes. It had been a hard pill to swallow, realising Adam was right. They might not have a traditional Dom/sub relationship, but they had the dynamic of one. The months of weekly play dates had developed into more. Not that Carl liked to think too hard about that. Or the number of months he'd been monogamous, not even having a play date at the club.

The introduction the month before of a list of things Adam wanted to try had got Carl's hopes up that maybe there was a chance Adam would be more open to the lifestyle. Carl was convinced that the debacle at work had trampled that hope right into the ground. All because his anger had got the better of him and he'd been blind to his boy's needs. The whole situation was out of his comfort zone and was enough to make his blood run cold.

When he'd explained what had transpired to Nathan while having yet another sparring match, Nathan was only too keen to point out the obvious to Carl while pummelling him into the ground. Anger was a wasted emotion, and it had no place in his BDSM lifestyle. Yet one glimpse of the guy manhandling Adam, and Carl had been consumed by a murderous rage. A rage so strong he was lucky he'd got out of the building without doing something that he could have got arrested for.

The tension mounted as neither spoke. Adam's tapping foot and narrowed stare spoke volumes. Carl tried to remember whether there was a back door to the flat. There was a chance Adam would try to make a run for it. If he did do a runner—not that it wouldn't be fun to play a game of chase—but Carl wanted to be ready.

No longer happy to stay silent, Carl spoke softly, but with a hint of steel threaded through his voice, "I won't ask you again. Where have you been for the last couple of nights?" Carl watched for Adam's reaction and was stunned by the sudden flood of tears filling his eyes as he crumpled towards the stairs behind him.

Carl dashed forward, and his heart raced as he just managed to catch Adam before he landed. His nostrils flared at the subtle scent of Adam's aftershave and musky sweat. Arms bulging under Adam's dead weight, he shifted and concentrated on getting a better grip. He lifted Adam up and slid his forearm under Adam's legs while the other cradled his shoulders.

The sound of sniffling caused a sliver of panic to roll up his spine and his muscles to tighten. *Please don't do this to me, please.* He pleaded silently but to no avail. It would seem, Adam couldn't read his mind and buried his head into Carl's chest, dampening his T-shirt with soul-searing, racking sobs.

Carl scurried down the hall to the lounge, doing his best not to bang Adam off the walls. He flicked on the tall lamp by the door. Eyeing the room, now bathed in soft light, he shuddered. The room never failed to give him the heebie-jeebies; the colour choices on the walls were horrendous. The previous owner had gone with vibrant pink, dark greens, and black. Adam's choice of black leather and chequerboard patterns fit the décor, believe it or not.

He opted for the chequer-patterned, two-seater sofa facing the bay window, and sat down on the uncomfortable couch. The moment he did, Adam snuggled right into him and wept in earnest.

He glanced at the top of Adam's blond-brownish hair, his eyes growing bigger by the second. His hands lifted and hovered over Adam's trembling back. *What the hell am I supposed to do?*

Tentatively, he patted Adam's back. At a loss for words, he murmured nonsense. His cheeks heated, grateful they were alone, so no one could listen to him.

"Tell me what's wrong," he encouraged, his hands more confident as they stroked soothingly.

When Adam's head lifted, showing his swollen red eyes and puffy, cherry-red lips, Carl had to swallow hard past the lump in his throat. "The woman who is more of a mother to me than my own… is… dying," Adam hiccupped, resuming his sobbing.

Not sure what to say to that or even if he should ask questions, he chose to hug Adam closer and continue to rub circles over his back.

Adam's weight pressed against him. The reassurance of holding Adam and knowing he was safe allowed the tension of the last few days to melt away. He ignored the sense of completeness that filled him at just sitting quietly and cuddling when he'd never been of a mind to do that with anyone else before.

Every day, Adam taught Carl something else about himself. A resigned sigh escaped before he could stop it. He pushed aside his own anxiety, knowing now was not the time to analyse what was going on between them.

He gently held Adam, rocking him, listening to the decreasing sounds of his sniffles and sobs.

Bleary-eyed, Carl lifted the last box of meat onto the counter, waving off the delivery guy. He waited till the man was out the door before letting loose a string of curse words. Rubbing at his lower back, he grumbled loudly. When he'd stepped into the restaurant an hour earlier, his back had been complaining bitterly. Now the fucker ached worse than a toothache.

He couldn't believe he'd fallen asleep with Adam on that Godawful uncomfortable sofa. He had woken to find his boy draped over him like a human blanket. Uncomfortably hot and with a body that had been stiffer than a surfboard, he'd had to crawl off the couch.

His hands fell away from his back when rubbing made no difference. He eyed the boxes. Boxes he was well aware weren't going to move themselves. He ground his teeth together, lifted a couple, and took the few steps to the walk-in, stainless steel fridge. Sweat beaded his upper lip, and the muscles in his back protested.

To take his mind off his aching back, he recalled how peaceful Adam had been with his nose stuck in the pillow he had used, a small smile curving his plump lips. It had taken all of his willpower to leave. Only the thought of having to explain why he'd not been there to receive their planned meat delivery got him out of the house. He'd found a scrap of paper and left Adam a note pinned to his front door so he wouldn't miss it.

He had hardly had time to get home, shower, and change before he'd needed to get back in his truck and hightail to the restaurant, and now he was paying for it. The lack of stretching out or a caffeine fix made him wonder if he was going to survive the day.

He rolled his shoulders and hefted up the next two boxes. He clamped his lips together, praying he'd be able to get a caffeine fix and soon.

Two hours later, he stood next to the eight-ringed gas burner, seasoning the sauce in the pot. His attention was not on the task at hand at all but rather on Adam, who'd bustled into the kitchen a few minutes earlier. The tentative smile he offered before heading to Seb's office left Carl flustered.

His flushed and overheated skin was, as far as he was concerned, down to the steam coming from the pots on the stove. How could it be anything else? He was over forty and not some bloody teenager swooning over a pop idol.

He eyed the sauce, shaking his head.

He shouted to Billy, "Can you check this. I'm trying something new." The discussion around his seasoning of the sauce distracted him from mooning like a lovesick fool over Adam. Moments later, Carl stared yet again through the glass office window. Adam showed no signs of leaving any time soon.

He rubbed at the back of his tense neck, his gaze fixed on Adam's short, highlighted hair, which was cut and styled to perfection. His angelic face beamed at Seb. The dark circles from the previous night were significantly less today, and for some reason, Carl hoped that was because of him. His gaze swept down Adam's lean, corded body. A body he had slowly been teaching to love the darker side of his life.

He'd twice mentioned in passing to Adam about piercing his nipples. The thought of tiny hoops hiding under Adam's tailored outfits was enough to cause Carl's cock to twitch in agreement. His eyes lingered on how Adam's plump arse filled the taupe-coloured drainpipe trousers. The tailored cream shirt fitted like a glove. The jacket, which no doubt matched the trousers, would be hanging on the back of Adam's chair in reception as was his habit when there were no patrons in the restaurant.

A conversation suddenly popped into his mind about Adam's flat. Carl's brows drew together. The casual comment about how Adam had bought the apartment hadn't registered at the time. Carl calculated its cost in relation to where it was situated in London. His eyes widened before they narrowed on Adam, giving his clothes and shoes a closer inspection. Carl knew quality, and Adam's outfit screamed it.

He considered what Adam's salary was, and though it was good, it wasn't enough to afford a flat in Notting Hill and designer clothes.

"Chef, you okay? You've been staring into space for the last five minutes," Billy asked, concern lacing his voice.

Carl brushed off the concern. "Yeah, I'm fine." He paused, trying to come up with a valid excuse for standing like the moron Adam had called him the night before. "I was thinking about what could be added to make this smoother to the palette." Happy he'd come up with something valid to excuse his behaviour, he averted his flushed face.

The reminder of Adam's cheek the night before had him chewing over a suitable punishment to dole out. His eyes gleamed with speculation. Tugging at his lower lip, he considered the possibilities. Over the last few months, since the night he'd used the paddle on Adam, he'd taken to adding a few extra things to his gym bag.

He eyed the locker room door and wondered if he'd have time to get to his bag and find the perfect toy to make Adam beg. Not overthinking it, he called Billy. "Keep an eye on my sauces, please. I'm just going to the bathroom." Billy nodded, and Carl all but skipped to the locker room.

After checking the room was empty, he clicked the lock and pulled out his bag. He lifted it onto the bench in the middle of the room and rooted through it. His hand landed on a small anal hook. The small metal ball at the tip was not big enough to cause Adam a problem. There were two strands of metal chain attached to the end, which were long enough to go up a person's back and over the shoulders. This allowed the two clips on the other end to attach to the wearer's nipples.

His fingers stroked the cool metal. Would this be too much? An evil glint came into his eyes, remembering Adam's behaviour before his breakdown. Carl understood that Adam had been upset, but he still needed to understand where the line was. He'd most definitely crossed it when he'd called Carl a moron.

He chuckled gleefully, pocketing his toy along with a couple of small packets of lube. He tidied his bag away and strolled back into the kitchen. He glanced at Seb's office, pleased to see Adam was still in there.

When Adam walked out two minutes later, he was ready for him. "Adam, do you have a minute? I need to give you some receipts I left in my bag for the new blender I bought."

Feeling pretty smug to have been able to use a valid excuse, Carl hid his smile when Adam followed naively. The moment the door shut at Adam's back, Carl turned and stretched around him to lock the door.

Adam's widening eyes drew out the wolfish grin that Carl had kept hidden "Now, do you know what happens to cheeky boys, Adam?" The shake of his head had Carl continue while he delved into his trousers and pulled out the anal hook. He opened his palm to let Adam get a good look.

"Err, what do you think you're gonna do with that," Adam asked in a squeaky voice.

Carl sauntered forward. Sitting on the bench, he placed the toy down next to him and patted his knee. "I'm going to insert that nice little hook into your arse. Then I'm going to feed the chains up your back and attach those nice, stiff little clamps to your nipples. And you're going to let me because you'll take your punishment like a good boy."

Carl kept his gaze focused on Adam, wondering for a moment if it was a step too far. The slight hitch in Adam's breathing, flared nostrils and wide, wild eyes were enough to settle the butterflies in his stomach.

Adam's small hands moved to the rather obvious arousal tenting his trousers.

"Oh no, there will be none of that. The only one going to be touching that pretty cock is me." Without saying more, Carl held out his hand. Adam instantly lowered his hands and eagerly stepped closer to him. His head dropped in submission. Carl sucked in a breath, willing his clamouring pulse to behave. Fuck, Adam was breathtaking. He was well aware of how Adam struggled to be submissive. That action alone was enough to have Carl's heart and cock take notice.

With trembling fingers, he unbuttoned and removed Adam's shirt. Then he opened and slid Adam's trousers and briefs down his thighs. He spun Adam around, not giving him a chance to think about what was going to happen next. When he saw Adam's pert backside, Carl gave in to his baser instincts and nibbled on the pale globes of flesh. Inhaling deep Adam's clean scent, Carl took a bite. His teeth sank into the warm flesh. The sound of a mewling had him pulling back and chuckling. Adam's hips canted back and begged for more.

The urge to give in had Carl taking a calming breath before picking up the hook. The weight and feel of cool metal against the palm of his hand sent a thrill through him. Carl ripped open the lube packet with his teeth, eager to start. He squirted several drops onto the small metal ball. His fingers spread the lube over the smooth surface until it glistened under the overhead lights.

Using his feet, Carl spread Adam's legs as far as they would go. "Bend forward, boy, and put your hands on your shins." Not expecting a response, Carl encouraged Adam by laying his hand in the middle of his back. When Adam presented his backside, Carl groaned in appreciation of the flexing muscles.

Need washed over him in waves, wearing at his control. His teeth clenched together. He promised himself that the next time Adam presented his arse like this he would fuck him into the next week. He inhaled, using his free hand to pull apart Adam's cheeks, revealing his hairless pink pucker. Carl leant forward and swiped his tongue down Adam's crease, breathing in his musky scent. He pulled back and swallowed. "You are so yummy, Sugar Lips. In the not too distant future, I'm going to spend hours and hours devouring your sweet hole," he said huskily.

The hook gleamed as he teased Adam before easing it past his tight rim. The slight noise as it popped past the muscle was drowned out by Adam's long moan. Breathless whimpers followed and tortured Carl. His cock pulsed and throbbed with the need to replace the hook. He gave a resigned sigh and slid the hook deeper, not stopping until it was buried deep in Adam's arse. "Stand up carefully, Sugar Lips. It's gonna feel a little weird as the weight drops."

"Oh… oh… oh… my God. How am I supposed… to work… withthisinsideme," Adam panted breathlessly.

"It won't be for long." Carl sniggered. "Because once I attach the sharp-toothed nipple clamps, you'll be begging to come."

93

Adam's wail of distress was music to Carl's ears. An evil grin spread over his face as he stood and slipped the chains over Adam's shoulders. The chains sparkled as if threaded with hundreds of tiny diamonds. He stepped around Adam and admired how they glowed against his golden skin. Adam's pink rosebud nipples peaked almost in expectation of what was to come. Adam's body might be on board, but he wasn't so sure about Adam's head. Was he going to enjoy the initial sharp bite of pain?

They'd soon find out. "Take a breath." When he did, Carl placed the nipple clamps simultaneously on each erect nipple. Adam's howl and hip jerk, followed by several loud curses, were enough to have Carl want to forget his plan and give in to his boy.

He clenched his fists at his sides, working on keeping himself from pouncing. Adam undulated, his body jiggling. Carl was sure it was to make the ball inside Adam's channel rub on his prostate.

He lifted Adam's shirt. "You, Sugar Lips, need to take it easy, or else you'll end up with another punishment for coming when you don't have permission." He issued the threat while redressing Adam. He buttoned up the shirt, needing to cover Adam's adorned nipples before he forgot himself. He couldn't resist one final touch and brushed his fingertips over Adam's swollen bubs through the soft cotton.

Adam's hips canted forward. "Pleaseeeee… I… I need you."

The breathy moan, heaving chest, and hand moving towards the arousal in his trousers made him ponder whether Adam would last longer than five minutes.

He lifted Adam's chin and stared into his desire-laden, heavy-lidded eyes. "Can you do this for me? Can you hold on for one hour and make me proud, boy?" The word "boy" hung in the air.

The reference pulled him up short. This new dynamic was not something he was ready to analyse. Even when his heart beat crazily against his ribs, Carl worked to keep his emotions in check. His body derailed his thoughts. The painful throb between his thighs increased with Adam's needy expression and dazed nod of agreement.

He took a faltering step back, his hands dropping from Adam reluctantly. "Stay here. I'll grab your jacket." He all but ran out of the locker room. The driving need to leave work and take Adam somewhere he could give his needy boy what he wanted left him shaking. For the first time, he wondered who he was actually punishing: himself or Adam. It was a close call.

Chapter Thirteen

Adam

H OVERING AROUND HIS DESK, ADAM WAITED FOR RICHIE TO ARRIVE. He was aware he shouldn't be earwigging on Carl and Seb, but there was a lot riding on Richie getting the office assistant job. He couldn't deny he was a little happy that Carl was finding fault with all the other interviewee candidates.

As far as he could see, Richie was the best candidate, and if Adam could help him with any tips or hints he'd learnt from listening in, well, what was the harm? His hands rubbed together in glee. *I'm just being a good friend.*

He chuckled on hearing Carl's voice carry while complaining bitterly about the last candidate. It was when the talk turned to the next candidate that Adam's blood boiled. His eyes flew to the partition wall when he heard Richie's name mentioned. Adam's face turned mutinous listening to Carl rudely interrupt Seb.

"He's probably a right slacker, a dropout who spent all his time bonking and drinking himself stu—"

Adam roared as his temper flared, his instinct to protect his friend taking over. He barrelled around the wall separating the reception from the main dining room, his chest heaving. He stomped to the booth where both men sat.

His temper riding him hard, he got right into Carl's face and shouted, "Don't you fucking dare say that about Richie." He jabbed at the solid wall of muscle that was Carl's chest. "How bloody dare you talk about him like that. You have no fucking clue what Richie is going through. He is neither a dropout nor a loser. His mother is dying, you dickhead." Carl's eyes widened, but Adam carried on, "Yeah, that's right. He's had no choice but to defer so he could care for her."

As the red mist cleared, he forced himself to step back. He panted, a flush of mortification heating his neck at losing his temper in front of Seb. Adam turned away before the tears gathering in his eyes could fall. He stormed back towards the door, blinking rapidly.

He cursed under his breath and halted in front of Richie. *Aww, fuckity, fuck.*

"I can see I won't need an introduction now, will I, Pipsqueak?"

Adam's lips wobbled at the defeat he could hear in his friend's voice. Adam sagged when a hand landed on his shoulder. The scent of Seb's masculine aftershave let him know who'd followed him.

"Its fine, Adam. I'll escort Richard—or is it Richie?—into the dining room for his interview."

"It's mostly Richie. It's only my mum who calls me Richard, and then it's when I've done something she disapproves of."

Adam headed to reception, trying his best not to feel guilty for the added strain he could hear in Richie's voice.

He sat behind his desk, plonking his elbows on it and resting his chin in his hands. Staring morosely at the engraved glass door, he wished he was anywhere but there. He didn't want to have to face his best friend and explain what the hell had happened.

He sighed, considering how to talk his way out of this situation. His behaviour was bound to make Seb suspicious, especially after his earlier request for Adam to go and inform Carl of the arrival of their first interviewee. There was something about Seb's expression when he'd asked that caused Adam a moment of panic. He was positive Seb had somehow figured out what was going on between him and Carl.

He groaned, remembering what had happened the previous month and how he'd barely kept it together. He had not lasted the stipulated hour. He'd caved and demanded Carl remove the hook and nipple clamps after just forty minutes.

At the time, he had been convinced Seb was going to sack him. With his mind and body in turmoil, he'd made so many mistakes. *Hell*, he'd have sacked his own arse. First he'd inadvertently called a couple by the wrong name, twice. Then to add insult to injury, he'd sat them at the wrong table, only realising his mistake when they'd received their first course. To prevent a further disaster and desperate to hide his mistake, he'd got Scott to help rearrange several tables.

Seb's face had turned dark and thunderous when he'd entered the ordinarily serene dining and found it looking like a disaster site. Seb had chewed Adam a new arsehole. Right after, Adam had scurried to the locker room. The idea of enduring another minute more was too much to bear, or so he thought.

Adam shifted uncomfortably on his stool, vivid images replaying in his mind.

His arse clenched, feeling the warmed metal ball on the end of the hook filling his channel and driving him to distraction. The nipple clamps tugged on his oversensitive nipples with every step he took, running through the kitchen to the changing room, desperate to stop the torment.

He barely made it into the room before he heard Carl ask, "What do you think you're doing in here?"

Adam whirled around. He gasped at the sharp tug on his nipples and the metal ball shifting in his backside. He panted through the pleasure and pain. "I've had enough. This is going to get me sacked." He hated how breathless and anxious he sounded.

Carl's intense stare had Adam's hands fisting at his sides. The urge to lower his eyes was too much to resist, and his lashes fluttered down to hide the desire nestled within.

"Come here."

Adam dithered, unsure whether he could cope with any additional stimuli.

"Now, boy."

His feet moved at the commanding tone. His head might not like what was going on, but his body clearly hadn't got the message. Adam silently cursed his own lack of willpower. His lower lip poked out. "What do you want? Unless it's taking these torture contraptions off me, I'm not interested."

"Is that so? Then why is your cock fighting with your trouser zip, hmmm?"

Adam chose to ignore the obvious answer. Staying quiet, he waited to see what new torment Carl was going to inflict. His body, with its need for more, warred with his common sense telling him he'd had enough. His skin felt like it had shrunk two sizes for his body. He was convinced someone had stripped it off and stuck it into the dryer on full heat, then tried to redress him in something that would fit a child rather than an adult.

He got distracted from his crazy thoughts by Carl's hot chuckle whispering past his ear. It was the only clue he had as to what was coming next. His body trembled under the heat of Carl's tongue licking his ear and his teeth nipping the fleshy lobe. The sting lasted a second before he soothed the nip with his tongue. Adam shuddered. Several more bites were delivered along his jaw, ending up at the corner of his mouth. Desperate for Carl to kiss him, Adam turned his head.

He growled in disappointment when Carl retreated instead.

"Tut, tut. You know who is in charge here, don't you, Sugar Lips? Tell me."

Adam ground his molars together, his frustration growing. His aching, over sensitised body took charge of his mouth, and he answered without thinking, "You, Daddy." His mind screamed at him to take it back immediately, no matter how right it felt to say it.

Carl froze, and Adam had his own internal meltdown. *Why did I say that? Shit, shit, buggering shit!*

His pulse skyrocketed. He'd figured out ages ago that Carl was a dominant and though he occasionally called him boy, he didn't think Carl meant anything by it.

Adam blinked. His eyes widened to the size of saucers as Carl stepped into him. His breath backed up in his lungs.

"You want a Daddy, boy? Do you want a Daddy to take care of your every need?"

Carl's breathy request had Adam nodding eagerly.

Oh, fuck, do I?

He couldn't deny he'd been turned on by both the Doms and the Daddies he'd watched on porn sites. But he'd been convinced he liked the Doms more. Yet the Daddies seemed more geared towards a caring dynamic, which Adam yearned for.

He'd realised pretty quickly he wasn't naturally submissive. His parents' behaviour towards him over the years had seen to that. It had conditioned him to be the exact opposite. Adam heaved a sigh when his body reacted negatively to where his thoughts had taken him.

When Carl's eyes narrowed, Adam's stomach tangled into knots at the possibility of twenty questions.

Carl gripped Adam's chin, forcing him to meet Carl's gaze. "I'm getting the impression there is something going on in your pretty head. We'll leave it for now, but we will be coming back to revisit what you really want. Now, as you've been such a good boy, I'll let you come." The evil glint in Carl's heated stare was enough to make Adam's arousal pulse with renewed life, especially when Carl had put a strong emphasis on the word "boy".

Adam's gaze followed Carl as he sat on the bench and beckoned him forward. Adam went willingly, his cock more than on board with what was about to happen.

His nipples throbbed at memories of the last time Carl had taken nipple clamps off him. The teeth on those clamps had been tiny compared to the ones adorning his body now. Oh, fuck. Sweat gathered on his upper lip at the thought of the pain. Carl unbuttoned his shirt.

He trembled at the sensation of the warm air caressing his exposed, sensitive tips.

"Arrrrrghhhhhh," Adam ground out through his clenched teeth. His whole body pulsed and withered. Wetness soaked through his trousers as Carl mercilessly tugged the clamps off his nipples. "Oh, fuck... noooooo... make... itstop," Adam cried. The flood of sensations short-circuited his brain, and his

cock ached and thrummed in extreme pleasure as it released pulse after pulse of cum.

Adam's channel clenched and released several times, trying to expel the hook. His knees gave out, and he collapsed forward onto Carl, a panting, quivering mess.

Adam cursed his vivid imagination when he heard the door rattle open in front of him, bringing him back to his senses. He gave his lap a look of disgust before he made his mouth lift into a pleasant, welcoming smile. "Welcome to La Trattoria Di Amore." All the while he was talking to the beautiful couple in front of him, he conjured up the most disgusting things he could think of to make his body behave.

The couple took the seat Adam offered them on the brown leather sofas, which had been placed in reception for customers who needed to wait a few minutes for their table. He got them settled before hurrying into the dining room.

He explained to Carl and Seb that they needed to vacate the dining room for the customers. It was only then he realised his daydreaming meant he had no clue what had happened during Richie's interview. He offered a bright smile to Richie and swept his gaze over both men, trying to gauge if it had gone well.

When Seb talked about filling in paperwork and guided Richie towards the kitchen, Adam waited till they were out of sight before giving a fist pump and bum wiggle. He skipped with excitement to find the wait staff finishing the lunch setup, already thinking about how great it was going to be to work with his best friend.

Fuckity fuck! He hesitated before opening the door to the little staff room where the guys had their break. The visit with Marian and her lawyer washed away the buzz of excitement. How was Adam going to keep secrets from Richie if they were such in close quarters? *I never thought about that, did I?*

Richie knew Adam better than anyone, and they'd never kept secrets from each other.

Yeah, right!

"Oh, shut up, this is different," he mumbled, chewing his lower lip between his teeth. Richie's ability to read Adam made it nigh on impossible to hide anything from him. He released a groan at his misfortune and his inability to keep anything secret. *I'm fucked, big time.*

The urge to complain was squashed like a bug when he reminded himself that Richie needed this job.

Adam opened the door and stepped into the room, smiling at the guys scattered about lounging on seats. "The dining room is all yours, guys."

The five men glanced his way before they got up and cleared the remnants of the meal left on the table. They gathered up their stuff while they bantered good-naturedly with each other. It never failed to surprise Adam how Seb liked to hire cute gay waiters. They had been with Seb for years. And though Seb never discussed his personal life or his sexuality, Adam felt his choices reflected his own circumstances. Though he kept that thought to himself.

The uniform of form-fitting black trousers, vibrant maroon shirts, and black waistcoats showed off their trim figures. None of the men were above five foot five. Adam was pulled from his observations by Scott addressing him. Scott, who he would say was his closest friend at work, had the weirdest eyes Adam had ever seen. They almost appeared colourless, the grey was so pale. They gave him an ethereal appearance, especially when you added to the mix his jet black hair and milk bottle white skin, which never seemed to tan. Scott went a little pink and then would return to his usual lily-white complexion.

Adam often wondered if he'd like to be that white. His skin had a tendency to tan the moment it was exposed to the sun, always giving him a sun-kissed look he quite liked. And he was vain enough to acknowledge that Carl seemed to like it too, judging by the amount of time he spent caressing it.

"Adam, are you planning on coming out on Sunday? You missed the last two nights out on the bang. It's not like you unless you have a new boyfriend." Scott wagged his dark brows, fluttering his long eyelashes.

Adam blushed. *If they only knew!*

Their boss's clause of not dating co-workers had been the topic of many discussions on the nights out. Nights Adam arranged as a monthly catch-up and get-to-know-your-colleagues-type situation. After some staff left and complained about being moved between the different sites, he'd suggested it as part of a staff incentive to Seb, with him paying every third month as a kind of bonus. They'd initiated the nights out about a year ago, picking Sunday when all the restaurants were closed.

It had started out with just a few staff at first, but now it was a big occasion. The staff from all three restaurants attended. The usual was a meal out and then clubbing. It allowed everyone to get to know each other and stopped there being any anxiety transitioning between sites when staff needed to switch venues to help out at short notice.

The reason for his non-attendance at the last two nights out was not common knowledge.

"Scott." He paused, considering how to explain about Marian. He'd never clarified about his personal home situation, more from embarrassment than anything. His family owned hotels worldwide and were always on the local news. He couldn't escape their presence outside of work, but he did his best to keep it out of his work life. "My best friend, Richie… has a personal type situation happening that's real crap… so I'm spending my days off with him," he hiccuped the last part.

Scott nearly bowled Adam over when he bounded over, hugging him tightly. That's what he loved about Scott. He wasn't a man of many words, but he could give you the best hugs that conveyed exactly the right amount of support. Adam held on for a minute, inhaling his sweet scent, before stepping back, swallowing the ball that had lodged in his throat.

"You know you smell of sugary sweets, right." He chuckled wetly.

"Yeah, I know," Scott said with a shrug. "Who can resist all the cakey goodness that Carl creates." Several catcalls and some good-natured ribbing followed them as they headed out to work.

Adam sucked in a sob and walked into the dining room.

The day he'd applied for the job was, to his mind, the best decision of his life besides befriending Richie. Uneasiness swam past the happiness at what he knew was coming his way. He shook off the melancholy that wanted to trample him like a pack of wild horses.

A smile plastered on his face, Adam sauntered back to reception.

Chapter Fourteen

Carl

CARL LOOKED IN THE SHOP WINDOW, SEARCHING THE COLOURFUL array of gleaming gifts displayed. He hardly noticed the bitter cold biting at his bare face as waves of panic tried to choke the life out of him. He was sweating bullets. He shoved his clammy hands deep into his old donkey jacket pockets and hunched in despair.

He grumbled to himself and glared at the bright, sparkly window as though it were to blame for him standing outside it.

When he'd left Adam's warm bed that morning, he had been smugly satisfied after their night of debauchery. Before leaving for work, Adam would have put on the brand-new coffee machine he'd bought. He'd complained about Adam's lack of coffee maker just a few weeks earlier, only to find one in the kitchen the next day. Carl had blithely gone in search of a mug of steaming consciousness.

A smile spread across his face, but it faltered when he remembered what had got him out of the house. On the way to the kitchen, he'd paused outside the lounge room door, intrigued by the scent wafting from inside. The night before, he'd been so late arriving, they'd headed straight for the bedroom. His need to get Adam naked was his priority. So he'd stuck his head around the door, and that's when his troubles had started.

Santa's grotto had nothing on Adam's over-the-top homage to Christmas. He still recalled his laughter at seeing the decorated room.

Every surface, including the carpet and walls, was covered with something related to the season.

The scent of pine had drawn his attention to the giant Christmas tree sitting in the front window. The floor underneath was stacked with more than forty presents. Amused at first, he'd strolled over and glanced at several of the labels, thinking they were either for Adam or gifts for his family.

Imagine his surprise when they all contained his name, every blasted one of them. He'd all but run back upstairs as if his arse was on fire. He was grateful Adam wasn't there, or he might have witnessed his massive panic attack. He'd hyperventilated, he was ashamed to say, and his legs had given way, forcing him to sit on the bed.

It was only then that he'd calculated how long they'd been having their weekly play dates. Play dates that sometimes didn't involve any play at all and were more like cuddle dates while watching movies and eating crap. When he'd considered how many of those types of date he'd had in the last six weeks, since Richie's mother had died, Carl's heart trembled.

He'd not been in the restaurant when Adam had received the call from Richie, so he had been unaware something had happened until after he returned. Everyone was in a flap about Adam leaving in a tearful mess. Carl had gone in search of Liam, the waiter who on occasion stepped into Adam's role, to find out what was going on. The real surprise had been how fiercely he needed to go and make sure Adam knew he was there for him. It floored him. But he'd been thwarted by a full restaurant and Billy on a day off, so had no choice but to stay at work.

In all the years he'd worked as a chef he'd never once resented it, until then. Being unable to do what his heart craved was devastating. Calling Adam resulted in no answer, so he had left a voice message and then sent a text, wanting Adam to know he was there in spirit, if nothing else.

He'd waited impatiently till the end of service, asking his staff to finish off. He had rushed to Adam's, only to find his house empty. As he didn't know Richie's address and didn't have a valid excuse to ask Seb for it, he'd been left to deal with the blistering emotions that threatened his normal composure all by himself. Not being able to support Adam when he needed it most left him feeling more impotent than he'd ever felt in his life.

This morning, legs shaking as he sat on the bed, he had taken stock for the first time in months, and that reality scared the bejesus out of him. Adam had become the centre of his world, quietly filling a space in his heart Carl didn't even know was empty. He couldn't think of a life without Adam in it. The months of play dates had bled into so much more. And now, nearly a year later, Carl realised he'd made a huge error in judgement.

He remembered all the broken promises he'd made with himself to talk to Adam about the lifestyle. No matter how many times he'd promised himself he'd open up and explain his connection to the BDSM community and his club, he'd found ways to avoid it. He wasn't sure if it was to do with the number of times Adam slipped the honorific "Daddy" into their play. He wasn't convinced Adam was even aware he did it. Usually it occurred when he was in such a state of arousal Carl was pretty sure Adam couldn't even remember his own name, never mind what was coming out of his mouth.

That begged the question, why hadn't he stopped him? The warm, lovey-dovey feelings that accompanied the term were not something Carl was used to in relationships. That alone should have been a warning bell, and if he was honest, he'd heard it but chosen to ignore it.

Like I can overlook how many times I call him boy or how I see Adam as my boy and not my sub.

"Oh, shut up," he mumbled, glancing around to see if anyone was paying any attention to him. He sighed, gazing back at the gleaming window.

Shit on a stick.

He liked, *no*, he loved the feelings Adam evoked. And the Dom

Daddy persona was something he was growing to relish, though not something he'd ever considered. He'd always enjoyed the darker side of BDSM. His innate understanding of a sub's needs and the fact that they are not dissimilar to those of a boy had him tuning in to Adam's.

Though Adam loved a little pain and some aspects of play with him, he shied away from the more hardcore parts that Carl loved. The submissive aspect of the dynamic was a significant part of BDSM for him, and Adam rebelled against it. He wondered if Adam's avoidance of talking about his family was part of the reason he fought against being submissive. There was something there, but he couldn't get to the root of it.

In reality, they were both tiptoeing around each other, not stepping outside the invisible boundaries they had inadvertently created by keeping their relationship to themselves. And it was something that needed to change, but how?

No closer to finding a solution, he'd forgone his coffee and got dressed, with thoughts of Adam and Christmas crowding his mind. Now, several hours later, bagless and frightened he wouldn't find a gift, he stared at the jewellery in the bright window. He examined the sparkling items, trying to recall what Adam liked. His eyes landed on the tiny platinum hoop earrings, and his pulse skipped a beat as he imagined what they'd look like attached to Adam's nipples.

Mind made up, Carl trudged through the few inches of wet sludge to push open the door to the high-end jewellery shop. As he stepped in, a wall of warm, perfumed air hit him, and he let the heat soak into his frozen body. He warily eyed the carpet beneath his feet. The rose gold darkened as his dirty boots sunk into the deep plush pile.

He glanced cautiously at sales assistants, a shudder rippling up his body. He hated these types of places. They made him feel self-conscious of his size and demeanour. He tried to shrug off the urge to turn and run. Unbuttoning his coat, Carl nodded to the bored security guard.

The place smelled of money. He reluctantly stepped up to the busy counter. The gleaming glass cabinets were full of expensive jewellery that would make your wallet cry for mercy. The anorexic-looking sales assistants were all dressed in the same form-fitting, above-the-knee, cherry-red skirts, and floaty, cream blouses. The five-inch heels made him wonder how they managed to stand for eight hours and keep a smile on their faces. He glanced at the sullen-looking sales assistant who was free, and winced. *Smiley. In your dreams, matey boy.*

He blew out a noisy breath, stepping towards the dour-faced woman who gave him the heebie-jeebies. She looked down her pointy nose at him, which was a feat in itself, considering he was probably a good eight inches taller than her.

He could tell by the dismissive way she eyed his clothing that she found him wanting, but he refused to show that he was intimidated. He knew if she got a look at the top line of his bank account, she would be all over him like a bad rash, so he supposed he should be thankful for small mercies.

Stealing a breath, he stood to his full height. He offered her his best "don't mess with me" grin. "Can you help me," he asked sugary sweet, making sure to tower over her so she'd have to look up rather than stare down her nose at him.

"Yes, sir, what can I do for you today?"

Though the response was pleasant enough, her eyes were saying "go away, you heathen" as clear as day.

After the shitty morning he'd had, he really wasn't in the mood to be fucked with, so he got straight to the point. "I wish to look at the platinum hoops in the window."

Her little gasp and eyes darting to the security guard got his back up. He wasn't stupid. The silly cow was acting like he was going to rob the place. *Fucksake!!*

He couldn't resist and clicked his fingers in her face. "I don't have all day." He struggled not to laugh when she nearly jumped out of her Jimmy Choos. Sending him daggers, she said nothing as she rounded the counter and glided to the window. The urge to wind her up just a little got the better of him.

He shouted loudly after her, "Oh, and the bracelet with the cute charms that interlock. I'll look at that as well." This time he didn't hold in the laughter when her back went rigid and she threw a rather alarmed look in his direction.

When she came back with the trays of jewellery, Carl let her off the hook and got to the business of considering what he wanted. His mother had a thing for charm bracelets, and this one was good. You added the charms into the band so nothing dangled down.

He picked up the three bracelets and ignored the saleswoman clucking under her tongue when he brushed the metal with his fingerprints. His eyes narrowed on the rose gold bracelet. Adam would love the colour. Carl's lips pursed.

Sod it.

Not overthinking it, he picked several charms and two bracelets, one for his mum and the other for Adam. Carl also bought the earrings. His next stop would be to his tattoo parlour to make an appointment for Adam to get his nipples pierced.

"I'll take all these, please," Carl said, paying the woman no mind.

Lost in thoughts of how sexy Adam was going to look wearing the jewellery, Carl missed what the nasal woman had said about the total. "Sorry, what did you say," he asked.

"I said that will be two thousand seven hundred and thirty pounds, sir."

Her tone spoke volumes. She clearly thought he couldn't afford it when he'd asked her to repeat herself. A broad smile slid over his face. Pulling out his wallet, he quickly calculated if he had enough cash. He'd only been to the bank the day before. His habit of keeping a chunk of money in his wallet for "just in case" moments was a blessing.

He counted out the fifty-pound notes, feeling a level of satisfaction as her eyes widened and her face flushed to match her skirt. "There, I think you'll find that's correct." He offered her the cash, not waiting to see what she'd do. He snatched the bag up off the counter and strolled out the shop. His euphoric mood lasted all of about ten seconds when he got outside and remembered how many gifts were lying under Adam's tree.

His breath ghosted the air as he huffed and barrelled down the street. People jumped out of his way as he hunted the shop windows. He was desperate for something to catch his eye, praying for more inspiration than the two gifts he'd bought.

Laden down with several heavy bags, Carl struggled to hold on to them while he rummaged in his coat pocket for the truck's key fob. He unlocked the cab and placed the bags onto the back seat. He grinned at the pile of bags. He climbed in and started the engine, relishing being out of the bitter cold as the heat hit his face.

Pulling out into the traffic, he wondered if he should go home first or go to Adam's?

He checked the time, and seeing that Adam wouldn't be home for another couple of hours, he headed home. He drove straight into his garage and used his remote to shut the door behind him before climbing out and grabbing his shopping. With his arms full of bags, he walked through his garage into the kitchen.

Inside, he flipped on the overhead lights, and brightness filled the dim kitchen. He plonked his bags down, then headed for the massive triple door fridge, his thoughts on getting a drink. After enduring the trauma of Christmas shopping, he deserved one.

Fancying a crisp and fruity wine, Carl opened the side that held his wine and beer, selecting a bottle of Orvertio. He went to the large glass-fronted cabinets down the left side of his bespoke kitchen and grabbed a wine glass. As he placed the wine bottle and glass on the countertop, he noticed just how dusty it was.

He glanced around his self-designed kitchen. Layers of dust covered every uncluttered surface. The oak and glass combination he'd used in the design hid nothing. It wasn't something he'd considered when he'd gone for oak-framed cabinets with glass doors; not that he regretted it. Far from it. He loved the simple design.

The chunky cabinets seemed more refined with the glass fronts. The carpenter had worried about seeing inside the cupboards that it would make the room feel cluttered. He'd argued there'd never be any clutter, so what was there to worry about?

He liked order in his kitchen. And that was obvious. Everything had a place, and though some thought it was a little anal, the chef in him demanded it. What had Adam made of it all?

His eyes widened. He chewed his lower lip between his teeth. His mind searched for when Adam had spent any time in his home. He came up blank.

Well, shit.

How the hell have I not noticed this?

That might be because I've been too interested in getting Adam naked and tied up in pretty knots.

The inner voice had his body warming to pictures of Adam tied to his large bed. The sound of the glass he was still holding hitting the oak counter startled him. He shut down his thoughts. How was he going to rectify this?

He pondered while pouring a glass of wine. He leant back against the counter and eyed the shopping bags as he sipped at his wine. The flavour burst over his tongue, and he hummed in pleasure. An idea formed.

Carl placed the glass down, and swung towards the fridge, and opened the food section. He grumbled at the empty shelves. Next he opened the freezer door. A smile lit his face as he snatched out various tubs and checked the labels. He placed three back, keeping out the other three, then headed to his oven. It was a massive thing, taking up a third of the far wall, but he loved it. He set the temperature and decanted the food from the tubs into his trays before placing it into the oven.

He glanced about for his coat, only then realising he'd yet to take it off. Sniggering at himself, he delved into his pocket and took out his phone. He sent Adam a text.

Sugar Lips, you want to come to mine for dinner this evening? C

He dropped his phone on the counter, stripped off his coat, and went to hang it up in the hall. He'd taken no more than two steps when his phone rang. The song *Dangerous* by David Guetta filled the kitchen, the ringtone he'd picked for Adam. He moved back, dropping his coat on the counter, forgetting about the dust.

Lifting the phone, he swiped to answer. "Hey, Sugar Lips."

"Dinner, as in actual food, and not me as the menu." Adam's high-pitched screech had Carl pull the phone away from his ear. He stuck his finger into his ear, waggling it in the hopes it would help with the ringing.

Adam shouted, and Carl gingerly placed the phone back to his ear. "Please stop screeching. I like my eardrums intact." He wasn't sure whether Adam heard or not as he continued to chatter nonstop.

His amusement died when he registered what Adam was saying. "Why are you asking me to dinner? You haven't bothered before. This is so not you. We've been doing this weekly stuff for months and months, and you've never invited me to your home before. Are you planning on dumping me? Is that it? Oh my God, you are. I know you're a decent guy and wouldn't do that over the phone. Shit, it's that, isn't it?" he cried in anguish.

Carl growled. His temper grew as he realised how selfish he'd been by not inviting Adam before. "Adam, shut up. I'm not dumping you. I'm simply asking you to come to dinner. I thought it would be a nice change to do something that resembled an actual date. You know, like proper couples have." Done. He'd laid it out there. He'd made sure Adam understood that he saw them as a couple.

His breath backed up in his lungs at the sudden silence at the end of the phone.

Shit, shit, shit.

Carl felt the colour drain from his face. Had he totally misjudged Adam's perception of what they'd been doing? The silence lengthened. Carl's lungs screamed at him to take a breath. The air whistled past his lips when Adam finally responded.

"Really? You want to be my boyfriend?" The anxiety he heard in Adam's breathy response was enough to melt away any barrier he'd used to protect his heart.

He mentally slapped himself upside the head, recognising that he was done for.

Chapter Fifteen

Adam

ADAM RAN THROUGH HIS FRONT DOOR, HARDLY TAKING THE TIME TO shut out the cold behind him. He ran for the stairs, his coat going flying before he started on his suit. Adam was down to his underwear by the time he hit the bathroom, an array of clothes left in his wake.

Shimmying out of his skin-tight, pink briefs, he leant into the shower cubicle and switched it on. His heart continued to trip in his chest, racing with excitement at the prospect of a proper date with Carl.

Boyfriends.

A dreamy sigh escaped before he could stop it. The moment of fear he'd felt when Carl invited him to dinner was long gone. He just wished Carl had waited and asked towards the end of his shift. It was nigh on impossible not to let the cat out of the bag and explain why he couldn't get the massive grin off his face. Oh, he'd wanted to share, but the reality of his contract was never far from his thoughts lately.

The deeper his feelings for Carl grew, the harder it was not to shout it from the rooftops. Though he had been cautious about putting an actual label on what they'd been doing, he'd been aware for quite some time that it was more than a casual fuck buddy scenario.

When Carl increased his visits after Marian died, Adam had sat and done the maths. He'd been shocked by how oblivious he'd been to the length of time they'd been having their clandestine meetings.

Nearly a year. Fuck.

It was the longest relationship he'd ever had, regardless of its non-relationship status. *Not anymore,* the voice reminded him.

He grinned like a loon at the empty bathroom. He stepped into the shower and grabbed his body wash. Adam did his best to clean himself and hurry at the same time, which was no mean feat for him. He'd said he'd be at Carl's no later than nine-thirty pm, but he was already running a little behind.

Why was it that when I have somewhere to go, someone always tries to stop me to talk?

In this case, it had been Richie. He'd been struggling for weeks since his mum's death. Not that Adam could blame him; he'd been fraught himself. They had been muddling along together, each working to keep the other upbeat. Though he'd noticed Seb was doing his level best to support Richie, and it was kinda fun to watch how the attraction between them was growing.

Smirking, he wondered how long it would take before Richie decided to ask Seb for what he really wanted from him.

His smile dimmed as he thought about Richie's honesty when he'd talked about his need for a Daddy. Adam, on the other hand, was being a total fraidy cat. Not only had he failed to share about his relationship with Carl, but he had also failed to mention his own craving for a Daddy.

A Dom Daddy no less, *yeah.*

He had figured it out a few months back, and he was aware he'd slipped up sometimes, calling Carl Daddy. The fact that Carl never brought it up during or after the event made it harder for Adam to talk about what he wanted. Add in the lack of definition around what it was they were actually doing together, and it left him clueless as to how to broach the subject.

That won't wash as an excuse any longer.

"Oh, shut up," he muttered.

He rinsed the soap off his body, his mind circling back over the last month and a half.

Something had shifted between them six weeks earlier. Carl's one weekly visit morphed into several sleepovers, and he wasn't even sure how it had happened. The quiet support Carl offered while he grieved was invaluable and not something he'd considered he'd receive. Not that Carl was a horrible person; he wasn't.

Carl was, however, very intense when they played together, but tended to avoid personal conversations when they weren't messing about.

So what was tonight all about? And why now, out of the blue, had Carl asked him to dinner at his home?

Adam skipped out of the shower, soaking wet and dripping all over the floor. He grabbed a towel and swiped at his body half-heartedly, distracted by thoughts of what Carl constituted as a date. He wasn't sure what to envision as he went straight to his wardrobe, threw open the massive doors, and eyed his clothes.

Carl was a casual type, so he supposed dressing up would make him just look daft, and he didn't want that. He pulled out a pair of electric-blue skinny jeans that he knew made his bottom look particularly edible. In his drawers, he searched for a plain black cashmere jumper. He turned to the bed and halted. He huffed, blowing his wet fringe out of his eyes.

"Why the fuck didn't he bother making the bed?" he asked the empty room. He continued to complain, dropping his clothes on the chair nearest the bed before he straightened the navy striped sheets and matching duvet. He stepped back and glanced around the room. The dirty glasses from the night before were still on the table.

His brows rose.

Carl was typically anal about cleaning up and making sure things were tidy. So it begged the question, what was different this morning?

He caught sight of the alarm clock next to the bed and cursed. He hurried to dress and style his hair, the worry about why Carl was suddenly acting differently forgotten, and he rushed to get out of the house and to Carl's on time.

He pulled up outside the house Carl had given him directions to. He wasn't sure what he'd expected, but it definitely wasn't this modern brick and wood home. The outside of the building was illuminated to allow him to examine the exterior. His eyes widened at the triple garage that seemed more suited to a family than a single man.

Soft lights glowed in the downstairs windows, offering a cosy welcome to the contemporary, two-storey house. He hadn't really considered Carl's financial status until now, but it suddenly became apparent how well off he was. Houses in this part of London fetched well into seven figures, and he should know. His parents' home wasn't that far from Carl's.

A sigh escaped Adam's lips when he remembered the unanswered email he'd got the day before from his parents' personal assistant, Marcus. The occasional demand he received, to attend some family gathering or event, always sent him into a deep depression, so he avoided them at all costs. He hadn't seen his parents since last New Year, which had resulted in yet another epic fight, and he had hoped they'd given up on him. Sadly he was disappointed, given that they wanted him to attend their Christmas luncheon this year.

The idea of using work as an excuse had been quashed this evening by Seb. His plan to shut the restaurants for Christmas and stay open for New Year had been met with cheers from everyone bar Adam. His valid excuse for not attending what would be a painful event had flown right out the window.

Why his parents insisted Adam attend these functions, he'd never know.

This is self-inflicted crap.

He pretended not to hear the voice of reason; a voice that, for some reason, sounded an awful lot like Richie's. He hunched into his wool coat and huffed out a big breath, absently watching it fog the cold glass.

He never understood why they'd hated his sexuality with a passion that rivalled none. They despised him because they couldn't change it, and they'd made no secret of it. His teenage years had been a myriad of different therapists "to correct his deviant thoughts and behaviour." Their words, not his. Not that any of it had worked. They just didn't get that it was as vital to him as breathing. And that lack of foresight had caused a rift as wide as the Grand Canyon between them. It had, however, had one positive. It had given him a new family.

Adam's breath hitched, and grief sat like a lead weight in his stomach as he thought of Marian. She and Richie had not once judged Adam for who he was. If it wasn't for them, he wasn't sure he would have survived his teenage years. He'd spent the majority of those years hiding out at Richie's whenever he could, just to avoid his home life.

His family were one of the wealthiest in the country, yet that appeared to be the sum total of their contribution to his life: money. Love never seemed to be on their busy agenda, and then if you took into account his sexual orientation, his worth plummeted like a stock market crash, never to rise again.

Releasing a shrill screech, he bounced on his seat. The loud tapping at the window and Carl's face looming out of the darkness nearly gave him a heart attack. He clutched his clammy hands at his chest, feeling his heart hammering against his ribs.

"You planning on sitting out here all night," Carl said, loud enough for Adam to hear through the door.

He got out of the car with as much dignity as he could muster. He was sure Carl was laughing at him. "You know you could give a person a heart attack, creeping up on them like that," he said, huffing loudly.

He tried not to drool when he copped sight of Carl in his low-slung ripped sweat pants and long-sleeved fitted T-shirt that hugged every damn muscle he had. Adam turned his back on him, wishing he'd chosen another pair of trousers. He glanced down, not missing his cock clearly fighting with the fabric of his skinny jeans.

The writing was already on the wall, so he ignored his growing problem and stretched across the passenger seat to retrieve the bags he'd brought with him. He did his level best not to think about stripping Carl out of his clothes and licking every gorgeous inch of him.

His trembling fingers grabbed the bags off the seat. Then he shoved the bags to Carl. "Here, do something useful." He gave an undignified snort at the "humph" Carl let loose as he felt the weight of the plastic bags.

"Come on, big boy. I know those muscles aren't just for show."

"Yeah, but they prefer to be lifting and throwing you around." Carl paused, poking his nose into the bags. "Not carting wine, beer, sweets, desserts, crisps, and snacks. What the fuck, Adam? Are you worried that I won't be able to feed you," he asked indignantly.

Adam grinned back at Carl's flustered, flushed face. "Nope, not at all. But I was taught you don't go to a person's home empty-handed."

He shrugged, carrying on and then wishing he hadn't when his mouth ran away from him. "I know you've been spending quite a bit of time at mine, so I thought I'd bring some of your favourites in case you hadn't had a chance to shop." He was waffling, growing more and more embarrassed by the smile crossing Carl's face and lighting his dark eyes.

Adam clamped his mouth shut and stalked past Carl, nose in the air.

He made his way up the drive and to the open front door before he noticed the lack of snow on the path. He glanced around, seeing Carl was just as anal about keeping things tidy outside as he was in.

The scent coming out of the front door drew Adam inside. He sniffed up the heavenly aromas coming from somewhere inside the house and licked at his lips.

Carl stepped in behind him, crowding him. The smell of Carl's body wash competed with the fragrant food. Unsure which made his mouth water more, Adam shifted to give Carl room to get past.

"Come on. The kitchen's this way. You must be starving."

Carl didn't wait for an answer, and Adam watched his retreating back with uncertainty. His trainers moved soundlessly down the glowing wooden floor, but Adam straightened his spine and followed at a slower pace, taking his time to explore Carl's home.

The first thing he noticed was that everything gleamed and that everything was tidy, making him feel like a slob. He glanced along the hall to the couple of open doorways leading off the hall.

Pale cream walls complemented the wooden flooring. A small squat oak table sat at the bottom of the staircase. It was chunky and solid, much like its owner, with a beautiful multicoloured Caithness glass bowl sitting on it.

He glanced into the first room on his right. His eyes widened. Though modern, he couldn't get over the homely feel the room presented. The urge to go and stretch out on Carl's enormous deep brown sofas was almost irresistible. There was also more solid oak furniture, which Adam would bet his last quid was handcrafted. He caught glimpses of some pictures hanging on the walls, but he was side-tracked by the photos he spied of Carl, hanging outside the room on the wall leading upstairs.

He stepped closer to the staircase, peering up at the ones that depicted Carl's career. He craned his neck, his feet itching to go up the stairs and have a closer look at the photos of Carl when he was younger.

"What you doing, Sugar Lips." Carl's enquiry drew Adam to follow the sound of his voice.

He stepped through the doorway Carl had gone through, and stopped dead. "Oh, mother of God, your kitchen is a thing of beauty." Adam gasped in surprise.

The gleaming oak must be Carl's favourite by the amount he had already seen throughout the house. The oak shone under the spotlights, showcasing the handcrafted cupboards. The glass-fronted cabinets sparkled, and he thought about the old adverts for window cleaner. They almost blinded him with the gleam. He was almost embarrassed to think about the state of his own kitchen compared to Carl's. Everywhere he looked, he was met by polished glass and wood. Nothing was out of place, even inside the glass cupboards.

"You know no one can compete with this level of tidy, right?"

He forgot what he was saying the moment he spotted the glass wall, his feet already moving towards the back of the room. The whole of the wall was glass and had him wishing it was daylight so he could see out. "Does the glass fold open, or do they slide back on each other?" he asked excitedly. He squinted, trying to see the details of the garden, past the lights reflecting on the glass.

Living in a flat, he didn't have the option of having anything more than a patio door into the little courtyard he shared with Rupert. He signed in envy, turning back to Carl as he answered.

"They slide into the walls themselves, so it opens up the back of the house and makes the garden feel part of the room," Carl said, a rosy blush coating his cheeks.

The casual way Carl tried to pass off his home didn't match the flush spreading up his neck. Adam peered up at him, trying to figure what Carl would have to be embarrassed about. The place was spotless and immaculate. Never mind the fact that it was stunningly designed.

Adam strolled closer, tilting his chin to look at Carl, keeping his gaze locked on the bigger man's. "Did you have a hand in designing the house"—Adam waved his hand about the room—"and this kitchen? Because I have to say it's beautiful. Your eye for detail is amazing, but I bet you gave your designer a few headaches."

He sniggered at Carl's eye roll.

"Let's just say they said they'd never work with me again," Carl grumped, breaking eye contact to fiddle with the pots bubbling on the stove.

Adam let him be and went to sit on one of the tall stools that sat on the far side of the cooker, around the centre aisle, so he could watch Carl work. His stomach gurgled, and Carl chuckled.

"It will only be another minute. I just need to dish up."

Adam groaned aloud at the sight of the bubbling, meaty stew that Carl took out of the oven. It was Adam's favourite. The creamy, tangy fragrance of the red wine sauce increased the noise level of his hungry stomach. He rubbed at his belly, willing it to behave as laughter rippled out before he could stop it.

His cheeks flushed under Carl's flirty wink as he placed a full plate in front of him. Adam wanted to devour the food. It might have only been several hours since he'd eaten, but it didn't feel like it as his mouth watered. The meat looked tender. The creamy scalloped potatoes and array of colourful vegetables had him lifting his cutlery before Carl came to sit next to him.

"Fuck, I didn't even offer you a drink. Sorry," Carl said.

Adam didn't think of it so much as an apology but more of a complaint, judging by the angry tone of Carl's voice. He shrugged off the sliver of hurt, offering a bright smile. "I'll have whatever you're drinking... Oh, shit... maybe not. I'm driving..."

He wasn't sure what he'd said to cause the sour expression on Carl's face, so he shut up, not wanting to make things worse.

He didn't have to wait long to find out.

"What do you mean you're driving... I... thought... you'd be staying."

Carl's hesitation and uncertainty were things Adam wasn't used to. To reassure him, Adam jumped off the stool and launched himself onto Carl's lap, nearly upending them both.

Adam clasped his hands around Carl's neck, sinking his fingers into the silky strands of hair he found there. He tugged Carl's head down so they were nose to nose. "Of course I want to stay, silly, but you never said it was a sleepover-type date." He rubbed his nose against Carl's in a sweet Eskimo kiss. Easing back, he offered a sultry smile, speaking with a sexy drawl. "Though I might have packed an overnight bag in my boot. You know...just in case."

Adam fluttered his dark lashes and offered up his lips for a kiss. He inhaled sharply at the mysterious smile Carl gave in return. His cock thrummed in anticipation, right as his lips were claimed.

Chapter Sixteen

Carl

CARL DROVE THROUGH THE EMPTY STREETS WONDERING, NOT FOR the first time in the last week, how he'd ended up forgoing Christmas with his parents in his childhood home in Suffolk. Something he loved to do when work permitted.

With Seb and him deciding to close for Christmas, he'd pre-warned his parents he was coming home. Then Adam had spent the night at his house, and all his good intentions had flown right out the window.

He cursed his own weakness.

When Adam had stayed at his home the previous week, Carl had come to a few realisations. The two that stuck out were how selfish he'd been with Adam, not taking the time to get to know him other than on a sexual level, and the lack of discussion around expectations, boundaries, and most importantly, their contract.

Since his introduction to the BDSM community, he'd been a stickler for these. However, from the very beginning of the relationship with Adam, that had gone out the window. Why had he chosen to ignore it?

Adam is different. And so are the feelings he evokes.

Carl pursed his lips. Indicating, he switched lanes, doing his best to concentrate on the traffic with his mind full of Adam.

Adam didn't need to spell it out that he'd never be a submissive full time or that he'd be unhappy sitting at his feet. *No,* his boy wasn't built for that. He wanted someone to take care of him and give him a little extra kink in the bedroom. Adam wanted a Dom Daddy.

A year of play dates to figure that out!

Carl kept his eyes on the road, resisting the urge to roll them heavenward. *I know what I want now, so what does it matter?*

A permanent commitment. He shivered in the heated cab as the reality of that sank in. Adam had used the term boyfriends, but Carl wanted more than that. With a stomach full of butterflies, he'd come to realise that while Christmas shopping. He wanted what they'd unknowingly been building together. A life with a boy, his boy, his Adam. But not part time. He wanted a forever-type situation.

The only thing was that he didn't want to frighten Adam off. When Adam had asked him to clarify what dinner meant at his home, the term "boyfriends" seemed the least threatening. He understood that it was only the start, which would become clearer once Adam received the personalised gift he had purchased. A gift that would ensure there would be no mistaking what he wanted.

Before that first real date, he had calculated how it was going to go. Feed Adam his favourite food, ply him with wine, and then get him talking; simple. He had, however, failed to consider Adam's insecurity. After some tense moments after Adam arrived, Carl had managed to get them back on track. Or so he'd thought. He should have suspected then that things weren't going to go to design.

He'd stupidly never considered that he would have to share, to the same level he wanted Adam to. So when Adam agreed to talk about himself and then demanded the same from him, Carl had seen no way out and reluctantly agreed.

The need for several glasses of wine to get himself to calm the fuck down was the beginning of the end. What was it they said about loose lips sinking ships? *Yeah, that had been him.* Why did you have to mention the playroom in the spare bedroom? Why for Christ's sake?

Adam had acted as if he had ants in his pants the way he'd jumped up. Excitement had poured off him as he'd danced around the kitchen counter to drag Carl off his seat and show him his sacred space. Was that when shit had gone south?

Given the possibility that Adam might have been a little overwhelmed by his equipment and toys, Carl had worked to play the "whole having a playroom in his house" thing down. Then Adam had acted like it was the most normal thing in the world and demonstrated how knowledgeable he was.

His hands tightened around the steering wheel. Why had he thought Adam wouldn't do research?

They'd been playing for months, even if it erred towards the lighter side of BDSM. Paddles, nipple clamps, dildos, penis wands, cock cages, and who could forget the anal hook. He was well aware of Adam's thirst for information and how he liked to figure stuff out. Why would a trip to the darker side of life be any different? He didn't have an answer.

Recalling Adam's progress around his playroom, Carl rubbed at the back of his neck. More and more aroused with every second that passed, Carl had stood transfixed. Adam's small hands touching his toys had been too much, and before he could stop himself, Adam had been naked and tied to his paddling bench. Using a soft suede flogger to bring the blood to the surface of his skin, he had warmed Adam's backside until he'd begged to be fucked.

Yep. A total lost cause after that. I'd have agreed to anything to make my boy happy.

His defences were already lowered, but they were ripped to shreds when Adam talked so blithely about how his family had treated him as a child, as they lay curled up in bed.

He cursed till the air was blue. His heart ached for the lost boy who didn't understand why he wasn't loved. When Adam had let slip that he'd been summoned to Christmas luncheon, Carl had been totally screwed. The writing on the wall, the confession all but guaranteed, he knew he would agree to anything to protect his boy from those heartless bastards. There was no way he was going to let him face his family alone, regardless of how they might react to his presence.

He muttered half-heartedly about his own misfortune and ignored how his cock pulsed at the memories of how his boy had paid him back for his gallant offer. His knuckles whitened. He did his best to focus on the road and not the party happening in his pants.

He was relieved to pull up outside Adam's several minutes later and not have caused himself or anyone else an injury. Adam's bright blue door flung open before Carl could unbuckle his seat belt. His gaze fixed on the figure emerging from the door, carrying several bags. He gulped, his tongue suddenly feeling ten sizes too big for his mouth. He wiped at his chin, not convinced he wasn't drooling all over himself.

The three-piece suit in navy fitted Adam to perfection and showed off his willowy frame. The tapered jacket was buttoned up, and a crisp, white shirt and navy silk bow tie completed the outfit. It should have looked nerdy, but on Adam, it looked anything but.

Carl rubbed his sweaty palms down his suit trousers. He knew before he'd dressed, at Adam's request, in a suit that he'd never be able to compete. Now he realised he wasn't even in the same ballpark. Adam in a work suit was gorgeous, but this Adam was absolutely stunning and made Carl itch to claim him as his own, in every sense. The word "mine" roared inside his mind as he imagined Adam walking down the aisle dressed in something similar.

As the thought hit home, Carl stilled at the wild beating of his heart.

Marriage!

Holyfuckingshittingbuggeringhell!

His mind blanked for a second as it registered what his heart wanted. His mouth dried. *Forty-two years old and now you want the whole kit and caboodle?* Love, romance, and marriage, with a side helping of kink. *Yes, please!* And that right there was the truth. His stomach surged up, choking him for a second. He dragged in several breaths, letting this new truth take hold. *Well, I never. Holy hells fire!*

Previous visions of a life with a sub were ground to dust. In their place, a new picture formed, of his boy taking pride of place at the centre of his world. The piece of jewellery he had at home, now more than ever seemed to fit with his heart's desires. Desires that had already shown themselves. He had just been too blind to notice.

He chuckled.

I'm so fucked. Marriage for Christ's sake!

If Nathan had any clue how Adam had him wrapped around his tiny fingers, he'd never hear the last of it. And that begged the question, what to do about the club. He still hadn't mentioned it to Adam. Was discussing it now the right thing to do, or would it muddy the waters?

No closer to an answer, Carl leaned over the seat to open the door for Adam. Deep lines marred Adam's forehead, and the smile he offered didn't reach his eyes. A sense of unease unfurled inside Carl. He took the bags off Adam and placed them on the back seat.

He turned back and hefted Adam up into the truck before he could climb in. Carl ignored the grumbling at his manhandling and twisted in his seat, pulling Adam onto his lap. He held firm and lifted Adam's chin. The misery in his boy's eyes was enough for him to want to say fuck it and carry him back inside. Then he remembered how adamant Adam was about attending, after he'd explained they'd only try to make his life more difficult if he didn't go.

"Okay, this fake smile shit isn't working for me. I want to see the real you, the boy who wants to make his Daddy proud." The heat of Adam's gaze intensified the moment the word Daddy left his lips. Not wholly convinced rushing his plans was a good idea, he hesitated to see how Adam would respond. No matter how right it felt to finally express his own need, he wanted Adam to acknowledge what he wanted. He held his breath, and his gaze locked on Adam.

Blatant arousal sparked in the depths of Adam's eyes, but the stilted words forced Carl to focus. "Do you... do you mean a Daddy... or a... Dom... Daddy?"

It took a moment to register that Adam's hesitation wasn't done to separate the two terms, but that he was, in fact, asking if Carl meant a Dom Daddy. His head tilted as he looked deep into Adam's eyes. "Do you want a Dom Daddy?" Could he have his cake in effect and eat it too? Was Adam offering him a world where he didn't need to choose?

The soul-searching and a bolt of lightning that had just hit him said it didn't matter. He was happy to have Adam, no matter what option he chose.

When Adam's eyes clouded with worry as he hesitantly nodded, Carl rushed to reassure. "I would love to be your Dom Daddy."

The smile beaming up at him was hard to resist, so he didn't. He moved swiftly, giving Adam a punishing kiss, branding him as his. Pulling back, he smirked at the debauched look on Adam's face.

"Come on, the sooner we get there, the sooner we can leave," he said, gently helping Adam into his seat. As he buckled his seat belt, he made sure to tease Adam's cock with the back of his hand, then sat back, grinning at the whine of disapproval he got for stopping.

He switched the engine on and put the truck in gear. Keeping his hands occupied, he did his best to ignore the throbbing coming from between his legs. "Right, give me the directions." He listened, his eyes glued to Adam.

"Fuck, we're practically neighbours," he growled.

"Yes, Daddy. But just think how quick we can get back to your house and then play in your playroom," Adam responded, grinning from ear to ear.

As all the blood in his body decided to pool in his lap, Carl shook his head to clear his vision. He lowered his hand and pressed down hard, attempting to alleviate the painful ache.

Even if it made him desperate, he couldn't argue with his boy's logic. "You are going to pay for that with a punishment when we get home, Sugar Lips," he threatened.

He groaned at the giddy excitement displayed on Adam's face.

Yeah, that worked as a threat. Not!

He huffed out a breath, focusing on the road and willing his body to get a grip.

A while later, Adam indicated he should pull over. He stopped the truck and glanced with some trepidation at the security gate and surrounding twelve-foot wall, blocking the view of the house. "Your parents live here?" He knew it was a stupid question, but he felt the need to clarify, if only for himself.

The stilted nod he received in reply had him looking back at the house. He wasn't sure what he'd imagined, but it sure as fuck wasn't this. "What do your parents do?" A question he was sure he should have asked long before.

"They own hotels all over the world," Adam answered timidly.

Carl swivelled his head round, and he pinned Adam with a hard glare. As the dots connected and Adam's surname hit him like a sledgehammer, Carl sank back in his seat. "Holy fuck, you're not a Grainger. You're THE Grainger! Your family is one of the wealthiest in the world, and I'm only fucking finding out about this right now," Carl bellowed, flabbergasted. "Why the fuck would you need to work?"

His already thundering pulse turned into a skyrocket aiming for the moon as Adam explained. He listened to the matter-of-fact way Adam clarified how his parents put money in his bank account every month. Not because they loved him and wanted him to be happy. No, it was because they wanted to keep him out of the spotlight. To ensure none of their highfalutin friends would find out what an embarrassment he was.

His heart bled, and his hands itched to ball up and punch the fuckers in the face. Adam's teary expression was more than he could bear. He swore a promise right then and there. He'd make sure Adam knew he was loved in every way. His palms sweated at the thought of saying the words right then. His mouth dried. *Okay, maybe not quite ready to declare my feelings yet.* That didn't mean he couldn't use actions to express them, starting right now.

He released Adam's seat belt and hauled him back into his lap. He hugged him close, offering him his silent support while Adam cried into his shoulder.

He waited until Adam pulled back, his eyes red and swollen, and kissed his soft puffy lips. "We got this. You and Daddy are gonna knock them right off their perch."

Adam's wet chuckle and sparkling eyes had Carl grinning back.

"Let's go," he said, opening his door. "Hold on." He eased out of the truck with Adam hanging on. Then he lowered Adam to the floor, making sure to tease him just enough to stop the frown that was marring his beautiful face.

Adam let out an indignant snort as Carl stepped back and grabbed the bags off the back seat. "Come on, the sooner we get this over with, the quicker I can get you naked." He wagged his eyebrows and offered his empty hand to Adam.

An ominous grey sky loomed overhead as they walked towards the security gates, hand in hand, and Carl wondered if it was an omen. An hour later, he was convinced it was. The meal, though absolutely delicious and cooked to perfection, tasted like ash on his tongue. The snide comments and poisonous little darts Mr Grainger threw at Adam since they'd sat at the dining table in the ostentatious room made him sick to his stomach. His fingers clenched the cutlery as the need to stab Adam's father in the eye grew with each passing minute.

"Explain again who this man is, Adam. You say he's a chef." The disdain when he uttered the word "chef" had Carl lay down his knife, not sure whether his calm was about to be threatened, yet again.

"I have explained this, Father. Carl Bentley is a Michelin-star chef and co-owns three restaurants. He is also my boyfriend," Adam said defensively.

Carl hated the way Adam cowered under the disdainful sneer being thrown in his direction.

Fuck this.

"Do you need to see an ENT specialist?" he asked with a rapier smile, his jaw aching from the strain of keeping his voice even.

When he received a blank expression from the man who looked far too much like Adam for his liking, he went on to explain. "It's just that you have asked my Sugar Lips"—he let that hang in the air for a minute, working hard to not act on Adam's choked sob—"that very same question several times. He has explained who I am and what I am to him, three times." Carl held up his meaty fist displaying three fingers. "So I'll ask again. Do you need an ENT specialist? Because I happen to know several who frequent our restaurants" He hardly resisted the urge to laugh when Adam's father choked on the sprout he'd just popped into his mouth.

Carl turned to Adam, sitting on his right. "I think it's time we left. I'm sure I left something cooking on the stove." He knew it was a crazy thing to say, but he was past caring. The relief on his boy's face was enough of a reward.

He stood, not waiting for anyone to say anything, and pulled Adam with him.

They got to the door before Adam's father spoke. "Stop right there."

Carl flicked his head around, keeping tight hold of Adam's hand. Carl's lip curled, and he gazed at the dining table.

The delicate white lace table cloth covered with silverware, Dalton china, and crystal goblets would have made for a lovely setting for a meal, bar two things: the two other people sitting at the table. They might look all polished and shiny on the outside, but it was a veneer to hide the crappy people they were deep down. To his mind, they were the same as those people who had stained, uneven, and rotten teeth who choose to use dental cosmetics to hide them. The surface might gleam, but underneath they still had the same awfulness going on. There was no amount of cosmetics that could hide what was beneath the façade of these two arseholes.

He gave Adam's mother a passing glance, seeing her glazed, not so sober expression. He wondered if it was how she survived.

Shaking off his observations, he responded curtly, "Yes."

"You won't get a penny of his money. I've made sure to tie it all up, so he can't let his deviant behaviour ruin his life." His father sneered.

Carl took a deep breath and willed himself to keep calm. Hearing a sob, he glanced at Adam. The shaking shoulders and quiet sobs were hard to witness, but it was Adam's head lowering in defeat that tore away any vestige of hope he had of holding on to his temper. He squeezed his boy's hand and bent down to whisper in his ear, "Stay here. Daddy will be right back." The trembling fingers and tear-drenched eyes did nothing to help the situation.

He released his boy and stomped back to the table.

His heart thundered. He hauled Adam's father up by the lapels of his expensive suit, crushing the silk fabric. He towered over him, getting right in his face. "Now you listen here, you arse wipe. I couldn't give a flying fuck what you do with your money, and neither does my Sugar Lips. I have more than enough for both of us. He will want for nothing. I didn't even know about the money until today, because un-like you, I care for him for who he is." For effect, he shook the man hard, pleased when his perfect teeth rattled together. "Now if you've quite finished being a poor excuse for a human being and parent, we are leaving. Please don't bother getting back in touch unless it is to apologise and grovel to your son for his forgiveness." He finished on a snarl and threw Adam's father back into his chair. He was slightly mol-lified when the chair skidded a few feet, and Mr Grainger had to flail his arms to stop the chair from tipping over.

Carl marched to Adam, ignoring the torrent of verbal threats be-ing fired at his back. Past caring what anyone thought, he lifted his sob-bing boy into his arms and encouraged him to wrap his legs around him. Holding him close, Carl stalked out of the room and past the scurrying housekeeper, who was trying to keep up with them. With a nod of thanks when she opened the door with what looked like ap-proval lighting her eyes, Carl walked out the door.

Once they were outside, he buried his face in Adam's neck, inhal-ing his fresh scent.

He lifted his head when his pulse rate finally dropped, and he could see past the rage burning inside of him. Their eyes connected. "You'll never have to step back inside there unless it's your choice. They will never get to speak to you or treat you like that again," Carl promised.

He barely restrained his anger, and he hoped Adam realised it wasn't directed at him. When Adam snuggled wordlessly into his chest, he heaved a sigh and tightened his arms.

As he headed down the drive, his only thought was to ring his parents and thank them for being the people they were. And ask them to share their love with the one person who needed it most: his boy.

Chapter Seventeen

Adam

ADAM MADE A BEELINE FOR THE EMPTY BOOTH HE'D SPOTTED AS HE entered the club. The guys followed behind, shouting over the base of the music. Twisting his body to get past the table and into the booth, he tried not to wince as he sat down. His hand hovered over his chest, careful not to actually make contact. The offending material of his silky, fitted top abraded his nipples. He'd picked it in the hope that the satiny material wouldn't catch on the swollen tips of his pierced buds.

Who the fuck knew pierced nipples would hurt so much? Not him, that was for sure. The excitement that had reached fever pitch that morning in the shop had faded into obscurity the moment the metal pierced his flesh.

Who had he been kidding? *There is no way in hell Daddy's touching my nipples.* Not when the merest touch made the fuckers ache like a bastard. He wanted to bitch, but the one person who'd forced this on him wasn't there to complain to.

No. Carl had other plans for tonight. He had wanted to ask what they were, but Carl's closed-off expression kept him from asking. Though that hadn't stopped the questions from taking up squatters rights in his head.

The little red-and-black business card with "The Playroom" blazoned across it, which he'd inadvertently found in Carl's bedside cabinet, taunted him. The Internet search on The Playroom provided him a whole new perspective on what Carl might be doing. Two and two made four in Adam's mind, especially given his knowledge of the room in Carl's home. His insecurities ran amuck. It was as if the world's worst cleaner had got into his mind, spent hours messing about, and then left with the place looking like a bomb had hit it. The untold anxiety was enough to have Adam bouncing from happy to plain miserable. Was Carl a member of the club?

Adam sighed dejectedly, refusing to acknowledge how hurt he was that Carl wasn't being forthcoming. His mouth moved into a pout against his will as a sulk tried to take hold and ruin his night.

Stop it. Daddy is allowed to have a life away from me and keep the details of it to himself.

The disco lights danced over his wrist. Warm memories of Christmas day overshadowed his qualms. When they'd arrived at Carl's home after the disaster of Christmas lunch, he'd whipped them up some delicious treats. Neither of them had eaten much of the meal at his parents' house, and Adam was happy to let Carl distract him, and oh, boy had he.

After they'd eaten, Carl had retrieved a large children's hemp sack full of Christmas presents, with his name on it. Totally speechless, he had been at a complete loss how to react to someone going to so much effort for him, and he'd sniffled and warbled like a fool.

His parents had always got their housekeeper to shop for his presents. When he'd turned eight, they'd poo-pooed the idea he'd needed gifts and given him cheques to bank. They'd said it was a waste of effort to buy gifts that would just be tossed aside for something new the very next day. How they'd figured that out when they'd never bothered to buy him anything he could cherish he'd never understood.

Shaking off the sour thought, he allowed a smile to form as he stroked the bracelet on his wrist. He'd cried buckets over the sack, and it was only Carl's alarmed expression that had spurred him to pull himself together. The time they'd spent after, opening gifts and laughing at the silliness of some of their choices, had been the best Christmas he had ever experienced.

That being said, it didn't stop a part of his Christmas gift from giving him a reason to moan and complain. He knew damn well it was a mistake to agree to attend the monthly work night out when he'd only had the piercing done that morning. But he hadn't wanted to stay home alone, and with Carl out God knows where, he'd agreed to Scott's badgering.

Adam stroked the bracelet one last time, about to lower his wrist, when Scott shouted over the music.

"Oh, that's pretty. Did you get that as a Christmas present?"

Scott was already leaning over Theo, grabbing at Adam's wrist before he could snatch it back. He didn't respond to Scott's question, choosing instead to try and pull his arm free. Regretting it immediately, he winced and blew out a heavy breath as the movement jostled his aching nipples. A sense of dread settled in the pit of his stomach as he gently shifted in his seat, trying to shake Scott off. Scott was having none of it though, holding on tight as he twisted the bracelet this way and that, squinting to see the details.

Eyes widening in alarm, Adam choked back a sob. The charm with a heart and "boy" written in the centre of it was right there for anyone to see. His arm tensed the second Scott looked up. His expression was one of comprehension as he mouthed "boy."

Fuck. He knows what it means!

He snatched his trembling arm out of Scott's hand, pretending interest in the packed dance floor, where he could see most of the staff had fled. The very idea of dancing and someone banging into his chest made him cower.

The seat cushion shifted, and a squeal of delight from Theo drew his attention back to the booth. He looked back in time to witness Scott sliding over Theo's lap. He groaned as the dancing lights clearly captured the intent on Scott's gorgeous face. Scott's compact body was dressed all in black tonight, and Adam had a moment to wonder if he wore black because it made his eyes even more alluring.

He watched with trepidation as Scott checked that Theo wasn't paying them any attention, and then leaned in towards him.

"You don't get to pretend I didn't see that charm, Adam. Come on, we're friends. I won't say anything. Who's your Daddy?" Scott whispered excitedly, directly into his ear.

Adam couldn't help wondering if the need brimming to the surface of Scott's face was connected to him or Scott's own want for a Daddy. Not sure he wanted to go there, he sat back and rubbed at his damp ear, sucking his lower lip between his teeth. Could he trust Scott?

The excitement and genuine joy on Scott's face released some of the knots forming in his stomach. More to the point, could he trust Scott with the secret of who his Daddy was? Scott's eager, puppy-dog expression said yes.

Is my desperation to share with someone clouding my judgement?

Uncertain of the answer, he gave Scott a wary glance.

"Come on, Adam, you know you want to tell me," Scott begged.

"Listen, just hold on to your horses there, and give me a minute," Adam asked. His mind raced faster than a kid on a bike freewheeling down a steep hill with no brakes. A breach of his contract seemed silly to worry about when he wasn't blind to what was growing between Seb and his bestie, Richie. They might be dancing around each other, but it wasn't going to be long before that changed. He sensed Richie's resolve mounting.

Just thinking about Richie made him cringe at the cowardice that kept him silent. He still hadn't explained to Richie about Carl, never mind what was going to happen at the lawyers the following week. Richie's mum's lawyer, Mr Carter, had contacted him only the day before. The time to fess up was fast approaching. What the lawyer was going to reveal might leave him without a best friend. The urge was there to hide away with his Daddy and not come out till all the shit had blown over.

It's a self-induced shitstorm, so that ain't gonna happen.

He groaned at the voice of reason and the thoughts of what Carl would do when he explained all this to him. Burying his head in his hands, he glared down at his crotch when it got on board with a potential punishment.

Scott tapped on his lowered head, and he glanced up. Scott offered an apologetic smile. He was pretty sure Scott had completely misconstrued what was going on, which was confirmed when he spoke.

"It's all right. You don't need to tell me anything. I won't hold it against you, although maybe your Daddy will." Scott chuckled.

Had Daddy shown up after all? Adam spun his head around to search the busy club. His shoulders drooped when Carl wasn't there, but he quickly realised he'd made a mistake when Scott followed his gaze.

The air whistled past his teeth, and he was convinced Scott could see a flashing sign over his head declaring, *"Adam is dating a work colleague."*

The thought got stuck in his head and wouldn't let go, causing him to flush.

Scott's eyes narrowed on him. "You're dating someone from work, aren't you?" Scott shouted over the music.

Adam froze and then quickly glanced at Theo before releasing a sigh. Theo sat seemingly oblivious to the drama unfolding right next to him as his body jiggled to the music.

Scott, unaware of the shitstorm he was creating for Adam, crowded into him. "It's okay if you don't wanna talk about it. I shouldn't have blurted that shit out like that. I wouldn't thank you if you did that to me," Scott said apologetically.

Adam rubbed at Scott's sinewy forearm. "It's okay... and... you're right," Adam mumbled, his eyes darting around. "Carl's my Daddy."

Clutching at his chest as his eyes bulged out of their sockets, Scott collapsed back against the seat. Disbelief was written all over his face. "Holy fuck," he gasped out.

"Yeah, I know, right?" Adam giggled, and then he was lying against Scott, howling with laughter. The awe in Scott's voice was just too much. He howled even harder when Theo rolled his eyes at them, shaking his head.

Adam rubbed at his leaking eyes, his gaze fixed on Theo, who was shifting uncomfortably. He took a second to check what he was staring at, and his eyes landed on Matt's blond head, which gleamed colourfully under the strobe lighting. His muscled body swayed seductively against Greyson. Adam moved his gaze back to Theo. The tightness around his jaw was a dead giveaway that he was pissed. But that begged the question, why?

Distracted by Theo getting up and storming off in the direction of the toilets, Adam missed the first part of what Scott said.

"What's his problem? He's been moody all night. It's not like him."

Adam glanced at Theo's retreating back, shaking his head. "Who the fuck knows? I've got my own problems. I don't need to borrow trouble from anyone else, that's for sure," he shouted over the music. A mournful sigh followed.

Scott raised his brow, offering a sympathetic smile.

Adam downed his drink and opened up. He spilt his guts faster than a fish being gutted with a knife. He played down the kinkier side of their play. No one needed to know that he loved to be tied down and have all sorts of toys and contraptions attached to his body. He tried not to let his mind drift to what Daddy had promised to do when his nipples had healed.

Adam shifted. His cock sure was on board with where the conversation and his head were leading him. The use of the honorific Daddy stroked him in ways that should have had him heading straight for the psych's chair. Yet the knowledge Carl wanted to be his Daddy, fuck, it made Adam all shades of hot.

After he'd finished talking, he allowed Scott to pull him onto the dance floor against his better judgement. When he got home several hours later, he felt lighter for having shared his secrets. The only problem with sharing was that he'd somehow associated it with needing plenty of cocktails and dancing. The alcohol sloshed merrily around his stomach as he moved. He groaned. His body was more than happy to remind him of the two solid hours of dancing he'd done.

The taxi driver took his cash, and he gingerly exited the cab. His body demanded he should lie down right now, regardless of the wind whistling through his thin, sweaty clothes. He stumbled up the path, and on reaching the front door, he punched the security code into the locked box that stored his keys when he went out. "Oh, shitting buggering hell," he wailed.

His eyes narrowed on the empty box, and he slammed the tiny door shut. The memory of where he'd left his keys after he'd gone to find painkillers flooded past all the alcohol. They were still sitting on the damn kitchen table.

He turned around. The taxi was still idling at the curb. He made a dash for it, complaining with every step. He screeched when the engine revved. "Stoppppp." He yanked open the door of the slow-moving car, panting and cursing. "Shit. Sorry. Can you take me to my…" He struggled to stop his mouth from saying Daddy. He swallowed and started again, "Can you drop me at my boyfriend's, please?"

At the nod, he slid back into the warmth of the car, giving the driver the address. He settled back, hoping that wherever Carl had gone, he was home now.

Chapter Eighteen

Nathan

"WHAT THE FUCK IS EATING YOU TONIGHT, CARL?" NATHAN ASKED. "Months you've been acting odd. Then the last six weeks, it's like you disappeared off the face of the planet." Eyeing his friend, he tried to figure out what the hell was going on. Carl looked the same. His dark hair was swept back off his face with a leather bandana, and his massive chest was bare but for the leather harness. His black leather trousers and black boots finished off an outfit that screamed dominant, but there was something off, and Nathan couldn't put his finger on it.

He wasn't sure if it was to do with Carl's sudden reluctance to do a demonstration. Or that he, by Christ, had forgotten he'd agreed to do one tonight for the clubs patrons. They'd been advertising this for months. The packed room full of Doms and subs looking forward to the show meant Carl had to get his shit together.

The club only planned demos every two months, so the level of expectation was high. Nathan had learnt to build anticipation, thus creating greater interest and excitement, much as you would do to bring a sub pleasure. Tease and then tease some more.

Nathan's gaze roamed the room. His eyes landed on Saul, Carl's choice of a playmate for the night. Saul's blond highlighted hair glowed under the fluorescent lights on the dance floor, making him easy to see in the multitude of moving bodies. Though he was small, he was never hard to spot in a crowd.

The bleached hair and flamboyant outfits suited his personality. He was bold and brash and made no excuses for who he was. Tonight's hot pink leather shorts with a zip up the crease of his bottom for easy access matched the tiny leather halter top that covered his small chest but left his back bare. Nathan's eyes narrowed on Saul's choice of outfit. Carl was going to whip him without Saul being fully naked. Why wasn't Saul getting naked?

It was always a pleasure to see Saul's firm corded muscles twitch and writhe when he was strapped to the St Andrew cross on centre stage. And tonight should have been no different, but for whatever reason it was.

Nathan shrugged off the thought. It was Carl and Saul's decision, and it had nothing to do with him. Carl would still be using his bullwhip on that lovely pale skin. Nathan's body thrummed with pleasure, and his hands twitched. The urge to swap places and play with Saul was strong, but Nathan couldn't afford to get entangled. Never mind the fact that he was no expert at using a whip.

He glanced back at Carl, ignoring how his own leather trousers had become snug. "Are you going to talk to me, or do I have to go and get Ferron."

Carl nearly spun his head a full three hundred and sixty degrees as he searched the room faster than lightning could hit. Nathan roared with laughter, continuing to do so when Carl threw him a disdainful glare. "You can relax. He's not here." He choked out past the laughter, "He finally got himself a Dom. Though surprisingly, not from here." Nathan's laughter trailed off. The little niggle which kept surfacing was back. Ferron—the last time Nathan had seen him—appeared nervous in ways Nathan had never seen before. His innate senses told him something was off, but when he'd questioned the sub, he'd brushed off his concerns. Nathan had let it be and hoped that whatever was troubling the young man wasn't serious.

"That's a fucking shit thing to do, man." Carl rubbed at his bare chest. "Why would you threaten me with Ferron? You know he doesn't understand the word no, no matter how many times I've told him in the past." Carl tilted his head, "I'm glad he's found someone to tame him, though."

Nathan gave Carl a speculative glance. He leant forward, sensing something was off when Carl's brows drew together and deep creases formed on his forehead.

"I'm dating someone, and it's serious," Carl said matter-of-factly, like he hadn't just dropped a bombshell.

Nathan shook his head, not sure he'd heard correctly. "You've what? When? Who? How don't I know about this?" He fired the questions off in quick succession, not giving Carl a chance to answer. "They can't be from here, or I'd know."

Carl held up his large hands, warding off any more questions, and laughed. "Give a man a chance to answer. Fuck, what's with the twenty questions? Half the time I struggle to get you to join in a conversation."

"Fuck off. This is monumental. The king of 'I don't date and I'm never going to settle down' all but has rainbows and fucking fairy dust hovering over his head," Nathan blustered over the top of Carl.

"I do fucking not, you dick," Carl raged back.

"Yes, you do. And stop avoiding answering my questions. Who is he, how long have you been dating, and why haven't I met him," Nathan asked, his eyes glued to Carl. The way Carl sank back against the booth, his gaze wandering the room rather than looking at him, got his back up. "What aren't you telling me?"

Carl

It had been inevitable they'd end up having this conversation. As soon as he'd received Nathan's text asking why nothing had been sorted out for the demo tonight, he knew it would be coming. He just hadn't realised how hard it was going to be to confess. Carl sucked in a breath.

Dating for over a year and not sharing that with his best friend, *yeah*, how to explain that? A big sigh escaped when he glanced at Nathan, sending up a prayer that he'd understand.

"First, let me just say it wasn't my intention to keep this from you." Seeing Nathan gearing up to interrupt, he held up his hand and rushed on. "Please let me finish. Then you can have a go at me for being a shitty friend."

He sat forward, taking a gulp of water to wet his dry mouth. Staying put, he rested his elbows on the gleaming wood table. "Remember when I came in months ago and you kicked my butt, and I mentioned a guy being manhandled at work?" Nathan nodded. "Well, it's the same person. I'm sure I've mentioned Adam Grainger, the guy who manages the flagship restaurant and oversees all three locations." The narrow-eyed speculation Nathan wore made Carl gulp.

He absently rubbed his shaky fingers up the condensation on the glass in front of him. "It started around fourteen months ago. We had a little run-in, which resulted in me giving him a paddling. I didn't plan it, but somehow that evolved into a weekly play date. Then last October, the woman who for all intents and purposes was Adam's mother died." Carl shrugged off a rising unease. Something that usually resulted from talking about his feelings. "Things changed for me. I found I wanted to be there for him. It cut deep to watch how he grieved and seemed so lost. It was his best friend's mother who died, so Richie couldn't support Adam, for obvious reasons. So I kind of stepped into the breach. Then things got a little shady when Adam occasionally called me Daddy during our play dates, and I found I loved it."

Carl paused as his friend's eyes widened. He picked back up his drink and swallowed deep. "Then I had a moment of clarity just before Christmas, figuring out what it was that I wanted from him."

Carl shrugged at the obvious question on Nathan's handsome face.

"Yes, I want to be his Daddy, but with a difference. I want to be his Dom Daddy, and though he doesn't know the extent of just how dark my kink is, I think I can make what we have together work for both of us. Because, man, nothing is going to stop me from claiming him permanently, whether that be with a collar or a wedding ring or both. He's mine." He growled out the last part, unsure who he was trying to warn off.

He sat back and waited Nathan out, trying to gauge his reaction. His accelerating heart rate dipped when he registered the look of delight on Nathan's face.

Then Nathan's question brought him up short. "Have you told him about the club or your involvement? Surely, coming here tonight to do a demo is going to be an issue for him? It sure as hell would be an issue for any other sub or boy in a relationship with their dominant."

His face heated at the hard stare his friend was giving him, and he tried not to squirm. "Yes, I know that," he ground out. He lifted his arms in frustration and clasped his hands at the back of his neck. He pretended not to notice the group of subs in the next booth nearly face-planting in their eagerness to get a better look at his bulging muscles.

"I'd made a promise to you months ago to do this demo, way before I'd made a commitment to Adam." He wet his lips, noting his own lack of enthusiasm. "I can't let you down at short notice. If my head had been in the right space, I would have asked you to rearrange or get Nigel or Isaac to cover. But as your text this morning was the reminder I needed, it was too late to do anything." He turned to observe the packed room.

Resignation filled him, and his stomach dropped to the floor at the reality of having to do the bullwhip demo with Saul. The only positive was that Saul, a pain slut, was the perfect sub for the demo. He'd be a pleasure to work with and perfect to get the crowd going.

He moved his gaze back to Nathan as he huffed out an exasperated breath.

"Fuck yeah, Carl. It's too late to cancel now. Shit, we'd have a riot on our hands. I've been promoting this event like crazy to assess what interest we'd have in opening up the second floor. The new subscriptions have tripled over the last few months." Nathan carried on filling him in on the business details. He discussed the future open evenings for men who were interested in learning more about being a sub, going into detail about the ratio of Doms to subs. He then went on to explain what that meant and how they needed a new influx of subs to even things out.

Only half listening, Carl let him drone on. His thoughts were distracted by what he was about to do. How was he going to explain this to Adam?

When lights dimmed and the music dialled back to allow the announcer to speak, Carl stood up. He nodded at Nathan absently, sliding out of the booth. He prowled up to the centre stage, and let his chaotic thoughts and anxieties about his Sugar Lips slip to the back of his mind. Then Carl worked to get his head into his Dom mindset.

He stepped onto the centre stage, more than a little happy that there were two subs helping strap Saul to the cross placed smack bang in the middle of the stage. The rear pockets of Saul's shorts were unzipped to reveal his creamy backside, leaving Saul's shorts in place.

His brows rose, but then he recalled Saul's request that they stay on. Saul had been explicit. He would only unzip the pockets to reveal his arse. His genitals were to stay covered. Carl hadn't questioned why, more than happy not to see the evidence of Saul's arousal.

He hoped that when he explained all this to Adam, this fact would go in his favour.

Pissed to find his mind was wandering back to Adam, he shut off his train of thought and paid attention to the two men removing Saul's tiny halter top. The unmarked, fine musculature of Saul's beautiful back tapered down to his slim hips and full bottom, and Carl itched to mark it.

He clenched his fists at his sides while he waited for the subs to finish. He swallowed the bile burning the back of his throat, working to shut out the guilt at doing this with someone other than his boy. In a vain attempt to rationalise, he told himself that Adam wouldn't cope with this level of his kink.

The three steps to check on Saul felt like he'd walked a mile. His chest heaved as he ensured Saul was secure and happy to continue. Once he reaffirmed his safe word, he stepped back and accepted the whip from Nathan, who had followed him onto the stage.

The music was muted, and the crowd became still and silent. He ran his hands down the leather, his fingers checking that it was soft, oiled, and supple. Nathan stepped off the stage, and the air of expectation and anticipation built. He gave a devilish smirk to the crowd before masking his face and turning to Saul.

The three deep breaths he took centred him.

"Thirty lashes, Saul. If it becomes too much, use your safe word." When he received an affirmative, he got into position.

"Count for me."

"Yes Master."

The crowd seemed to hold their collective breath. Carl felt the weight of the whip as he flicked it through the air, testing it. The whistling sound as it cut through the air had Saul's body twitching. The only outward signal Carl could see of his anticipation. Not wanting to prolong the mindfuck, Carl let the next lash hit its intended target.

Saul's loud mewl followed by "one" made Carl's blood sing. He forced the guilt away and swung the next lash. Saul's body swayed, fighting to escape his binds, but the count continued. The fine layer of sweat gleaming of Saul's now lined back and inability to hold still showed how hard he was working to keep it together.

When he got to ten, Carl paused and checked in. Saul's nod and solid erection in the front of his shorts had him stepping back and delivering the next ten lashes. The crisscross pattern he was creating on Saul's skin was, to Carl's mind, art personified.

He stepped in again, checking Saul was still with him and giving his arm a much-needed break. It was aching with the exertion. The months of absence from this kind of play was telling. He rubbed at his biceps, listening to Saul's slurred response to his question with some amusement. Was Saul going to make it to thirty?

A sense of satisfaction overcame Carl as Saul's body and mind stopped fighting the pain around lash sixteen. He was sure Saul was now letting the endorphin rush take over. He moved back into position, not failing to notice the crowd were transfixed.

The scent of arousal was dense in the room and acted as an aphrodisiac to his senses. He inhaled and used it to centre himself once more, putting all his power behind the next lashes.

His cock thrummed in appreciation of Saul's screaming wail, and his body flexed into rigidity as the scent of his climax filled the air. Pleased that he had not only given Saul the ultimate head rush but also managed to time it with his final lash, Carl offered the crowd a wolfish grin.

He signalled to the two subs waiting to aid Saul, and they hustled forward to help him down from the cross and off to the aftercare room. Saul had once again surprised Carl. He'd refused to let him give aftercare; instead he'd picked these two subs to help him. Though this was not unusual, Carl had been a little perplexed, especially when Saul had declined to explain why he didn't want Carl to aid him.

The few times in the past he and Saul had played, Saul had never refused him. Was Saul sensitive to his reluctance?

He rolled his broad shoulders, shrugging off the wheres and why fors. He sighed, suddenly feeling all of his forty-two years. The muscles in his right arm and shoulder throbbed as he walked off the stage, following Saul to make sure he was okay.

He checked out the clock behind the bar, and his eyes widened. "Shit," he muttered.

A flicker of hope that he could go and surprise Adam died. The disappointment on his boy's face when he had changed their plans had him wanting to make amends. Only he didn't think showing up at three am was going to gain him any brownie points. He sighed in disappointment.

Chapter Nineteen

Adam

H E GLANCED AT THE DARK HOUSE, GETTING A SENSE OF EMPTINESS AS the taxi pulled up into the deserted drive. He got out, asking the driver to wait. He gave the dark windows and closed garage a full look before ringing the doorbell. The distant chimes rang four times inside, what he had already figured, was an empty house. He gave up after ten minutes, knowing Carl wouldn't have slept through the sound of the bell.

He cursed his own misfortune as he got back in the taxi.

"Where to now, mister?"

He chewed on his fingernail as a harebrained idea flashed into his head. The lack of conversation about where Carl had gone tonight and the little card that sat in his bedside cabinet gave Adam the stupidest thought. Could Daddy be at that club right now? His stomach revolted at the very idea, but for some reason, the thought wouldn't let go. *I'm being ridiculous.* But even as he thought it, he was giving the driver the address of The Playroom. He sat back and caught the driver's frown in the rear-view mirror.

"You know that's a BDSM club, right?"

Adam pretended he wasn't the colour of flamingos and nodded when the guy turned to face him. He kept his mouth shut at the driver's muttered comments about deviants and oddballs. Relief flooded him when the driver shifted to face forward and started the engine.

The taxi took him back the way he'd just come. When they pulled up outside the unobtrusive building, he realised he could have walked there from his flat in around ten minutes. His lips pursed. *Wow, how close was the club to my home.*

He got the sense that if he asked the man to wait, this time it would be a "hell no," judging by the way he was eyeing the building as if it might bite him. The cash was snatched from his hand before he could offer it. Huffing indignantly, he slipped out of the backseat and hardly had a chance to shut the door before the taxi took off.

The wave of chilly air hit him, and a shiver shuddered up his spine. His gaze swept the empty street as he clasped his clammy hands together.

What club didn't have people hanging around at this hour?

Not au fait with this type of club, he shrugged off his anxiety and walked up to the big black door that gave no clue as to what was inside. He opened it and peered inside.

The entrance way was empty as he stepped inside, and he was pleasantly surprised to note how upmarket the place was—not at all seedy. The black-and-red-decorated walls were bold and complimented the black wooden furniture. The large unmanned cloakroom was stuffed full of coats and at odds with the lack of noise or people. *Where was everyone?*

He moved silently over the thick red carpet. This was so far out of his comfort zone. He fidgeted, uncertain what he should do when there was no one there to ask. He rubbed his damp hands down his trousers, nostrils twitching as he inhaled. The scent, one he thought smelt a lot like leather and arousal, increased the closer he got to the closed door.

He paused. His hand descended on the door handle in front of him. *Is that really what I can smell?* With a sweaty palm, he gripped the metal door handle and inched open the door in front of him. His heart hammered against his ribs. Incredulous that he was actually going to do this, he sucked in a breath and peered through the crack.

All his senses were assailed at once by the visual of a whip flying through the air and striking the back of a small man strapped to a St Andrew's cross. The man withered and moaned in what sounded like bliss. Adam lowered his free hand and grasped his sudden throbbing arousal. He exhaled. The erection under his fingers was more than a little intrigued by the show.

A soft voice counting out after each lash struck floated with ease over the silent, mesmerised crowd. Every person appeared to be transfixed on the show happening on the stage.

Adam's gaze landed on a man standing several feet in front of him. By the way the man was dressed, his outfit matching the colours of the club foyer, Adam would bet his last paycheck he should have been manning the entrance. That it went in Adam's favour was neither here nor there. He was convinced the owner of the club wouldn't be happy to know the guy had left his post to enjoy the action. It didn't matter how close to the door the guy was. Unless he had eyes in the back of his head, he wouldn't see anyone coming in uninvited.

Adam's attention turned to the dimly lit room and the spotlight highlighting the stage where everyone's attention was focused. His gaze moved to the two men on the stage. His eyes slid from the man being whipped to the wielder of the whip. He slapped his hand over his mouth to stop the cry from escaping. His eyes flicked open and closed rapidly as he hoped to dispel the image.

My Daddy. That's my Daddy.

How did I miss that?

Daddy!

As bold as brass, Carl was standing on the stage, making another man moan and cry in pleasure. The litany continued. *My Daddy, my Daddy.* His fears at finding the card and then checking out the website were laid bare, along with every insecurity he had. Up until now, they had been sitting inside, waiting for a chance to worm their way to the surface, desperate to show their faces and reveal his dirty inner secret. Who could love the unlovable?

His arousal fled. Adam stepped back as his mind valiantly tried to tell him this was all a big mistake. His heart ached at the betrayal.

Why hadn't Daddy told me about this?

You know why.

You've never been good enough for anyone. Daddy was just playing with you.

To stop the sob, Adam rammed his fist in his mouth. He swung round and ran out of the building, glad that no one had seen him. He would be beyond mortified if Carl found out he'd been there, and got upset.

With the use of his coat sleeve, Adam swiped at his wet face and sniffed up. He ran down the road towards his home and kept on running. There was no hope of escaping how similar he was to the man strapped to the cross.

Had Daddy picked him on purpose?

Was Daddy imaging it was me?

He panted breathlessly. "Stop... that... Fuck him... you're... worth-morethan... that." He hardly made sense of what was pouring out of his mouth as he continued to run. Sweat streamed down his back, even with the icy wind whipping through his open jacket.

On reaching his flat, he was a breathless, sweaty mess. Then he re-membered what had started this nightmare in the first place. He sat down on the freezing concrete, winded and wheezing. Sobs broke in between the panting. He glanced up through streaming eyes at Rupert's window. He slapped his forehead, wishing he'd remembered two hours ago before life had kicked his butt that Rupert had a spare key for emergencies.

Hiccuping his way up the steps to Rupert's door, Adam reluctantly knocked. Hoping against all hope he wasn't a complete mess. He shoved his hand through his hair and wiped at his face, all the while praying he could keep it together till he got inside his own flat.

Three days later

Adam hid under the duvet, pretending he didn't hear the banging on his front door. It was his day off, and he'd planned on spending it sulking in bed. He'd spent the last couple days licking his wounds and acting like there was nothing wrong when it was actually the complete opposite. It felt like his world was falling apart. No matter how many times he'd told himself he should be used to this, it made no difference. He had years of practice at hiding his feelings, and he was putting it all to good use. He just hoped he could keep it up and act like this indefinitely. *I have to if I'm gonna survive.*

He blinked back the tears.

The avoidance game, now that was where he might fall down. His parents were excellent at this particular game. He'd never had to try and keep his feelings hidden for long. He hadn't been prepared for Carl to be so tenacious. Over the last few days, he had received several angry voicemails and more texts than he could count. Each was shoutier than the last.

He had refused to answer any of them, arguing with himself that he wasn't the one in the wrong.

I'm not.

He argued with the voice inside his head.

If I didn't tell Daddy what was wrong, how can he explain himself?

He rolled over, ducking his head under the pillow, hoping to drown out the voice of reason. When he couldn't take a proper breath, he lifted the pillow and threw it across the room, flopping onto his back.

His ears perked up at the sound of more banging. He glared at the mirror above his head. The reflection showed dark circles under his haunted eyes and mussed hair that even a bird would struggle to find a comfortable position in.

A growl rumbled low in his chest as he rolled off the bed and went to the bathroom. He shut the door in an attempt to block out the din coming from downstairs, switched on the shower, and stripped out of Carl's large T-shirt.

He stuck his nose up in the air, paying no attention to how comforting it was to have Carl's scent and clothing touching his naked skin. His lips blew out in frustration. *Three days.* Adam sighed, wondering how much longer he could dodge Carl. At work, he had made sure they were never left alone, knowing fine well he'd break if Carl managed to get him on his own.

The problem with being on his own was that he had way too much time to think about what had happened. He still wasn't sure what had upset him the most. Carl touching another man in public, albeit with a whip and not his hands, or that it wasn't him strapped to the cross, getting his arse whipped.

The visual triggered a whole-body shiver and his cock to plump and fill. His body strained, and his cock stood erect and begging. Adam sighed, glaring down at his traitorous groin.

I didn't ask your opinion, did I? Fucking blasted thing has a mind of its own.

And wasn't that part of the problem? His body seemed to be on board with the idea of Carl whipping him, whereas his head was saying "fuck no." It was a total mindfuck, and until he got his head and body on the same page, Carl could go and take a running jump off a bloody cliff for all he cared.

The following day, he kept his head down, doing his best to act cheerful when all he wanted to do was run and hide. He had spent hours the day before trying his best to come up with a good reason to delay this morning's meeting with Seb and Carl. Whilst getting dressed, he'd complained bitterly to himself at his inability to come up with anything.

He was about to enter the kitchen when he heard Carl shout at Seb, heralding his late arrival. The relief that Seb hadn't arrived on time was short-lived. He heard Carl through the kitchen door insist they have the meeting. Adam nervously chewed his thumb before walking back to his desk to collect his files. He took a deep breath, willing his pulse to stop playing gymnastics inside his veins.

The walk into the dining room was far too short. He gripped the files to his chest as if for protection and plastered on a fake smile.

Two hours later, pain throbbed at Adam's temples. The nonchalant way Carl was acting as he joked about Seb calling Richie "boy" would have been funny if it didn't stick in Adam's craw. Not once had he made eye contact with him.

The few minutes Seb had disappeared for had been the tensest of Adam's life. And that was saying something with his shitty parents. The fact that Carl sat staring at him, his dark intense eyes firing question after silent question, left him a trembling mess, to the point he had to get up and go and find Seb.

Adam cursed his body's reaction to the passion sizzling between them. When he'd returned with Seb in tow, it had taken all of his willpower not to sock Carl in his gorgeous grinning gob. Carl sat laughing and joking with Seb as if he didn't have a worry in the world and then sauntered off into the kitchen like his shit didn't stink.

He ground his teeth together as he stacked the paperwork back into their folders with trembling hands and then stomped back to his desk.

Could this day get any worse? His jaw bunched. The sight of Luke Mason standing outside the locked door, foot tapping impatiently, was the last thing he needed. This guy was the biggest pain of all.

A professional smile slipped over his face before he unlocked the door and worked on remembering that it was the patrons who paid his wage. He led Luke into the dining room and gratefully fobbed him off on Seb.

A few minutes later, his smile fell when he looked up into the face of Richie's father. "What do you want? Richie is busy," he hissed.

"I need to speak to my son. I'll wait." The amicable tone did little to veil the underlying tension radiating from his stiff posture.

He gave Mr Bellinger a hard stare before he walked away to grab Richie. He followed his friend around the partition to the front entrance, where they were greeted by a belligerent scowl that made Richie's cheeks pale. He stepped closer to Richie, feeling a surge of protectiveness for his friend.

"Hello, Dad. Long time no see. What can I do for you?" Richie snarled.

Adam gave an internal cheer at Richie finally standing up to his lying, cheating dick of a father.

"I think you have forgotten yourself and who you're talking to." The disdainful tone made Adam's temper boil to the surface.

The heated conversation carried on. Adam listened and placed his hand on Richie's shoulder, squeezing in support.

Mr Bellinger blustered, "How dare you be disrespectful to me? You had such potential, and now look at you. You're such a disappointment." Richie wilted under the onslaught, making Adam forget his earlier reminder to himself about being professional.

"Hey, fuckface, you back the fuck up there a minute. A disappointment! How fucking dare you say that? He did everything for his mum, more than any son should have to. Where were you when your son was cleaning up the vomit or having to help his mother to the bathroom and wipe bits no son should ever have to see? Disappointment. You're the biggest disappointment of all," Adam ranted.

The rage at the injustice his friend suffered overwhelmed him. All sense of reason flew out of the window the moment Mr Bellinger had uttered those four fateful words. He could hear his own father spouting that very same crap at him.

Lost in his own anger, he wasn't aware of anyone else until he heard "Adam, enough" come from Seb, a second before his feet left the ground, and he was flipped over a strong, familiar shoulder.

His world spun as Carl swung around on his heel, holding him in a fireman's lift. Anger burnt through him. He ranted and pummelled his fists against Carl's broad back, before kicking out, aiming for his groin.

A squeal escaped when Carl's arms got unbearably tight around his legs. The anger drained from him on seeing the mortified faces of the kitchen staff. He buried his hot face into Carl's shoulder at the stark reality of what he'd just done in front of a restaurant full of people. Holy fuck!

The locker room door shut behind them, and he was wordlessly lowered to the ground. The abject misery on his Daddy's face was enough to have him slump down onto the seat.

"I'm not sure what the hell was going on out there?" Carl paused and gave him a searching look.

A sense of unease made Adam remain silent, positive Carl wasn't finished. The layer of mortification and humiliation at being thrown around in front of people he knew died at Carl's next words.

"I was worried for you, and I hated to hear you that upset and angry. So much so I found myself doing something I've never done before. I lost control, and all I could think about was taking you away and protecting you." A sheepish look crossed his face as he continued, "Carting you away was probably not the best thing I could have done. I'm sorry for that. With all that being said, Sugar Lips, I'm still going to tan your arse for attempting to kick me in the balls. Right after you explain what that was all about."

Adam shifted his arse, already anticipating what was coming, and quickly explained what had happened. Only when he'd finished did he see the furrows on Carl's forehead disappear, pride shining from his eyes.

"I'm sorry, Daddy. I didn't mean to kick you in the balls or try too. I was just so angry and upset. I could hear my own father saying the same thing to me and"—Adam shrugged his shoulders—"I just lost it."

"Then I'll forgo the spanking," Carl said as he sat and pulled Adam onto his lap.

Large arms encased Adam's shoulders, and he cuddled into Carl's chest. He inhaled the scent of spices that he always associated with Carl, and his heart rate settled. Back on an even keel, he registered what Carl had said. A slither of disappointment wheedled its way under his skin, and he glanced up at Carl. "I think I still need the spanking, Daddy. I did try and hurt you."

The rumbling chuckle emanating from Carl vibrated through his body and brought out a grin.

"Well, if you think you need a spanking, then who am I to argue?"

The devilish light in his eyes should have warned Adam something was up, but before he could think about it, his trousers were undone and dragged down—the inevitability of what was coming left him breathless with want. His body was already priming itself for what was going to happen when he was flipped around and was lying over Daddy's lap.

The sound of flesh hitting flesh rang through the room. The noise ramped up Adam's arousal, and the pain was bordered on too much, and yet it still wasn't enough to meet his growing need. His throbbing cock, trapped between his Daddy's legs, was desperate for attention. He tried to rock, only to find he couldn't under the heavy arm pinning him down. His begging and pleas fell on deaf ears.

The heat in his arse cheeks morphed into a beast that wanted to eat him whole. His body felt like one giant nerve. He undulated against the rough cloth beneath him, attempting to alleviate the frantic need clawing inside of him.

His pucker clenched in expectation as his legs were released, but he whined in distress as Carl placed him back on his own two feet. His weeping cock dripped onto the floor, not in the least bit cowed by the spanking. His body begged for the release it wanted so badly. A release, it suddenly dawned, he wouldn't be getting. The light in his Daddy's eyes now made sense.

"You did that on purpose," Adam accused as he yanked up his trousers and shoved his not so happy cock back into his too tight trousers.

"Err, Sugar Lips, you asked for a spanking." Carl laughed as he strolled to the door before looking back over his shoulder. "I always give my boy what he asks for. And I think you'll find what you asked for was a spanking. You didn't say anything about coming." With that parting shot, he winked at him and walked out the door, whistling.

"Fucker," Adam mumbled under his breath, doing his best to will away the erection that was still attempting to fight the restraints of his trousers.

The realisation he was going to have to face Seb and Richie was the bucket of cold water he needed. Feeling a little like a naughty child, he sighed and went to face the music.

Chapter Twenty

Nathan

NATHAN GROUND HIS TEETH TOGETHER. CARL WAS EVIDENTLY NOT IN the mood to listen to his angry rant about firing the prat doorman. The guy seemed to have decided that spending more time in the club than actually manning the reception was okay. Last night had been the fourth time Nathan had caught him. The first time had been the night of Carl's demo, and this was the final straw.

The moment Carl fully tuned Nathan out, he released a quiet sigh. Carl's skill at zoning out was unrivalled by anyone Nathan knew, and it irked just how well he could just shut everything out.

As far as Nathan was concerned, this conversation needed to happen. They were in business together, as much as Carl liked to leave the day-to-day running to him, and they usually talked this shit through. Carl evidently thought differently.

He stopped talking, wondering how long it would take before Carl noticed. He leant back against his office chair, eyeing his friend. Carl's dark hair was a mess, presumably as a result of his hands raking through it, and his bulging muscles flexed under the thick wool jumper and dark jeans he was wearing. He fidgeted in the chair opposite Nathan, lost in his own thoughts.

Nathan chewed over the information he'd been about to share before Carl had ignored him. The security feed from the demo night had perturbed him. To see a young man walk straight into the club unobserved and watch what was happening was jarring. A flush of fury burned through Nathan at the thought of the doorman allowing it to happen. They had strict protocols to prevent unwanted attention. Enough was enough. The guy was out. His shoulders bunched at the idea. The rules were there for a reason.

His eyes narrowed on Carl, considering what he should do about the other piece of information he'd discovered. He had been about to share it, but Nathan decided on another avenue. He would respond to a particular application form from a certain Adam Grainger, which he had received via email a few days earlier.

An invite to one of the open nights for new subs was, to his mind, very fitting. The intrigue on Adam's face before he'd noticed who was wielding the whip had said he'd be more than happy to play in the club. Would his Dom Daddy be pleased with that, though?

Nathan steepled his fingers, resting his chin on his hands, formulating his response to Adam while waiting for Carl to realise he'd shut up.

Carl

Carl lifted his hand and raked his fingers through his hair, letting them rest at the nape of his neck. He scratched. He had a feeling he was something missing when it came to his boy, and it wouldn't leave him alone. His gut was speaking far too loudly to be ignored, but he was struggling to connect the dots.

Two weeks and still he had no clue as to what the fuck he'd done wrong. One minute his boy was all sweetness and light, and then he'd turned into the devil incarnate. If he wasn't fighting with someone, he was spoiling for one. And for the life of him, Carl couldn't get him to talk about it. The fight at the restaurant the previous week with

Richie's dad showed just how angry his boy was. He'd seen him lose his temper before, but that had been a whole new level of anger.

The need to get Adam away from the situation, and fast, had him reacting rather than thinking things through. Seb had given him a telling-off that had burned his arse, but he'd been far too worried about Adam to care.

The leather chair squeaked under his weight as Carl shifted. He dwelled on the spanking he'd given to his boy and the dripping arousal he'd caused. That evidently wasn't the problem between them. The renewed visual of his boy's leaking cock was more than enough to eradicate any worries there. Unfortunately his body reacted to the image. He snarled at his lap, his body rebelling at the enforced dry spell it was enduring. To take his mind off his tightening jeans, he brought his attention back to Nathan.

The silence and watchful expression Nathan wore as he stared at Carl over his clasped hands had him offering a sheepish grin. "Sorry, my head is all over the place at the moment." He sighed, ignoring just how much of an understatement that was. "What was it you were saying about the demo night?"

Nathan shook his head. "Nah it was nothing. Forget it. Have you figured out what is wrong with your boy? And why are you here? It's not like you to come in on a Sunday afternoon," he asked, speculation in his eyes.

Carl shrugged. "I had a stocktake to do with Seb, and it appears my boy has other plans. Not that he told me. I heard him telling one of the wait staff," he huffed, his mouth moving into a pout against his will.

Nathan jabbed a finger at him, laughing. "You're fucking pouting."

"Am not," Carl growled.

He jumped up out of the groaning chair and stalked to the door. He flicked a look over his shoulder. "A lot of good you were to me," Carl said. With that, he stormed out and headed for the back entrance. He rushed to get out of the biting wind whistling around him. He eyed the thick, heavy clouds and wondered if winter would ever finish.

When he arrived at his house, he parked in the garage and roamed through his house, not sure what to do with himself. Even if he wanted to do housework, which he didn't, the place gleamed like a freshly minted coin…there was nothing left to clean. Having avoided spending any time at the club over the last couple of weeks, for reasons he didn't want to dwell on, his house had got all of his spare attention.

The pleasure he usually got from spending time in his home evaded him. He made his way upstairs and into his playroom, switching on the lamps to illuminate the room.

As he walked around the room, his fingers trailed over the sleek wood of his spanking bench, followed by his St Andrew's cross. He'd ordered a bed for the room. It had been delivered the previous week but still lay against the far wall, unassembled. When it had arrived, he'd been in a rush to get to work, and with everything between him and his boy taking all his attention, he had forgotten all about it. Needing to do something to distract himself, he set about assembling it.

A few hours later, sweat dripped down his forehead and soaked his hair. Carl cursed his own stupidity for buying a queen-size solid oak frame and not paying for the delivery crew to assemble it. He plopped his arse down on the wooden floor, eyeing the half-assembled bed in defeat. His chest heaved from the exertion of trying to hold the frame and screw the bolts into place. He wiped the sweat from his soaking forehead with his woollen sleeve. Why hadn't he taken off his bloody jumper before he started?

He sat forward, yanking the offending item over his head, and flung it on the floor. He hauled his arse off the floor and went in search of a drink. The muttered threats got his already overheated body revving hotter. This was his boy's fault.

When they resolved whatever was wrong between them, *because they would, mark my words,* Adam was going to pay in the most delicious way.

The thought sustained Carl through the following week as Adam continued to behave like a spoiled brat. Still no closer to coming up with an answer as to what was wrong with his Sugar Lips, he was slowly losing his patience.

It was like they were playing a game of chess, only Carl was playing blind and deaf, with no clue if he was checkmated.

He huffed out a breath when Seb distracted him by asking him to check the last items off the list as correct. He tapped at the computer, inputting the information onto the spreadsheet. Carl kept the complaint about having to spend a second Sunday on the trot doing a stocktake to himself. Seb's morose expression was why he'd offered to help in the first place.

There had been a shift in Seb's attitude over the last few weeks. He was more forthcoming and friendly in ways he'd never been before. It had lulled everyone into a false sense of security. Then bam, this week he was back to his old self, only worse. He was moodier than a hormonal teenager, upsetting the staff left, right, and centre, and it had to stop.

So Carl had bitten the bullet and offered to do the stocktake so he could ferret out the reason, only he was failing miserably. He wasn't actually trying too hard, though, lost in his own misery.

Scott's teary face sprung to mind from the previous week, after Seb had chewed him out for no valid reason. Carl groaned in defeat and set aside his own miserable state of affairs. Half an hour later, he followed Seb home, sat on his hideously uncomfortable couch, and took the drink Seb offered.

The perplexed expression on Seb's face made Carl wary.

"Have you heard of Daddy kink?" Seb asked out of the blue.

Hand jerking, Carl did his best to keep his face blank. Uncertain where Seb was going with this, he gave a nod and waited.

Carl listened without interjecting as Seb talked. He walked in front of Carl, thankfully not paying any real attention to him. A mask of indifference slipped into place as he worked on not expressing how close the topic of conversation was to his own personal situation.

His pity grew for what Seb had endured at the hands of his bigoted father. To his mind, no one should judge another for their personal choices. The thought barely had time to register as Seb dropped the next bombshell.

Carl's brows rose. Had he somehow misjudged his friend? His pulse pounded in his ears. He struggled to digest what Seb was saying without judgement.

"I found Ellie out the back of the restaurant three years before you came to work for me. He was starving and searching for something to eat. He was fourteen and homeless. I was a little stunned at how those frightened eyes called to the Daddy in me. I knew he was underage, but I didn't have the strength to shut the door on him. When he passed out with hunger, right there in front of me, I found myself with an armful of boy. I didn't think twice. I took him home. I checked out his story, and fuck, Carl, his mother was a piece of work. To this day, he doesn't know I went to see her. After I'd spoken to her, I knew damn well I wasn't going to tell him. I knew I'd never help him go back to that fucking bitch and her awful husband. So I kept him with me and took care of him the best I could."

"Please tell me you didn't have sex with an underage boy," Carl blustered.

"Fuck you. You know me better than that, I would hope. No, I fucking never. What happened between us happened after he turned sixteen and was consensual. I kept my hands to myself, even though he tried to push the issue," Seb answered angrily.

Carl let out the breath he'd inadvertently been holding. He wanted to say he hadn't doubted Seb there for a second, but he'd have been lying. The honesty shining in Seb's eyes and the conviction in his words helped settle Carl's dancing stomach.

He let Seb finish without further interruption. It was when he talked about Richie that he couldn't contain himself. His eyes rolled, and he roared with laughter. "You think you're hiding what you feel for Richie?" he choked out through the laughter. "Seb, I hate to tell you, but a bloody blind man could see you have strong feelings for Richie. Do you even know how many times you've slipped up over the last few weeks and called him boy? I'll tell you: loads."

"Oh, shut up. I have not," Seb blustered with uncertainty.

He continued to laugh as Seb stood and roamed the room, his hands shoved into his trousers.

He rubbed at his face, giving himself a moment to settle before speaking. "The problem as I see it is you're too worried about what others think. You're a grown-up. Take responsibility for that, and fuck anyone who doesn't like it. When Ellie left, you were miserable. Then over the last few months, it's like someone switched the light back on inside you. You stopped existing and started living. So let's keep that in mind. What do you want, Seb?"

Seb didn't hesitate. "Richie. I want him to be my everything."

"Then stop hiding. If you must, go find Ellie and hash out whatever is holding you back. Then go and claim your boy for all to see. Show him you mean it." As soon as the words left his mouth, he realised he was also speaking about his own situation. A sense of relief washed over him. How could he have been so blind?

As he shook off his stupidity, the beginnings of a plan pieced themselves together. Nothing was going to get in the way of sorting through whatever Adam's issues were. He was done with all this evading shit. It was time he acted like the Dom he was and showed his boy who was in charge.

An hour later he left Seb's house, with a plan. After checking what he had in the truck that he could use to break through his boy's defences, he headed to Adam's flat

He hummed in tune to the radio. Lewis Capaldi's song "Grace" played. *"Oh, how I long for us to find common ground. I got nothing but you on my mind."*

Those simple words touched his heart. He wanted to find that common ground with his boy. His earlier conviction solidified as he parked at the curb outside the flat. Adam's car sat in its designated space, and a predatory smile crossed his face.

He reached for his gym bag and chuckled. Gym bag, *yeah, more like kink bag.* When they'd started their play dates, he had gradually been adding new purchases. The bag now held more kink than clothes. Still chuckling, he got out and walked up the path.

A tiny spry man bent over the newly turned soil had Carl come to a grinding halt. He gave the light blue wintery sky a passing glance, wondering if it wasn't far too early to be considering doing any planting with the continuing nightly frosts. He might not be absolutely au fait with gardening, but he did know one didn't plant when there were still harsh frosts during the night.

He offered a smile. "It's Rupert, right? I'm not sure Adam's mentioned me. I'm Carl."

Rupert

Rupert gave the giant a passing glance, harrumphing in response, and carried on messing in the soil. He kept Carl in his line of sight, hiding a chuckle behind his dirty hand as Carl's eyebrows rose up his forehead.

"Err, right, I'll see you later, then," Carl said, uncertainty lacing his voice.

Rupert glanced up. "No point going up the steps. Adam walked to the shops to get me some milk a few minutes ago. He won't be back for another"—he checked his watch—"twenty minutes or so by my calculation."

The protectiveness he felt for Adam surfaced. From the very first time Adam had knocked on his front door to say hi, he'd grown to love him like a son. He had spent hours listening to Adam talk about his family, and he'd grown to hate them. He couldn't understand how they could despise such a wonderful boy, so he had adopted him.

He narrowed his eyes, his parental instincts coming to the fore. This had to be Adam's Daddy. He wasn't daft. What he was, was fed up listening to Adam whine about his Daddy. He'd caught Adam's slip-up more than once when referring to the giant. Rupert himself had had a Daddy in the past, but he'd died more than ten years ago, and now he was just happy to live vicariously through Adam.

He'd waited for the pair of them to get their act together. Buoyed when Adam had informed him how his Daddy had gone to battle with his awful father, he had secretly cheered Carl on.

He loved having Adam as his neighbour, but he wasn't going to be selfish. His heart sank at the thought of Adam not popping round for his chats. He pushed aside his worries when his fingers brushed over the key in his pocket.

Adam's stubborn nature meant they could be going round in circles for ages, and to his mind, that just wouldn't do.

The silence stretched uncomfortably, and Carl fidgeted next to him.

He heaved a sigh and took matters into his own hands. He hoped Adam would forgive him. "I have a key if you want to let yourself in," he said abruptly.

He averted his face, hoping not to show the mischievous twinkle lighting his eyes. Carl jumped, a smile gracing his gorgeous face. Rupert pulled out his key chain and removed Adam's key from his keyring. He passed it to Carl, uncaring he covered Carl's hand in wet soil.

He waved off his thanks and watched Carl head into the house, crossing his fingers behind his back. *Please let this be the right decision.*

Chapter Twenty-One

Adam

BEFORE THE FRONT DOOR SWUNG CLOSED, ADAM GAVE RUPERT A strange look. Was it his imagination, or was Rupert acting stranger than usual? The moment his feet hit the garden path, he had all but snatched the milk from his hand. He hadn't even had a chance to give him his change as Rupert shoved him up his steps and through his front door.

He shook his head and laid the bag of shopping onto the stairs, then took off his coat and hung it over the bannister. He picked up the bag and walked down the hall to the kitchen. The warmth radiating from the heaters seeped past the icy cold that had penetrated his clothes on the thirty-minute walk.

He made his way to the kitchen, then stilled, listening intently. The creaking came again. He wasn't just hearing things. His pulse sped up.

He laid the bag onto the counter and spun on his heel, creeping back into the hall to listen again.

"Hello? Is there anyone there?" He cursed his own stupidity. *That's right, moron. Shout and let the burglar know I'm here.*

He rubbed his clammy palms down his jeans, undecided if he should go and investigate, or call for help.

His heart skipped a beat when another loud creak came from above his head. Air whistled past his lips in fright. His eyes wheeled as he searched for anything he could use as a weapon. Spying the umbrella stand, he tiptoed to it. He lifted out his brolly with a solid handle, hoping it would be sturdy enough if he had to use it on someone.

"You can do this. What are you, a man or a mouse?" Adam muttered, hating how his head screamed "you're a mouse."

He set his foot onto the first step and prayed he wasn't going to end up murdered in his own bed. His mind was frantic as he crept up the stairs, desperately trying to recall which stairs made the most noise.

When he reached the top, he let out the breath he'd been holding, his lungs screaming for air.

A voice assailed him from his bedroom.

"Stop fucking about out there, boy, and get your backside in here."

He squealed and dropped the brolly, which clattered to the floor. Clutching his chest, he tried to keep his balance and not fall back down the stairs. Pulling himself together, Adam wasn't convinced he wouldn't have been happier facing a murderer than an angry-sounding Daddy.

Reluctantly, he stepped through the open doorway and stopped as a wave of dizziness swept over him.

The sight that greeted him left him breathless and aroused to the point of pain. His hand moved to his aching cock of its own accord.

"Tut, tut. What have I told you about touching, you naughty boy? Daddy didn't give you permission, now did he?" Daddy said, moving to stand in full view.

His mouth felt dryer than dust, and his hand dropped, even though it was the last thing he wanted to do. For the first time in his life, he was frightened that he was going to come in his jeans, untouched, just from looking at someone.

Daddy was dressed in what looked like butter-soft black leather trousers and an obscenely tight white T-shirt. Adam's legs went to jelly while his eyes devoured every bulging and flexing muscle on display. So taken with what his Daddy was wearing, it took a moment to register the state of his bed. The four posts now held leather straps around each post.

A shiver rippled up his spine as he gulped.

His gaze went to Daddy. "What…" He licked his lips when the words got stuck in his throat. "What are they for?" He pointed to the bed with a trembling finger. Then wished he hadn't asked when Daddy's near-black eyes turned molten. He shuddered under their intensity as they held him captive.

Daddy didn't answer him but issued a husky demand instead. "Strip."

With his clothes in a pile at his bare feet, he stood tall and willed the images of another naked man being whipped by Daddy out of his mind. He clenched his fists, his gaze lingering instead on the leather adorning the bed in front of him.

"Come here to Daddy, Sugar Lips."

Adam stepped to the bed, his breath coming in small gasps, his cock showing Daddy just how excited he was for him to start.

Then Daddy explained, in detail, what he was going to do. Adam's chest rose and fell in quick succession. His Daddy always took great pleasure in driving him to distraction by torturing him with the visuals.

What was there not to love?

He didn't have time to argue the point. His next breath seized in his lungs as he felt the rough pads of Daddy's fingers slide down his straining cock. Warm breath ghosted his cheek as Daddy whispered in his ear, "I'm going to use this lovely leather cock ring to stop you from coming."

When Daddy held out his palm to reveal what he was holding, Adam bit his tongue to stop himself from begging. Daddy firmly stroked his cock, and his eyes rolled into the back of his head. He moaned at the feel of the soft leather cinching around the base of his hard length. His cock pulsed and bucked, revelling in the attention and dripping all over Daddy's fingers.

Daddy wasn't finished and continued to torment him. "Now, you can't come until I let you. Let's get you tied to the bed, face up. We want to take full advantage of your mirror. We wouldn't want you to miss a thing, now would we?"

The evil little chuckle had Adam muttering under his breath, "It's not for my bloody advantage, that's for sure."

"What was that, boy? You wouldn't want to add to the already large number of punishments you've earned by not responding to your Daddy, would you?" The raised brow and devilish glint in his eyes had Adam's head shaking.

"Then get on the bed and behave," Daddy said in a deep husky voice that sent shivers down Adam's body.

Doing as he was told, Adam climbed up, trying not to act overeager. *Like Daddy doesn't know how eager I am.* The protruding cock wasn't enough of a giveaway?

He lay on his back and watched with some trepidation as his limbs were spread wide and secured to the bed. The soft leather bound around his wrists and ankles left him feeling vulnerable and more exposed than he'd ever been in his life. His lungs sawed, desperate to get some air in them by the time Daddy had him completely under his control.

The uncertainty he could see on his face in the mirror above the bed troubled him, and he worked to relax his tensing muscles. The moment he felt them release, they tensed right back up when the mattress beneath him shifted.

His eyes widened at the visual of Daddy straddling his body. The leather Daddy wore didn't hide the substantial arousal pressing against the zip of his trousers, and Adam's mouth watered in anticipation of wrapping his lips around Daddy and sucking him dry.

"You want to suck Daddy's cock." Daddy smirked.

He met Daddy's gaze, shivering under the intensity as he nodded. The smirk on Daddy's face conveyed a message loud and clear. He wasn't getting anywhere near Daddy until he'd finished tormenting him. The thought was confirmed when Daddy shifted back. Adam moaned and lifted his hips. The soft leather brushing his weeping cock teased him mercilessly.

When Daddy pulled back, Adam could see pearly liquid smearing the leather.

Daddy glanced to where Adam was staring and shook his head. "You will have to clean that now," Daddy growled.

Adam's hips bucked, and his aching cock throbbed as licks of pleasure spread up its turgid length. Panting like a dog in heat, he scented leather and musk. He sucked in several deep breaths, working on not hyperventilating. Eyes scrunched tightly shut, he willed his body to behave against the overwhelming sensations bombarding him.

Sticky leather touched his lips, and his eyes flickered open while his tongue already sought the treasure it had been offered. He lapped at the wet leather, the taste of his own cum and Daddy's leather exploding over his taste buds. He mouthed Daddy, desperate for more. His mouth widened as his lips latched on to Daddy's hard arousal. The taste acted like an aphrodisiac, and saliva dripped off Adam's chin as he sucked in desperation.

"No, no, Daddy. More please," he begged shamelessly as Daddy moved away.

"Now, what have we discussed before, boy? Where will begging get you?"

Adam didn't respond. He swallowed as he spotted the wicked glint aimed in his direction. His heart rate picked up alarmingly, and his cock jerked and dripped onto his stomach. That damn look meant trouble.

The bed shifted. His premonition turned into a reality.

"Do you know what this is?" Daddy asked.

Adam's gaze was fixed on Daddy's large hand holding the ball gag above his face. Eyeing it with trepidation, Adam was not entirely sure whether he was happy with what was about to happen.

"Let me explain how this works. The use of safe words is vital, but when you have a ball gag in, you can't speak. So instead, Daddy will give you a piece of cloth to hold on to." As Daddy explained, he put the white square in Adam's hand. "If you need to safe word, you simply drop the cloth, and I'll stop."

While he carried on explaining how it was going to work, Daddy worked to fasten the ball gag with the leather straps at the back of Adam's head. The taste of leather filled his mouth. His tongue sat under the ball, making it impossible to move. His mouth filled with saliva, and he struggled to swallow. Coughing, he shook his head, eyes wide and begging. Panic gripped his throat, and he struggled to suck in a breath. Was he going to suffocate?

"Stop that now. Take a breath. Come on. Easy now," Daddy soothed, his large warm hands stroked down his wet cheeks. "You need to swallow normally. You are not going to suffocate. Breathe through your nose. That's it."

He kept his gaze locked on Daddy, working on controlling the surges of fear at having his mouth filled and stretched.

"Just imagine it's my cock covered in leather, boy."

The moment the picture materialised in his mind, Adam's body relaxed. He could do this. He allowed the weight of the leather ball to sit against his tongue while he concentrated on breathing through his nose.

He grunted and jerked, his eyes flying down to where Daddy's hands were tugging on the platinum hoops adorning his nipples. He tried to evade when Daddy gave them another solid tug. Adam mewled, his chest dancing under the onslaught, saliva dripping out of his mouth.

"They look so pretty. I knew when I bought them, they'd look stunning on your body. But I have a feeling they'll look even better when I attach my chains to them."

Adam quivered at the sensual promise in Daddy's voice, but then his nostrils flared. The slight tug was followed by the feel of cold metal resting on his sternum. His eyes automatically went to the mirror, where his own heavy-lidded, desirous expression looked back at him.

Dazed, he watched Daddy's hands work to attach the glimmering chains to the hoops in his areolas. When he moved back, his leather-clad arse slid over Adam's cock. It pointed towards his feet. It looked obscene. The flushed purple head dripped between his spread thighs onto the green cover below. Adam's lungs sawed in and out, and his whole body shuddered.

"Now, what shall we do next," Daddy asked with a wicked gleam lighting his eyes. He shifted off the bed, causing Adam's cock to slap back up and stand to attention. He gave a mournful sigh or would have if not for the gag. He closed his eyes to shut out the visual of him undulating against the bed while his whole body thrummed with neediness.

"Boy, eyes open," Daddy said, tugging hard on his nipples.

Adam's eyes fired open as he withered against the sheets.

"That's better. Now. Where was I? Ah. Yes, I remember how you liked the penis wand the last time we used it. But this time, I think you need to have your beautiful asshole filled as well."

"Arrrghhh," Adam garbled past the gag as his hips thrust up. His thighs quivered while attempting to shut and ease the throbbing ache spreading from his clenching hole, around his sac, and up his cock. The pool of liquid gathering at the base of his cock tickled his bare skin. The sensation of wetness sliding down his balls was like a wet kiss.

His eyes crossed before rolling back into his head. He begged senselessly, the garbled words indecipherable.

"What, my lovely boy? Do you need something? Do you want Daddy to fill your needy hole?"

Adam lifted his head, nodding frantically.

"Hmmm. Well, now, Daddy thinks you need to wait. Maybe as long as you made Daddy wait for a response to his messages." He tapped his lip, "Oh, that's right you never answered them. Should Daddy leave you hanging, as you did him?" he rasped next to Adam's ear.

Daddy licked a path down Adam's neck, over his collarbone, and down to his swollen nipple. Adam braced, but nothing helped when Daddy bit down hard on his tender nipple and tugged at the chain attached to the other. His body arched up, the air leaving his lungs in a rush. His eyes squeezed tight to shut out the visual above his head, which was only adding to the agony.

More saliva slid down his chin, and his eyes watered under the onslaught of pleasure and pain. His whole body felt raw, as if someone had taken a scouring pad and rubbed at his skin for hours.

Daddy continued to attack his nipples till they felt triple the size. Only when he released them both did Adam open his blurry eyes and meet Daddy's heated stare. Adam squirmed anew.

There was no point in trying to talk. He'd sound deranged. And he wasn't wholly convinced he wouldn't sound precisely the same without the gag. He couldn't recall a session like this before. Oh, they'd played, but those games now seemed tame in comparison to this. He wasn't sure he'd survive this in one piece. It was as if his Daddy was trying to take him apart piece by piece.

Adam had a moment to wonder why he hadn't bothered to fight his Daddy's demands or challenge him about what he'd found when he'd gone to the club.

The thought died at the sight of the eight-inch ribbed vibrator Daddy held in his hand. It was about the same length as his Daddy, the girth, on the other hand, was not. To Adam, it looked a lot wider and made his arse clench.

He shook his head, and his eyes convey a clear message—*no fucking way*.

Chapter Twenty-Two

Carl

THE WIDE-EYED EXPRESSION ON HIS BOY'S FACE HAD CARL ALMOST laughing out loud. Adam was clearly saying no to the vibrator he was holding up for inspection, but his gaze shifted to the handkerchief still clutched in his boy's tight fist. His eyes drifted back to his boy's face, and he gave him a sinful grin.

"As you haven't dropped your handkerchief, I'm going to assume you aren't using your safe word," he said, just in case Adam had forgotten he had the ability to do so. The last thing there should be with this kind of play were errors or misunderstandings, and with his boy new to this level of play, Carl wanted to be implicit.

When his boy glanced at his fist and his knuckles whitened, he couldn't stop a chuckle from escaping his lips. The fun aspect of their play gave him a secret buzz of excitement. Tantalizing his boy to distraction was his new favourite thing to do. Why had he never pushed him like this before?

He loved what he'd done with his boy, up to this point. The caring aspect of being a Daddy went way beyond anything he'd ever experienced in any of the Dom/sub relationships he'd been involved in. But while he'd been nurturing his Daddy side, he'd neglected the other part of him...his Dom.

The night at the club had been a stark reminder of what he enjoyed about being a Dom. And that side of him also needed to be set free on occasion. The free time he'd had thrust upon him, and while he'd been preparing for his boy's return, helped him realise he only wanted to be a Dom for one person, his boy.

The guilt swirling like a tornado inside him since the night at the club had left his stomach in a jumbled mess. His boy's hiding and lack of response left him considering if Adam had somehow figured out what he had done. He shook off the thought, considering it impossible. His boy had been on the other side of town with the other staff. He'd checked with Scott to make sure, and he'd confirmed Adam had spent the night with him and headed home in a taxi at one am.

His boy's twitching limbs drew Carl's attention away from his worries. *This is not the time, pull it together.* No, the time would come when his boy was mindless with pleasure. Then, Carl would start his interrogation. As everything else had failed to get his boy to talk, this was the only answer. If he enjoyed it in the process, *well, there had to be some perks, right?*

He picked up the lube he'd left on the side and made a production of lubing up the vibrator. Once slick, he switched it on to show what it could do. His mouth twitched as he bit his bottom lip, desperately trying not to let his humour show. Adam let out a series of little, mewled whines as he strained to close his legs.

Carl climbed back onto the bed and sat between his boy's legs. Adam's engorged purple cock was right in his eye line. Copious amounts of pre-cum slid down its turgid length, making it glisten in the glow of the lamps. His mouth watered for a taste.

I'll get my treat, later.

Barely resisting, his hand clenched around the vibrator, and his gaze travelled down to his boy's twitching pucker. His mouth now watered for a different taste, and this time, he didn't resist. He leant forward and blew over his boy's hairless, pink pucker, admiring how it clenched before sweeping his tongue over the wrinkled flesh. He groaned at the dark musky flavour on his tongue. Heady with the essence, he sucked and licked at his boy's rim. The tip of his tongue pierced his boy and worked to loosen the ring of tight muscle. He drew back but teased the puckered flesh with small licks until his boy humped against his face. Then he stabbed his tongue deeper, past the loosening rim, inhaling sharply as his senses were overwhelmed with the scent and taste of his boy.

The hip cants and nonsensical murmurings pouring from his boy made Carl's cock throb inside his leather trousers. He ground his hips against the mattress, willing his body to calm the fuck down. He dropped the lubed vibrator on the bed, needing both hands to hold his boy still.

The loud whining and trembling limbs as he pulled back had Carl's pulse racing. He sucked his fingers into his mouth and made a big production of getting them wet while his boy's eyes begged. His fingers dripping, he worked one into his boy's tight sheath while he clenched his own thighs with need. The tight sheath of muscles worked to suck him deeper, and unable to deny his boy anything, he pushed his digit in until his knuckles touched his boy's arse cheeks.

He lowered his mouth and spat on his boy's hole. It sounded so dirty and looked so depraved when the saliva slid down his boy's taint. Limbs trembling, his boy mewled and bucked. The desperation came off Adam in waves and increased Carl's own need. His fingers shook as he massaged the saliva into his boy's sensitive skin. Sinking two fingers past the loosened muscle and into his boy's channel, he gave him a moment to adjust before moving.

The feel of his boy's arse clenching made him chuckle. He pushed in fast and went deep, giving his boy exactly what he asked for. He replaced two fingers with three, and the howls coming past the gag were music to his ears.

He glanced up along his boy's undulating body. The sight had him clench his teeth. Adam's mouth gaped as far as the gag would allow, saliva running down his chin and collecting on his collarbones. The pain and pleasure were doing a number on his boy.

Not letting up, Carl wanted his boy to feel the burn and fullness.

He stretched his fingers, working on loosening Adam's ring for what was coming. He shifted, spitting again, and it dripped down onto the bed while he grabbed the lube. Once his fingers were coated, he worked to pushed in four. This time, he eased in slowly, knowing the stretch would be harder to deal with. This was the first time they'd done this, and he was sure his boy wasn't used to this type of play.

He was mesmerised by Adam's arse as it ate his fingers. An urge to fist his boy surfaced, but Carl stifled it. The patience for fisting was long since gone, but he consoled himself that there would be other times. He eased deeper, and only when he felt Adam's tense thighs release and the punishing grip on his fingers relax did he thrust.

His boy's cock bobbed up at the ceiling mirror, adding to the sticky mess as it leaked and dripped. Carl didn't think he'd ever seen a more beautiful sight. His boy's sweaty body strained, he was flushed from head to toe, his eyes were clenched shut, and his head was thrust back into the pillow. His fine neck arched while his body rippled continuously, his blue balls sitting tight to his body, and his engorged cock begged for release. He was stunning, riding the pleasure-pain barrier.

Breathless and desperate, Carl struggled to calm his thundering pulse as it deafened him. His free hand trembled as he picked up the vibrator, an urgent need driving him to move things along. He eyed his boy's stretched, slightly open pucker as he removed his fingers, and sent up a prayer that he was loose enough for what was coming.

The bulbous head of the ribbed vibrator was pressed against Adams hot flesh, letting him know what was coming. The sharply drawn inhale as Carl carefully eased in the first inch had him pausing. He glanced at his boy's glistening face and wide eyes. Sucking in a breath, he took hold of his own need to devour. The thread of his desire was unravelling, and he wasn't sure he had the strength to stop it.

His chest was heaving by the time Adam's head moved in encouragement. He sank the dildo deeper inside Adam's channel and frantically wished it was his cock. His boy juddered and quivered with desperation. The wanton desire in his heavy-lidded eyes played havoc with

Carl's control. He took a deep breath, the scent of arousal working against him. He snarled, and his jaw ached from the effort of showing so much restraint.

At the end of his patience, he sank the vibrator in as deep as it would go. His boy tensed and then shuddered while his hips worked to drive the vibrator deeper. Carl gave him what he wanted, sliding the dildo out and in. He repeated the motion twice more. Adam shook and moaned under the onslaught. Only when the babbling decreased did Carl switch it on. An evil grin spread over his face at the wide-eyed response. He upped the speed so the vibrations were strong enough to make his hand jolt.

His teeth ground together at the roar Adam released, his limbs frozen in a rigid pose. His cock, the only part of him moving, swelled and bobbed, frantically seeking its release. The penis wand Carl had planned to use lay forgotten on the bedside cabinet.

Carl left the vibrator lodged in his boy's arse and moved up his body. Saliva pooled in Carl's mouth. His eyes fixed on the turgid length bobbing in front of him. His mouth opened and lowered over the purple, weeping head. He sucked and sought the salty essence of his boy with his tongue. Carl moaned when his boy's cock hit the back of his throat, and Adam thrust his hips frantically.

Carl devoured him, swallowing every drop of his boy's excitement. His throat relaxed, allowing Adam to work his cock deeper. The solid flesh turned to steel, pulsing against the flat of his tongue. He slid his mouth up and down, working on sucking deeper each time. The vocal sounds above became strangled moans and cries.

Carl eased off, his gaze travelling up Adam's flushed, soaking body to his face. His hair was wet and stuck up in every direction. His eyes were red and swollen, leaking tears, and his chin was dripping with spit. His boy was at breaking point, and his heart stuttered at the sexy sight.

He sat up, wiping his mouth, and sidled off the bed. He stripped off his clothes and climbed back onto the bed between Adam's thighs.

He gloved up his cock and made quick work of spreading on the lube. He revelled in the extra stimulations, but he was already concerned he'd blow before he got inside his boy.

The vibrator thrummed against his fingers as he switched it off and slid it out of Adam's gaping hole. His heaving chest and grateful expression would have been funny if Carl wasn't feeling equally grateful, knowing what was about to be replacing the piece of rubber.

The dildo dropped to the floor. Uncaring where it fell, Carl moved over Adam. He covered his boy with his sweaty body, meeting his gaze and doing his best to convey how much his submission meant.

Cock throbbing in time to his pulse, it reminded Carl what it wanted. Nudging at Adam's slack hole, he lowered himself down. He hovered over Adam's gagged mouth. His shoulders bunched as he took his weight onto his elbows, not wanting to crush his boy. His fingers worked to unbuckle the gag. The moment he removed it, uncaring of the spit covering his boy's lower face, Carl slammed his mouth against Adam's. His mouth, hot and demanding, was met with equal enthusiasm.

Their tongues duelled for a moment before his boy submitted. Carl groaned and sank deep into his boy. The tight sheath left him breathless, the tight squeeze on the brink of being painful. He withdrew and thrust hard and fast.

The taste of Adam's scream in his mouth made his hips piston faster. The sound of flesh hitting flesh was lost under the clawing need to get deeper. Not releasing his boy's mouth, Carl lost himself in the taste and heat.

Adam's hot, tight sheath worked hard to suck the essence out of his body before he'd had his fill. Carl snarled into his mouth, need devouring him and making him lose all sanity. He gave it up willingly. His boy was his everything and nothing, and no one was going to take that from him.

Mine. Mine. Mine. The one word drove Carl to distraction. His pulse thundered as he roared into his boy's mouth. His hands tightened on Adam's face, needing to make him understand that this moment changed everything between them. Love surged to the surface, leaving him bewildered and lost in a sea of emotions.

Hard and fast he plundered. Their combined, noisy gasps and breathless wheezes got louder. Neither seemed willing to give up the other's mouth for more than a second to suck in some much-needed air. Carl was dizzy and deliriously drunk on his boy. His spine tingled, sensations firing up the nerves and short-circuiting his brain. His cock turned to steel, and his thighs tensed.

Wanting to release Adam's cock so they could come together, he pulled back, only to be met with an angry growl. His chest heaved as he gasped out "Shush... boy... just removing the cock ring... want you to come with..." He didn't get any further. His fingers had already slackened the leather, and his boy's cock erupted in spectacular style. Hot spurts of cum landed all over his hand and hit both their chests, covering them both. At the same time, Adam's channel clenched down. Eyes rolling into the back of his head, Carl released a strangled moan.

His cock was crushed in sizzling heat. His body reacted instantly. His cock swelled painfully hard and didn't give him a chance to take a breath. His hips slammed forward, his back arched, his mouth open. He snarled at the ceiling while his cock fired pulse after pulse of cum deep inside his boy.

His balls ached at the continued pleasure firing through his body, as Adam collapsed in a hot, sticky, sweaty mess on the bed. He heaved a sigh as his own body relented and released him from the grips of pleasure.

His gaze was riveted to his boy. Adam's languid expression caused his heart to swell in his chest. Adam's first genuine smile lit his gorgeous eyes. Carl's heart thumped against his ribs. The reality of why they were both naked and covered in cum pushed past his happy.

Lowering his body and resting on his elbows, he barely resisted sighing at what he was about to do. He cupped his boy's face gently. The need for the truth was too much to ignore. "Tell Daddy what's wrong." He wanted to shout at seeing the shuttered expression and lowered lashes blocking him. Instead he lowered his forehead to his boy's, staring deep into his eyes. The indrawn breath and shudder made his stomach jitter.

The sadness in Adam's expression was going to be Carl's undoing. The fucker would be able to wrap him around his little finger. The internal sigh rang like a bell tolling his doom.

"I can't fix it if I don't know what I did to upset you." He swallowed past the lump forming in his throat. "I need you to think about that for me. I'm not going to push. But I won't let you cut me out of your life the way you've been doing. And when you're ready to talk, then we can sit and have an adult conversation." He didn't miss the rebellious light sparkling his boy's eyes at the mention of "adult conversation," but he meant it. They were not children, and Adam might be twenty years his junior, but he was still an adult, and it was time he remembered that.

Carl kissed Adam's pouting mouth before pulling back. Adam winced as he withdrew, and a sense of satisfaction filled him, knowing his boy would be feeling him for days. He removed the condom, tied the end, and aimed it at the bin by the bed.

He untied Adam's legs next before crawling over him to reach his arms. He rubbed at his boy's limbs as he checked the bedside clock. The time they'd spent playing meant Adam was about to experience a significant bout of pins and needles. The thought had barely registered when Adam twitched. The complaints flowed as the blood flow returned to his limbs, but Carl worked to ease his boy's pain.

When Adam stopped complaining, Carl hopped off the bed. "Come on, we're a mess, and I'm starving. I hope you bought something good at the shops." He halted, his face aghast, sure he hadn't heard what he thought he'd heard. "What did you say?" he asked.

"I said I've got tinned ravioli. That should do, with some toast," Adam replied, shrugging at him as he walked towards him, bowlegged and stiff.

To see if he was serious Carl checked Adam's face. His eyes widened as he spluttered indignantly. "You can't seriously be considering giving me tinned, fucking ravioli. Me! An Italian-trained chef. You've gotta be having a fucking laugh."

His boy stepped into him, his small hands pulling his sweaty head down. "Nope." Adam giggled, laying a soft kiss against his mouth before lifting his head, smirking.

Frozen to the spot, Carl's mouth gaped open. He couldn't believe his boy thought he was ever going to eat pasta from a fucking tin. Whoever the fuck thought pasta even went in a tin needed bloody shooting. *Shit, pasta in a tin.* Carl shuddered. *Whatever fucking next?*

He grumbled at his boy, who had already disappeared out the door. He followed, complaining with every step he took. "Fucking pasta in a tin. Seriously, who thinks up this shit?"

Chapter Twenty-Three

Adam

A DAM EYED RICHIE'S RADIANT FACE GLOWING WITH HAPPINESS AS HE sat next to him on the garden swing. The smidgen of envy was quashed immediately while he gave himself a stern talking to. Richie had been through the wars with his mother and his evil ex. He deserved to be happy more than anyone Adam knew, himself included.

He took the glass off Richie and gave him a smile of thanks. The jug of cocktail mix Adam had made after arriving half an hour ago wasn't going to last long. Sipping at the chilled fruity alcohol concoction, he sat back in the garden seat. In companionable silence, he listened to the sound of leaves rustling through the trees and birds chirping.

The contented peace he always found in Richie's home eased the tension of the past few weeks. The visit happily coincided with Seb being at work and meant they could speak freely. With Adam hiding out, he felt bad for avoiding his best friend, especially after the last few weeks. Things had been stressful for Richie. The visit to the lawyer had been only the start when it had been revealed his dad was a bastard. Only out for the inheritance, he hadn't cared at all about what Richie was going through. Adam thanked his lucky stars how quickly Richie got over him becoming Marian's executor so that she could carry on protecting him. Then there was a trip to the Isle of Man, his dad was arrested for theft, and his ex-girlfriend got engaged to one of his ex-friends. And if that wasn't enough, Seb, or should that be Daddy, had moved into Richie's childhood home.

Adam fretted it was all a little rushed after everything Richie had been through. Surely Richie should take more time to figure out if living together was the right thing to do?

He gave Richie another searching look and sighed.

Who am I kidding?

Richie was head over heels in love with Seb and had been for some time. It was as plain as the nose on his face. They'd discussed Seb's past, which Richie had only shared so Adam could understand why Seb behaved the way he did. The new awareness of Seb's issues, and they were legion, proved how much he loved Richie. And when Seb acted like an arse, Richie dealt with it. Not only that, but he'd have made a great stonemason the way he'd chiselled away at the walls Seb used to protect himself.

Adam stifled a chuckle, recalling Seb's attempts at keeping a professional distance from Richie at work. To say he failed miserably was probably the understatement of the year, and in some ways, it had allayed Adam's fears. Are the worries for Richie a reflection of his own situation? Was he trying to push his own insecurities onto Richie?

Fighting the urge to bury his head in his hands, he clutched the stem of his glass. The more out of control he felt, the more he wanted to hide. Yet every day, he found there was nowhere *to* hide. Every which way he turned, Carl was there; his work, his home, there was nowhere to escape. The more Carl worked to break him down, the harder Adam dug his heels in, fighting against the inevitable. He wasn't even sure who he was fighting against anymore: himself or Daddy.

He glanced up at the clear blue April sky. The soft breeze caressed his hot cheeks. His restless gaze landed on the budding blossoms that hinted at the warmth of spring. The scent of freshly mowed grass had him turn his attention to the garden.

A grin spread across his face as he let his surroundings distract him from his fears for a moment. He glanced sideways at Richie, who sat quietly, watching him. Adam knew his friend was waiting for him to get his head out of his arse.

"You've been communing with nature again, haven't you." Adam giggled and took a sip of his drink.

"Yep. I noticed when Daddy fucked me on the grass, it's better short." Richie raised his voice to a high falsetto and carried on, "Even grass can tickle places it shouldn't, darlinggggg."

Adam coughed, snorted, and inhaled his drink up his nose. He choked and tried to ignore the burning in his nose as he put his glass on the ground. Wiping at his streaming eyes and rubbing at his nose, he didn't fail to notice that Richie, the fucker, his supposed best friend, was barely able to keep a straight face.

Adam pointed. "You did that on purpose," he accused in a hoarse voice.

"Of course I did. You keep having a go at me about the garden. What can I say? I like it. And I wasn't lying. Grass in those places does tickle." He shrugged.

Adam gawping had Richie continue.

"Daddy likes to commune with nature too," he said, giving Adam a flirty wink.

A grin spread across Adam's face at seeing Richie back to being his old self, only a much happier self, who joked and messed with his best friend like old times.

He shifted, winced, and then cringed. The urge to curse Carl sat on the tip of his tongue.

"Why are you wincing?" Richie demanded. "It's not like we've got to our usual drunken dancing gymnastics. And it's usually me wincing after we've danced around the house like fools. I tend to feel like I've aged to a hundred by the time you've finished with me. Hell, the last time we did that, I had to crawl up the stairs on my hands and knees to avoid standing on my noodle legs."

A wave of heat rode up Adam's neck and suffused his face. Eyes widening, Richie pointed at him.

189

Adam braced for what was coming and then wished he hadn't.

"What aren't you telling me, Pip? I thought we'd discussed this weeks ago, after the lawyer debacle, no more secrets. What aren't you telling me?" Richie eyed him for a second before asking, "Did something happen with Carl?"

Adam picked up his drink and gulped at his cocktail, hoping it would settle his nerves. He glanced away and looked at the flower bed sitting off to the side, next to the house. Praying for divine inspiration or better yet, a hole big enough to hide in, he worked on how to explain what was bugging him.

Richie

Over the years of friendship, Richie had learnt Adam would only talk to him when he was ready to. With purpose, Richie relaxed back on the swing and gave Adam the space to figure out what he wanted to say. He used his foot to sway the seat, hoping the small rocking motion would help relax Adam.

The afternoon sun warmed his face as he turned it skyward. Shutting his eyes, he allowed the sliver of hurt that still remained to surface. When Adam had finally confessed about his relationship, Richie had been floored. Wrapped up in his own misery, he'd missed what was happening in Adam's life.

As far as he could tell, Adam and Carl had secretly been dating for over a year. It didn't matter what Adam thought or called it. They'd basically been in a relationship. He'd argued as much with Adam. If he saw someone every week for more than a year, then what else could it be?

Adam could argue all he liked that they'd only really started a relationship around Christmas time, but it was bollocks. Carl might have taken a while to define what it was they'd been doing, but Richie wasn't stupid, and neither was Adam. He just didn't get why his friend denied it so vigorously.

Previous boyfriends Adam dated lasted no more than a few months, at best. This was very telling and unfortunately reinforced what Adam believed about himself. Adam's pick of undateable dickheads and money-grabbing pricks only strengthened his belief that it was his fault they didn't stick around, and no amount of talking could convince him otherwise. Even his mother, before she'd died, couldn't get Adam to accept the truth. And because of Adam's conviction that he was unlovable, he hid behind his snarky humour and devil-may-care façade, not showing his vulnerable side.

Significant insecurities about being unlovable all stemmed from Adam's dreadful parents and their attempts to brainwash him into thinking there was something wrong with being gay.

Carl had put paid to that at Christmas, though. Richie's lips twitched. *By Christ*, he'd have paid good money to see Carl face off with Adam's prick of a father. It gave him hope that Carl would be the one to break down Adam's walls and help him see that there was nothing wrong with him.

He opened his eyes and glanced at Adam, wondering how much longer he would hold out.

His fingers drummed on his leg, unsure what was going on inside Adam's mind as he frowned at the garden.

When he sipped at his drink, Richie kept his gaze on Adam. While Richie worked on drilling a hole into Adam's defences, Adam turned his head in his direction, humour lighting up his sea-green eyes.

"Why do I get the feeling you're secretly laughing at me, Pip? Come on. Stop avoiding talking about whatever the fuck has you looking like you got a stick shoved up your arse," Richie said with a cheeky grin.

"You know me too well. And who told you I have a stick up my arse," Adam quipped back, choking on his laughter.

Richie continued to stare his friend down, knowing full well how much Adam hated it. Saying nothing worked like magic on Adam and could make him spill his guts in minutes. *Fuck, it was a gift.*

Adam's eyes rolled, signalling his victory. "All right. Put the pleading eyes away. I give in," Adam said.

When Adam glanced at his lap with some concern, Richie shifted on the seat nervously.

"You asked for this," Adam said when he looked back up and jabbed his finger into Richie's arm.

"Hey, stop with the finger-jabbing," Richie grunted, pulling his arm away.

Adam didn't respond. Instead he picked up his glass and took a sip.

Richie wasn't sure whether he'd done that for Dutch courage or just because his throat was dry, but whatever the reason, Adam looked nervous. His stomach did jumping jacks. What else could Adam have to divulge that would warrant nerves?

They'd already discussed the similarity in their situations. Though initially it had been a little weird, Richie was excited at having someone to talk about his Daddy/boy relationship with. Someone who understood.

"I'm not sure where to start with all the crap in my head. So bear with me, okay?"

Richie nodded in agreement as Adam continued to talk.

"I know you told me about some of the sexy stuff you and Seb get up to. The spanking and getting tied up and stuff." Adam paused, taking another drink. "Well, Carl is a Dom. Actually that's not quite right. He was a Dom, and now he'd probably be classed as a Dom Daddy. He likes both aspects, or he does with me. Though I think he was just a Dom before me." Adam shrugged, licking his lips.

The confusion clouding Adam's face kept Richie silent. He offered a supportive smile and placed a hand on Adam's thigh. He rubbed his fingers in circles, hoping to ease some of the tension in the muscles beneath his hand.

"It's probably better I start at the beginning. One night I had a run-in at work with Carl, and he ended up paddling my arse. It turned out I liked it...a lot. Then Carl slowly introduced me to some of his toys and things like orgasm denial. But he never really went hardcore on me. And I never gave it any real thought. I'd researched BDSM and what it meant. I understood we were playing at elements of it. And to my mind, it was playing."

Richie tried his best to keep his mouth from gaping open, his mind shouting, "your best friend is into BDSM."

Adam shrugged at him like he was aware of the internal dialogue and continued talking like he wasn't blowing Richie's mind.

"There was never any mention of contracts or anything that really defined it to be a real BDSM relationship. And the problem was I was too chickenshit to ask Carl about it. There was a part of me that worried he'd maybe want me to be a real submissive, in every sense of the word. And though I love what he does to me, I don't want to submit in the way a true submissive would. There is no fucking way I'm kneeling at anyone's feet. I love being dominated, but I do not want to be subdued. That shit ain't happening," Adam said adamantly.

Richie moved his hand from Adam's thigh and instead took his free hand, clasping it tightly. He said nothing, hating the little lost boy look in Adam's eyes. He guessed where Adam's head went at the mention of being subdued. Richie's hate for Adam's parents had him sucking his lower lip between his teeth to stop the anger that wanted to escape. It was the last thing Adam needed. So he worked to fight back the burning in his throat, wanting to give Adam the same unbridled support he'd always offered so freely.

Adam

Adam chewed on his lip, his anxiety levels going through the roof. His pulse skipped so fast his body wanted to shake.

"The thing is, Richie, as the time moved on, it seemed silly to ask, you know? After six months, a year, it was like I'd missed the boat. Then out of the blue, he invites me for dinner, and things changed." He stared at Richie, swallowing the bile burning at the back of his throat. "Richie, shit, Carl has a playroom dedicated to BDSM. Who the fuck has a whole room and doesn't live the lifestyle twenty-four seven?" The moment he said it, he knew that was one of his biggest fears. The one he'd been shoving to the back of his mind since he'd seen the room. Witnessing Carl playing at the club with someone else had forced the reality in his face, whether he wanted it to or not.

"I don't know, Pip, but unless you ask Carl this, you're never gonna know the answer," Richie suggested gently.

Adam hadn't missed that Richie had reverted back to his childhood nickname this afternoon. Richie had recently stopped calling him Pip after he'd inadvertently used the nickname at work and caused some confusion about who he was talking about. Unable to sit still, Adam released Richie's hand. Resting his glass on the ground, he stood up, forgetting his current predicament. He groaned as licks of pleasure short-circuited his legs, and they trembled, forcing him to grab at the swing to hold himself up.

"Will you tell me what the hell is wrong with you?" Richie demanded.

Adam went to sit, but Richie was already up and moving to take hold of his arm, worry written all over his face.

"I'm all right, sort of. Carl's idea of a fun afternoon without him consists of a cock cage and a butt plug," Adam complained, his eyes crossing as he sat back down. Not sure whether to laugh or cry at Richie's wide eyes glancing at his nether regions, he chose to do neither, aware that he'd regret the movement it caused.

Instead, he cursed how exceptionally well Carl's ploy to break him down was working. Fuck, at the moment he would have confessed to anything, just so he could come. And that made him grateful Carl wasn't there to witness his weakened state.

Hadn't he taken everything Carl dished out? *Up to now,* his arse reminded him. His lips pursed at how his willpower was waning. *I can do this. I have to.* The need to get everything straight in his head bubbled inside him. Staying schtum was the only option until he knew what he wanted.

He sucked in a breath of fresh air, not liking his odds.

He sat up straighter and confessed his biggest fear. "Carl isn't playing at this type of lifestyle. He lives it. He has to have had subs that used that room before me and did things I'm never gonna want to do." Adam exhaled and met Richie's supportive gaze encouraging him to continue.

"I found something that confirms all my suspicions. I went to get something for Carl out of his bedroom drawer and found this business card with the name 'The Playroom' written on it. You know me, nose disease. I was intrigued enough that when I got home, I did an Internet search. It's a BDSM club." Adam braced, lowering his voice. "A club Daddy likes to visit and whips boys in."

"Wow. Hold the fuck up. He what!" Richie screeched as his eyes bugged right out of his head.

"Oh, stop that. It's not like that. It's consensual, and I'm sure Daddy's very good at it." He hated the underlying whine of distress he could hear in his voice.

"Fuck. Hang on. I need to get my head around this. I get the stuff about BDSM." Richie shrugged. "Well, sort of. But what do you mean he touches other boys when you two are dating. Is that normal? Because I'm telling you right now, that shit doesn't sit right with me."

"I'm not sure. We've never talked about that side of his life. As I said, I was too chickenshit to bring it up. And I only found out about the whipping shit a few weeks back. You know the night I went out with everyone from work and I ended up with no keys. I went to Carl's and found he wasn't in. I got the crazy notion after several cocktails, to go to the place on the card I'd found. Let me just say. Don't ever do that," he said mournfully, blinking back the tears that filled his eyes.

He swallowed the ball in his throat that was trying to choke him, and stumbled through what he'd found when he'd got to the club. "I didn't hang around after witnessing Daddy whipping the boy. Oh, and by the way, the boy looks a lot like me, making this whole situation ten times worse."

Richie stopped him. "Why worse? It's all fucking shit as far as I can see. There is nothing good about this whole situation!"

"Worse because I don't know if Daddy wanted it to be me on that cross and wasn't honest enough to ask me. Or that the boy and Daddy have been doing that type of thing for a long time, and that's why he's dating me. Because I look like him." Teary-eyed, he buried his head in his hands. He gave up the battle to hold the tears in, and they poured down his face.

"It made… me… realise how much… I have to lose this time around… I… love… him." He hiccupped out the last part, not looking at Richie for fear of seeing the condemnation on his face. Lean arms wrapped around his shoulders, and he found his face pressed into Richie's neck.

"What are you going to do?"

Adam lifted his tear-stained face, sniffing up. He gave Richie a forced smile. "I'm going to go to that club and get answers. And you're coming with me."

"There's no way Daddy would let me do that, not in this lifetime," Richie stuttered.

Adam let his humour surface, seeing Richie's face drain of all colour. "What Daddy doesn't know won't harm him," he said gleefully, tapping Richie's nose. "What is it they say? What the eye doesn't see, the heart won't grieve? I'm going, and you are coming with me." He spoke with conviction, hoping like hell that Richie would agree because he didn't want to go alone, and Richie was the only person he trusted with this.

When Richie gave a mournful sigh, he knew he'd won.

"How the hell are we gonna get in that club? Surely it's a private-type place," Richie asked.

Adam grinned with delight at the hope dying in Richie's eyes as he said, "Oh, you don't need to worry about that. We have an invite—"

Richie held up his hand, stopping him from carrying on. "Don't tell me any more. That way I won't have to lie to Daddy. Yours is not the only one who can come up with ingenious punishments."

Adam made a zipping motion over his mouth, his eyes alight with conviction.

Pray that if Daddy finds out what I'm up to, he's in a good mood because my balls will probably fall off before Daddy lets me come again.

He rolled his eyes at the voice of reason and prayed he'd cop a break.

Chapter Twenty-Four

Carl

CARL ROLLED HIS SHOULDERS, FEELING EVERY ONE OF THE KNOTS IN his tense muscles. He picked up the cloth and finished wiping down the stainless steel tops, glancing up at Lenny's shout.

"See you later, Chef. Have a good one." Lenny waved, bounding out the back door.

Carl waved and grunted back, his mind not really paying attention. He completed the mundane tasks, shouting out the odd goodbye as the kitchen emptied, leaving him to finish off. He'd taken to staying behind over the last few weeks when Adam was busy doing other stuff.

Tonight was no exception. Adam had made plans to visit Richie.

He scrubbed at the dirty top, his mind going to Richie and the previous day. For some reason, Richie's odd behaviour had set off alarm bells. He couldn't explain what caused it. Richie was always a little nervous around him. Yet for whatever reason, yesterday he'd acted like a skittish horse getting ready to rear at any opportunity. When he'd mentioned it to Adam, he'd quickly changed the topic. The look of guilt that he wasn't quick enough to conceal was enough to make Carl suspicious that his boy might have been talking about their relationship.

Though it was his general rule to keep both his private and his professional life separate, he was unconcerned about Richie knowing about his lifestyle choices. How could Richie know everything when Adam didn't?

Isn't it time to be forthcoming with everything?

He snorted at the counter.

"What's up with you? And what has that counter ever done to you?" Seb asked.

Carl sneered back and flicked Seb the finger.

"You look like you're trying to win a competition of who can make stainless steel gleam like a new pin. And by the way, you'd win hands down." Chuckling, Seb carried on, "If you ever decide to give up your day job, you'd make a great kitchen hand."

Well aware Seb was teasing, Carl ignored the jibe about the kitchen hand. They both had had their share of mucking in, cleaning up, and pot-scrubbing. When you were a novice chef, you didn't get much choice. It was put up and shut up if you wanted to get anywhere in this business. It was cutthroat and damn hard work. He fucking loved it. There wasn't a day he regretted the sacrifices he'd made to have this career. The dedication, the long hours, the gruelling heat, and the brutal head chefs. *Yeah, I fucking love it.*

He paused when Seb left him to it and strolled off towards his office with a bunch of files tucked under his arm.

It suddenly struck him how similar training to be a Dom and a chef were. They were pretty much the same. Only a Dom didn't have to deal with gruelling heat. What about a trainer using heat play to break him down? His body shuddered, not enjoying the memory. He'd understood early on there was a dedication required and the right mindset to understand that a Dom's pleasure was directly connected to their sub. The sub was the centre of it all, and without that, a Dom was nothing.

Fuck, fuck, fuckity fuck.

So wrapped up in his own feelings, he'd not seen the wood for the trees. His boy's need to feel like he was the centre of his world. Had he done that for Adam?

A great fucking Dom, aren't I? More like a dumb Dom.

"You dickhead."

"Hey, I take umbrage at that statement. Why the hell am I a dickhead?" Seb asked in the snooty tone Carl knew all too well.

He dropped the cloth and swung around, nearly colliding with Seb, having misjudged how close he was standing. "I wasn't talking to you." He pointed at Seb before turning his finger towards his chest. "I was talking about myself. Not that I meant to say it out loud."

The last month was evidently catching up on him. The restaurants had been manic, and he was convinced there weren't enough hours in the day to fit everything in. The new staff they'd employed didn't help as most were still finding their feet, which made him antsy.

Then there was the club. He huffed aloud, remembering he still needed to make time to speak to Nathan about his decision to stop doing the demos. Nathan, on the other hand, was a different kettle of fish. Carl wasn't big-headed. He knew he drew a big crowd and boosted their income. The money, though helpful, wasn't everything.

No, he couldn't give two shits about the money. What he did give two shits about was the need to get his Sugar Lips to talk about what was bothering him. Several times over the last few days, he'd considered confessing to his feelings, wondering if it would make a difference.

The L-word was there sitting, waiting, not so patiently, for him to man up. He wasn't convinced that using Adam's closed-mouth behaviour to cover up his own insecurities was working for either of them. *What if I confessed to my feelings, and then my boy didn't feel the same?* His stomach dropped at the prospect.

Stop it. I'm not blind. My boy loves me.

If that's the case, then why the fuck won't he talk to me?

Carl eyed Seb hovering next to him and chewed on his lower lip. There was no way Adam hadn't said something to Richie by now. How did one go about mentioning a relationship that had been going on for more than a year? It had to be only a matter of time before Richie slipped up and spilt the beans to Seb.

It had become commonplace for the staff to give little jibes about Seb and Richie's relationship. The contract would have been a deterrent to Adam's honesty in the past, but what about now? He gave a self-deprecating chuckle. The clause in the contract was a joke, and they all knew it. And it was something Carl wanted to talk to Seb about removing when they had their next sit-down meeting with all the managers.

He was pulled from his thoughts when Seb nudged his arm.

"You want to sit and have a drink?" Seb asked.

"Yeah, why not? Just let me go and wash the day off me," Carl said as he ambled off to take a shower. Twenty minutes later, feeling a little more relaxed, he sauntered into the dining room. The scent of rich food and expensive perfume had him glance around the now pristine room. A small thrill coursed through him at the part he'd played in creating the critically acclaimed restaurants with Seb.

His gaze moved to Seb, who was waiting for him in their favourite booth and that of their patrons. It allowed those sitting to view the whole room, and why it was also booked months in advance.

He sat and picked up the glass Seb pushed in his direction. His hand paused with the glass to his lips.

"Are you going to tell me how you found out about Richie's father's embezzlement, Carl?"

With a groan Carl eyed Seb. He'd been harking back to this subject for days, and Carl just wanted him to drop it. He shook his head and took a sip of the whiskey.

A look of determination crossed Seb's face.

Carl raised his hand and swallowed his drink. "As I've said about a million times, you really don't want to know. All I'll say is that I have friends in nefarious places." Carl snorted at Seb's look of disbelief. If Seb only knew who he mixed with on his time off, he'd freak out. He knew full well that even with Seb's proclivity for kink, he still fell firmly into the straight-laced category compared to him.

Distracted, he didn't immediately register what Seb was talking about.

"I wonder if the boys are having a good time tonight. My boy mentioned something about Adam having plans to take him clubbing." Seb sipped at his own drink before continuing. "My boy was worried he was going to be left alone because he thinks Adam is on the hunt for some action tonight."

The sound of his knuckles cracking broke the silence. Carl stiffened at the spark of humour in Seb's eyes.

"What do you mean hunt for some action?" Carl snarled, unable to brush off what Seb had said as if it meant nothing. He held on to the glass for fear he might jump up and throttle his friend.

At Seb's laughter Carl braced.

"You know fine well what action. Come on, we all did the club scene when we were younger. The main reason to go clubbing is to find a hookup." Seb shrugged nonchalantly as if he hadn't just pulled the rug right out from under Carl's feet.

Not satisfied with Seb's answer, Carl slammed his glass down and got out up to prowl around the tables. *Calm the fuck down and focus.*

Calm, what calm?

With Seb's loose lips, Carl wasn't positive he'd ever find his composure in the next century, never mind the next few minutes. He stomped to the bar, his eyes narrowed on the selection of spirits. He threw a glance over his shoulder, lifting his brow. "You want another?"

"Nope, one was enough. I need to stay sober for when my boy rings."

"You know you're cockwhipped, right?" Carl fired back.

Seb gripped his sides and roared with laughter. "Look who's talking," he cantered back through the laughter.

"Fuck off. I'm young, free, and definitely not cockwhipped," Carl stuttered, making sure to keep his face averted. The lie tasted bitter on his tongue, and heat crept up his neck and into his face. *Have I been too obvious about my feelings for Adam? Fuck's sake!*

No longer wanting a drink, Carl stalked back to the table without looking at Seb.

"Who do you think you're kidding, Carl? I may have had my head up my arse this last year and a bit, but I'm not blind. You've been eyeing Adam the same way Scott eyes your tiramisu."

"You seriously have to be kidding me right now. For fuck's sake, Scott has drool hanging off his chin when he gets within ten yards of my dessert. I am not like that," Carl snarled.

"I beg to fucking differ, my friend. So what gives between the pair of you?"

Carl remained silent, searching for a suitable answer. When he couldn't come up with one that fit, he shrugged. "I have no clue." He considered if he should just tell Seb what was going on. When Seb's phone vibrated on the table, offering him a reprieve, he released a sigh of relief.

Seb swiped at the screen of his phone and lifted it to his ear. Carl could hear the loud bass of the music when the call connected.

"Go outside, boy. I can't hear you," Seb shouted.

A few seconds later, Seb's eyes widened. He pulled the phone from his ear, he stared down at the silent phone.

"Shit, I've lost the connection. Listen, I'm gonna head to the club and see if I can find him."

Seb stood in front of him, rooting in his jacket pockets.

Carl's brows rose. "Which club did they go to?"

Seb glanced at him, a frown marring his face. "Emm, The Playroom. I've never heard of it, but Adam seemed to know it when he mentioned it to Richie."

The tiny amount of alcohol Carl had consumed roiled and burned up the back of his throat. His feet were moving before he realised what his intention was. He took hold of Seb's arm. "Are you sure it's The Playroom?" he asked with a sense of urgency.

His legs turned to jelly, and desperation rolled off him when Seb gave a tentative nod.

"Shit. Shitting hell. Come on. We need to get there and fast," Carl said as he dragged Seb with him towards the door.

"What? Why? What am I missing here?" Seb asked as he fought against Carl's grip.

Carl halted, releasing Seb's arm. Carl turned to face him. "It's a hardcore BDSM club. What the fuck is Adam playing at?" Not expecting Seb to answer, Carl marched to the door.

The sound of Seb giving chase and shouting, "How the fuck do you know this?" was ignored. The ringing in Carl's ears would have competed with the chimes of Big Ben as he ran to his truck, motioning for Seb to jump in when he caught up.

The engine roared into life as soon as Seb's door slammed shut. The tyres screeched as he pulled out, barely stopping to check for traffic. Normally he would have laughed at Seb grabbing for his seat belt as his body was thrown against the door, if he hadn't been so frantic to get to the club.

The truck juddered when he took the next corner far faster than he should. He gripped the steering wheel harder and did his best to keep the truck on all four wheels. His white knuckles stood out starkly against the dimness of the truck.

How had Adam managed to get an invite to the club? There were strict rules, and as far as he knew, they were never wavered from, ever.

"There will be hell to pay. Mark my words. If anyone has so much as laid one finger on Adam, they're dead meat," he snarled at the windscreen. Past caring what Seb made of it all, Carl had one goal. Get to Adam before he did something foolish and they both regretted it.

Chapter Twenty-Five

Adam

THE SUEDE INSIDE THE LEATHER TROUSERS ADAM WORE HAD SEEMED like a great idea, but now it was glued to his tacky skin. He rubbed his sweaty palms down his brand-new pink leather trousers. Why hadn't he chosen to wear something else? As he glanced around, the obvious answer didn't make him feel any less sweaty.

Lured by pink leather, he got a little carried away at the local fetish shop. With its array of outfits to suit every kink, it had been far too tempting. So instead of resisting, he'd purchased way more than he'd intended, including some fabulous black boots, with a heel he'd adored.

This was his one chance to see if he could embrace his Daddy's world. Adam's motto "go big or go home" bounced around inside his head as he dressed and decided to put on black eyeliner and lip gloss. He'd hardly recognised himself in the mirror, and Richie's gaping mouth and wide-eyed expression had been priceless when he arrived at the flat.

Adam wanted them both to be dressed in similar outfits, partly to ensure they looked like they fitted into the club scene. Richie, unlike him, would never be caught dead wearing pink leather, so Adam had bought him a pair of butter-soft beige leather trousers.

When he had shown Richie the leather trousers, the "fuck no" expression was to be expected. But after being persuaded to try them on and seeing how beautifully they fitted his arse, he had quickly changed his tune. Adam's humour at the whole situation had continued right up until they'd stepped inside the club an hour earlier. That's when he'd seen the error of his ways.

The Doms roaming around eyed them with far too much speculation. The sweat rolled off him as if he'd spent hours in a sauna. With Richie clinging to him like a limpet, he thought he'd be four sizes smaller by the time they left.

"Will you give me a break and stop trying to crawl up me," Adam hissed into Richie's ear.

"Fuck off. It's either that or leave. Do you see how these big fuckers are eyeing us up? I'm sure they think we're their next meal. And I've still not forgiven you for talking me into wearing fucking leather. If my Daddy finds out, he's going to have a fit. Seriously, I have a bad feeling about this, Adam," Richie murmured back.

The alcohol that Adam had thought would give him Dutch courage before they'd left the flat turned his stomach. How had he got into this bloody mess?

An icy dread froze him in place, his upset stomach all but forgotten. His arms now locked around Richie instead of the other way around. His gaze got stuck on the massive blond giant moving towards them. The men milling about the bar parted like the red sea to let him through.

The leather top, which had been loose when Adam entered the club, now seemed to cut off his air supply. His chest heaved. Thoughts crowded his mind, of participating in some of the activities he was doing his best not to stare at. That was impossible, given the massive mirrors behind the bar reflecting the whole room back at them. The mirrors made damn sure you didn't miss a single thing going on. Despite the sensory overload, Adam was a little mortified to find he was actually more than a little interested in and aroused by what was happening to some of the men on the small stages.

"There's a giant headed in our direction. What do you think he wants?" he choked out.

He heard Richie's put-upon sigh, but a memory surfaced, distracting him. It dawned on him that this was the club owner, Nathan Daniels. Adam's tongue glued to the roof of his mouth, unprepared for how stunning he'd be in real life. The picture on the Internet didn't do him any justice at all. It didn't capture the predatory nature in his tiger eyes or his prominent Roman nose. A square jaw covered with just the right amount of scruff to make a person wonder how it would feel scraping against their skin finished off what was a captivating face.

Adam could almost feel the power radiating off Nathan from across the room. His naked torso rivalled any bodybuilder he'd ever seen on the TV and made Adam wonder if he'd ever competed professionally. His firm chest, covered only by a harness, tapered down to surprisingly narrow hips. Long legs flexed with every stride Nathan took towards them. The black leather trousers were like a second skin, making Adam wish, just for a second, that he was those trousers. Everything about Nathan screamed power and control, and it made Adam tremble.

Nathan tried not to smile as he spotted the two petrified men, who stood out as newbies at the bar. It was only when he'd got closer that it twigged who the man in the fuchsia pink was. Carl's boy had taken the bait.

He chuckled under his breath, seeing exactly why his friend had fallen so hard. There was something alluring about Adam that drew the eye, and it wasn't just his beautiful face. It was more than that. There was vulnerability in his eyes that made the Dom in Nathan want to protect him and keep him safe. Then there was the spark of mischievous. It created a powerful punch that could knock a person right on their arse if they weren't careful.

Nathan hummed in appreciation, his gaze travelling up Adam's compact, leather-encased body. The boy had certainly dressed to kill. A laugh escaped when it struck him that if anyone touched the delicious man, Carl would probably kill them.

There was a moment of doubt, where Carl wondered if inviting Adam to the club might backfire on him, but he shrugged off the worry. Too late now, so he might as well have a little fun. Continuing towards the two men, Nathan kept his face amicable, offering a small smile. He stopped a couple of feet from them and held out his hand. "Hi, I'm Nathan, one of the owners of The Playroom. I haven't seen you two here before." His grin widened, knowing the effect it had. "So I'm taking it you're both here to see what we have to offer."

He bit his lip at the sight of Adam's shaking hand when he stuck it out with apparent reluctance. The man at his side squealed and clung tighter to Adam's side. Nathan took the small hand and squeezed. He let his fingertips caress Adam's knuckles a moment longer, seeing his nostrils flare and his pupils engulf his eyes.

"Err, yeah. I'm Adam, and this is my best friend, Richie," Adam stuttered.

Nathan released Adam's hand and focused his attention on the other man. Holding out his hand to Richie, he observed his stance and awkwardness, taking a guess at what his possible problem might be.

When Richie took his hand, Nathan tugged him closer. "It looks like you came prepared. I see you're wearing a cock ring. Do you have a nice little plug in your arse to go with it?" he rasped, putting enough sex into his voice to make Richie's eyes go impossibly wide.

Richie froze, telling Nathan his assessment had been right on the money. He lost his train of thought when Adam stepped between them, effectively dislodging his hand. Adam's enquiring brow lift caused a stain of red to fill Richie's cheeks. Richie was clearly uncomfortable, hopping from one foot to the next and looking anywhere but at his friend.

Evidently, Richie hadn't discussed what he was wearing under his clothes, and Nathan had to fold his lips together to trap the chuckle that tried to escape when he noticed Adam eyeing up his friend's crotch.

Realising he was to blame for Richie's discomfort, Nathan drew Adam's attention back to him. "So, what brings you here tonight, Adam? What are you looking to see"—Nathan paused for effect before adding—"and experience tonight?" He followed the question up with a salacious smile, and laughter bubbled at the back of his throat.

Adam looked at him like he was going to drag them up to the centre stage and force him to do something he didn't want. Then something shifted in Adam's expression, and he pushed back his shoulders and let go of Richie's arm. Adam took a step towards him.

"I'm not really sure. I'm not a true submissive, I don't think. I'm too..." Adam paused.

"Cocky, arrogant, feisty, free-spirited," Nathan supplied helpfully, enjoying himself immensely.

Adam chewed his lips before nodding at Nathan. "Yeah, I suppose all those. I'll admit I like to be dominated. But I would hate to be subdued, if you get my drift?"

As Adam continued to talk, Richie muttered something about needing the loo and strolled off. Adam paid no attention, too busy explaining himself.

Nathan listened intently to Adam talk about the aspects of play he did with Carl and how he'd like to try more intense scenes but was unsure how to broach the subject.

"I know my Da... boyfriend," Adam quickly corrected, "likes this." His hand waved around the room. "But he's never mentioned it to me. I... err... found out by accident."

Nathan gave him a knowing stare. The resulting blush covering his cheeks made him look adorable. He then let Adam off the hook. The same could not be said for Carl. Nathan was going to kick his bloody arse. He was a fucking Dom and therefore should know better. Where the fuck were the ground rules? What happened to the conversations to set out what was expected from both parties? Any Dom worth their salt did this at the beginning of a relationship. So that begged the question, why the fuck hadn't Carl?

Adam was left vulnerable and searching for answers that could lead to a whole heap of trouble. What if Adam had chosen to go to a different club where they couldn't control the outcome?

The disheartened sigh was barely restrained while Nathan tried to reason away his friend's lapse in judgement and his own growing anger.

Adam couldn't decipher what Nathan was thinking as he stared at him. A little unnerved, he fidgeted, his fingers working to squeeze into the too-tight leather pockets. When the silence between them lengthened uncomfortably, he sensed he might have said too much.

Seeking a distraction, he glanced around, searching for Richie in the crowd of people, wondering what was taking him so long. His mouth opened and then shut as he spotted Richie tucked in the corner of the dance floor. His phone was in his hand one minute; the next it went sailing through the air. Adam could see Richie's mouth moving from where he stood. When Richie raised his hands, Adam's attention was drawn to the massive Dom standing far too close for comfort. His dark, hairy chest would have rivalled a grizzly bear for sheer size.

Adam nearly swallowed his tongue in fright when the man continued to approach Richie, his meaty hands lifting to do God knows what. A predatory smile spread across the guy's face, and Adam screeched at Nathan, "Go stop the bear from mauling my friend." He shoved at Nathan, though it was like trying to move a mountain.

Nathan's bold laughter got his back up. About to lose his shit, he was thankful Nathan walked off to the dance floor. Wanting to make good on the promise he'd made to Richie not to leave him alone, Adam followed reluctantly. Why the fuck had Richie gone onto the dance floor in the first place? It was just asking for trouble.

"Isaac, stop playing around with the fresh meat," Nathan said at the larger man. "He's already claimed."

Isaac shrugged his linebacker shoulders. "Maybe, but fuck, look at him." He smacked his lips together and gave a leer in Richie's direction. "He's delicious, and I'm sure I could offer him a ride he'd never forget." The bear's roar of laughter made all the people around them stare.

Richie went deathly pale. Frightened he was about to pass out, Adam stepped into his body and wrapped an arm around his waist.

Nathan muttered something in the bear's ear, and thankfully he stepped back.

Adam pulled at Richie, but panicked fingers bit into his flesh. "I need to find my phone."

With the lights illuminating the ground, Adam scanned the floor. He spotted the phone in the corner of the room. He shook off Richie and went to retrieve it. When he returned, he was happy to see Nathan had stayed, and that he escorted them back to the safety of the bar and their waiting drinks.

Seeing Richie's glare, Adam sighed and picked up his drink to chug it back. He placed his empty glass down, resigned to going home. "Did you ring a taxi?" he asked, leaning into Richie's side.

"No, I rang Daddy…"

"You did what?" Adam screeched, looking about to see if anyone had heard him. His hand slapped over his mouth, and heat spread up his neck. Several heads had turned in their direction, including Nathan's, who'd stopped to talk to a man sitting two seats down from where they were standing.

Adam glanced back at Richie accusingly, hissing under his breath, "Why the fuck would you do that? We could have got a taxi to mine, and he'd have been none the wiser. Now he'll probably tell Carl."

"Listen, I already told him we were coming here. I'm not keeping secrets from my Daddy," Richie hissed back, his face turning a furious shade of red when Adam arched his brow. "Okay, I might not have explained exactly what type of club this was, but I did tell him where I was going."

The men around them were enjoying their little spat, so Adam took a minute to take a few calming breaths before lowering his voice to respond. "Let's see what Seb thinks…"

"And what do we have here?" A seductive voice enquired, making Adam's head whirl to his left.

He gulped, swallowing the pooling saliva in his mouth. All thoughts that Nathan was the most stunning man in the room faded. His eyes travelled greedily over the Adonis standing at the side of him, leaving him speechless.

He towered over them. Golden naked skin stretched over a swimmers build chest and narrowed down to sculpted abs. Every time he moved his stomach, muscles rippled, showing off the glorious eight-pack. The long, lean legs were encased in dark green leather that lovingly cupped his groin and offered the viewer a preview of what was underneath.

Adam inhaled, and a sweet musky scent overwhelmed his senses, making his head swim. Coal-black eyes, much like his Daddy's, held him captive. He was stuck to the spot. The man traced a roughened fingertip down his cheek before he leant in to him and whispered seductively in his ear, "You want to play with me?"

"No, he doesn't. So get your hands off him," Richie blustered.

The guy didn't drop his hand as his gaze turned to Richie. The toothy grin he gave to Richie wasn't at all friendly.

"I wasn't aware I had spoken to you?" A dark brow rose to make the point.

Adam's pulse skipped a beat when Richie persisted.

"You didn't, but he's not interested."

"I beg to differ," the man said, glancing back at Adam. "You want to play with me, gorgeous boy. I promise to make you sing with pleasure." He chuckled darkly.

Caught under the spell of his intoxicating promise and his

alluring charm, Adam shuddered. Then he stumbled into the bar and Richie as the hand on his face was torn away.

The next thing he knew, Carl had the stranger pinned to the bar, growling so loudly the whole club could hear him over the music. The one word rang clear as a bell. "Mine."

Chapter Twenty-Six

Carl

CARL AIMED FOR CIVIL AS HE MARCHED STRAIGHT PAST THE QUEUE OF men waiting outside the club, with Seb trailing behind. He nodded at Gary sitting behind the desk, before hurrying into the club.

His gaze swept the room, and his stomach dropped the moment he spied Adam at the bar. White-hot rage blinded him and took away his ability to suck any air into his lungs. He cracked his knuckles while thoughts of murder ran through his head.

Riveted to the hand that dared to caress his boy's face, Carl released a growl. The flush in Adam's cheeks and shy smile directed at Gabriel worked to rip any vestige of calm Carl would say he normally held. Like a cat with a roll of toilet paper, Adam's fluttering lashes and lustful stare took hold of his control and left a ripped mess in its wake. His jaw bunched and thrust forward. *Don't kill the fucker.*

He worked on keeping that thought at the forefront of his mind and tried to remember that he usually found Gabriel quite charming. *Just not when that charm was aimed at my boy.* The walk to the bar gave him no time to reset his head. All he wanted was to remove the hand touching Adam. With that filling his mind, he yanked away the hand touching what belonged to him and twisted Gabriel's arm up his back, shoving him into the bar. His boy staggered and fell into Richie, and a moment of regret filled him. Then he remembered his boy's flirty smile, and his anger boiled over. Like a volcano spraying its molten fire over everything in its path, his spittle sprayed Gabriel's face as he roared out one single word.

"Mine." He got right up in Gabriel's face, conveying exactly what he wanted to do to him through a steely hard glare.

Nathan turned at the loud shout, and his mouth dropped open. Too late to stop what was happening, he cursed loudly, "Fucking hell." He dived around Saul, who he'd been talking with, and hurried towards Carl and Gabriel, intent on stopping a full-on brawl. Not that he thought Gabriel stood a chance against Carl, but still.

Clasping Carl in a bear hug from behind, Nathan's arms bulged under the strain of holding him still. A sweaty layer filmed his skin as he used all his strength to restrain him.

"Let him go. He's got the picture, along with every other man in the place. Now calm the fuck down," he said directly into Carl's ear, willing the other man to see sense. Carl fought him for another minute before he finally released Gabriel.

When Carl's body relaxed a fraction and the angry posturing stopped, Nathan released him and stepped back. Wary, he stayed within easy reach in case Carl lost it again.

Nathan gave Gabriel an apologetic smile. "Have a drink on the house, and go find someone else to play with." He didn't sigh, even though he wanted to, when Gabriel offered Adam a flirty wink before sauntering off to the far end of the bar.

Frustrated at his part in debacle, Nathan rubbed at his face before giving the nosy bastards surrounding the bar and were trying to pretend they weren't glued to the show a "fuck off" glare. When they all fled, he turned and gave Carl a pointed look. Almost amused at seeing Carl hunch under his displeasure, Nathan hoped it sank in how fucked up the situation was. Losing his temper in their place of business was not cool. When Carl ignored Adam, Nathan held in yet another sigh. The tension mounted as they all stood, waiting to see who would speak first. Nathan's heart sank as he accepted that he'd helped to create the problem, so it was now up to him to clean up the mess.

He caught movement out of the corner of his eye, and his attention was drawn to a man standing behind Carl. His gorgeous face looked intrigued by what was happening, but there was a familiarity to it that had Nathan searching his memory for a name. His eyes narrowed.

Sebastian Smythe, Carl's other business partner. What is he doing here?

Nathan offered a curt nod and his hand. "I'm Nathan, and you're Seb, right?" Seb nodded, shaking his hand.

"It's nice to finally meet you," Nathan grumbled, giving Carl an angry glare, "I just wish it had been under better circumstances.

"Same here. Though I only found out about your connection to Carl about twenty minutes ago."

His tone made Nathan wonder if he wasn't the only one pissed at Carl, but he was too distracted by Richie's nervous, twitchy movements and constant glances at Seb to give it much thought. When Seb gave Richie a look that spoke volumes, Nathan realised they were a couple. He barely kept the smile off his face as he continued to chat to them for a few minutes to ease the tension.

"Does this mean I'll now get an invite to the restaurant?" Nathan inquired.

"You're more than welcome. What about next week? The evenings are fully booked, but I'm sure we could fit you in for lunch."

Delighted, Nathan grinned at Seb when they confirmed a lunch date for the following week. Waving both Seb and Richie off, Nathan chuckled at the contrition on Richie's face as Seb led him away. The smouldering glare Seb gave Richie said he might find himself having difficulty sitting down for the next few days.

As the men exited the door leading into the cloakroom, Nathan glanced at the two silent men standing by the bar. He pointed at Carl. "You, office, now!" His gaze swung to Adam. "You, trouble maker, are coming with us."

Adam stared longingly at the door Richie had just left through. When his boy glanced in Carl's direction, it took all his willpower to stay still and not throw Adam over his shoulder so he could teach him a lesson he'd never forget.

His boy sighed resignedly as Nathan commanded that they follow him.

"Come on. I said office, now. We're gonna straighten this out. And neither of you are leaving until I'm convinced it's resolved," Nathan said.

Nathan wittered about them being worse than a nursery school full of unruly toddlers. He rolled his eyes heavenward. How the hell would Nathan know about looking after a bunch of unruly toddlers?

He walked off and followed Nathan, casting a quick glance back to make sure his boy was following. *Why me, I ask? Why fucking me?* He paused, letting Adam walk around him so he was now in front, then gave the group of Doms showing more than a passing interest in his boy's tight arse wrapped in leather a "don't fuck with me" glare.

Only when he turned his attention back to his boy did he register what Adam was wearing. Gabriel touching his boy's face must have blinded him to everything because how the hell did he miss the pink leather? His mouth dried when his gaze travelled over his boy's spectacular body. The leather showed off Adam's attributes to perfection. He supposed he couldn't blame Gabriel from wanting to touch.

The anger still simmering below the surface didn't agree, and he struggled to swallow. His ears rang from the pulse pounding in his neck. The Dom inside him wanted to flex and show his boy who he belonged to. The deep-seated need wanted Adam strapped to the nearest surface, so he could have his wicked way with him, any way he chose.

With his restraint hanging by a thread, he dug his fingernails into his palms while he followed both men into the office. Stepping away from Adam, Carl barely held on to his control. He walked stiffly to the far chair and sat, the leather creaking under his weight. He kept his hands clenched in his lap and looked at Nathan.

"How the fuck did my boy get in the club without being a member?" he asked, anger lacing his voice. The wary expression Nathan wore made his eyes narrow. Suspicion wormed its way past his anger, but before Nathan could say a word, Adam interrupted.

"I applied. There's a form online. And when I completed it, there was an offer to an introduction night, so I asked for an invite," he offered in a belligerent tone.

Carl disregarded the loud sigh Nathan released, too busy snarling at Adam, who'd stuck out his chin in defiance.

"Right, you two, stop it," Nathan said, giving Carl a hard glare. "Enough. You need to pull your heads out of your arses and try honesty for a change, the pair of you. This is a BDSM club, not a bloody remake of Fantasy Island. Stop pussyfooting about. Tell each other what you want and move the fuck forward." He walked to the door.

"Don't mess this up," he said and excited the room.

Knowing Nathan was right didn't make it any easier when Adam stood defiant and looked anywhere but at him, his small chest heaving.

Carl got up and scooped up his boy, holding him firm. "Don't even think about kicking me," he said through gritted teeth when Adam moved his legs.

A warm breath huffed into his shoulder crease a second before arms slid around his neck. Carl took that to mean he was safe and walked over to Nathan's large leather office chair. A chair built for more than sitting on, it was as sturdy as they came. That was more than could be said for the one he'd just vacated. It barely held his own weight, and Carl wasn't taking any chances.

He sat and settled his boy so he straddled his lap, facing him. Adam's chin thrust out, and Carl took hold of it, looking directly into his eyes. The swirling emotions he saw there made it difficult to make sense of what his boy was thinking.

"Talk to me. Is the visit here part of what you've been hiding from me?" Carl demanded, a little harsher than he'd planned.

His boy narrowed his eyes in warning. "Daddy, I'm not the one keeping secrets, am I? You're a member of this club. And... and you've been coming here... whipping boys... while we've been boyfriends. And you're supposed to be my Daddy. And don't even think about denying it. I saw you with my own eyes," Adam yelled, an angry red flush covering his face while his eyes burned with accusations.

Carl dropped his hand and opened and shut his mouth several times, no words coming out. *He saw me, fuck. How? How was it even possible?*

This was why his boy was so distressed. *Oh, fuck, it was his fault.* His boy challenged him to lie, but Carl had no intention of denying it. His gut roiled at the untold anguish he'd unintentionally caused. He swallowed the bile at the back of his throat as awareness slid past the wall of misery. The emotions he'd felt at seeing Gabriel touching his boy's face surfaced. Was that how his boy had felt at seeing him touch someone else?

Fuck, why didn't I just tell him the truth? I was too chickenshit, that's why.

Self-recriminations weren't going to help now. His boy's chest heaved, and his strained expression held traces of fear.

"I'm not a member, boy. I own half the club." He waited for a beat for that to sink in, his eyes never leaving his boy. "Nathan asked me to do a demo with the bullwhip months and months ago, and I forgot all about it when things got serious between us. He texted me the day we went to get your piercings to remind me I needed to check in. It was too late to ask anyone else to step in. I was left with little option. I had to do—"

"Then why didn't you ask me to come with you, Daddy?" Adam wailed over the top of him.

He didn't have an answer. Truthfully, he hadn't even considered asking his boy. The selfish part of him didn't want to share Adam with the men at the club. If anything, tonight reaffirmed that more than ever. This level of possessiveness was new to him and hard for the rational parts of his brain to process.

Tears rolled down his boy's pale cheeks and cut at Carl's heart. He took hold of his boy's cold cheeks and wiped at the tears with his thumbs. "Please don't cry. You're cutting my fucking heart to ribbons," Carl begged.

"What do you think you're doing to me," Adam sobbed inconsolably.

"Buggering hell," Carl growled out. "I'm messing this up by not explaining myself properly. It's not that I didn't want you with me. I do. It's just I don't want anyone looking or even considering touching you. You're not getting that I wanted to rip Gabriel's arms off for daring to touch you tonight. Never mind rip his eyes out for looking at you like he wanted to devour you. You're mine, and I don't know how to cope with these possessive urges. I've never had them before with anyone. And it's making me crazy even sitting here, knowing Gabriel is just downstairs.

"And just so you know, I was going to confess what I'd done right after the event. But if you remember, you went into hedgehog mode, hibernating."

The wet chuckle eased Carl's thumping heart.

"Do you mean it? That you were going to tell me?" The quiver and look of disbelief in his boy's eyes continued to cut at him.

"Yes. Don't doubt it. I wanted to talk. Only, the walls you kept throwing up were stopping me, and I was trying to be a good Daddy and let you have time to come and talk to me." He sighed. "That didn't work out so well, did it? You went behind my back and came here to find... what... answers?"

He waited to see if his boy would be honest this time and tell the truth.

Chapter Twenty-Seven

Adam

ADAM WORKED TO KEEP CONTROL OF THE TEARS CLOGGING HIS throat and scrubbed at the damp lashes blurring his vision. He sucked in a deep breath, praying he wouldn't fuck things up any more than he had. He could hear the truth in Daddy's explanation and see the honesty shining in his eyes.

The urge to cuss at his stupidity for not facing the problem at the time was pushed aside. Too late for self-recrimination. The wound had already festered while he'd picked it to death over the last few weeks. Inadvertently, he'd allowed it to infect their relationship and the dishonesty spread till he couldn't see past it.

Adam straightened his spine. *Be brave. I can do it.*

"I came to the club the first night because I saw the card in your bedroom drawer, when you asked me to get you something. Then on the work night out, I got locked out of my flat, so I came to your home, and you were out. In my not so sober state, I got the crazy idea to check out the club and well…you know the rest," he rushed to explain, not wanting Daddy to think he'd been snooping.

"It's fine, boy. I don't think you'd be nosy," Carl reassured, rubbing his warm hands up his arms.

Adam sighed under the caress. He relaxed his weight against Daddy's chest, needing the contact to continue. "When I came to the club that night and opened the door and looked inside, I didn't initially notice you. I was confused for a minute, not understanding what I was seeing. It took a few seconds even to register it was you up on the stage. I was so taken by the boy's reaction to the whip that I missed the vital part. The man holding the whip was, in fact, my Daddy. Anyway, once I got my bearings, I ran. Then got so caught up in my head with why you didn't talk about it and that this was..." Adam hesitated, licking his lips. He willed himself to carry on, locking eyes with Carl, needing to see his reaction to the next part. "This was the real lifestyle you wanted and that you knew it wasn't what I wanted all the time. So you came to find it with someone else..." he trailed off, not sure what Daddy's furrowed brow meant.

Adam didn't have to wait long to find out.

"I love you."

Those three words dropped like stones into a pond, causing ripples to roll through his body as Daddy carried on talking.

"There isn't any lifestyle in the world that could match what I want and have with you. You're my boy, and yes, the Dom side of me wants to push you to try more, but only if and when you want to. Everything else pales into insignificance next to you. You're my heart, boy."

Adam opened and shut his mouth, but no words came out. His heart thudded against his sternum, fighting to burst out of his chest. Tears leaked down his cheeks. Emotions held his throat captive and surged through him. They tumbled and rode roughshod over his tender soul.

He hiccupped, sobbed, and cupped his Daddy's face, declaring, "I love you too, Daddy, so much. I didn't know how to keep it from swallowing me whole. It's so scary. I was terrified you didn't want me in the same way. That's why I've been avoiding talking to you. I knew the minute I started to explain it would all come out. Then I stressed that I wasn't enough...wasn't... loveable," he whispered the final part, unsure how Daddy would digest that nugget of information.

His breath got trapped in his lungs. Daddy's mouth swooped

down on his, giving him no time to think. Adam opened his lips, allowing Daddy to dominate his mouth. Carl's firm lips pressed against his own. The kiss was hot, wet, and sloppy, their teeth clashing together. Tongues danced sensuously against each other and made Adam groan. His screaming lungs cried out for oxygen. He didn't care. He couldn't bring himself to stop when he could taste Daddy's need in the hot demanding kisses. Who needed oxygen? Not him.

The kisses bled together, making him mindless with want. They took him apart bit by bit and put him back together with the love that fuelled the exchange. His body undulated against Daddy, the love firmly in the driving seat.

Breathless and needy, Adam ground down. The hard length pushing against his arse drove him to rock back and forth. Desperation clawed at him, and he roamed his hands over Daddy's jumper seeking to reaffirm this was real. Adam's chest heaved.

He mewled at the sudden release of his mouth. His dazed eyes sought out Daddy's. His fuzzy head worked on figuring out why they were stopping.

Daddy gave him a slow, sexy-as-sin smile. Adam's cock bucked in the tight confines of the leather, loving the sensual threat written on the face in front of him.

"Now we need to decide on a suitable punishment for my boy not being honest, don't we?" Daddy rasped.

The air left his lungs in a sudden explosion. Adam struggled to swallow, his gaze riveted to the meaty digit tracing down the front of the leather covering his cock. The pressure was not nearly enough, and Adam thrust forward wanting more.

"Tut, tut. That will not do. Daddy is in charge here. And I don't remember saying you could thrust into my hand."

Adam hated the amused chuckle his groan of despair elicited.

"Slide off my lap, boy."

Adam was released before he could argue. He huffed, but the wicked glint in Daddy's eye was clear. Do as he was told or suffer the consequences. Uncertain what they would be, Adam wasn't stupid enough to push it, *yet*. An idea took hold. Would Daddy take him downstairs and strap him to God knows what, to punish him? Adam wasn't wholly convinced he'd try and stop that from happening.

Vivid images caused licks of pleasure to stiffen his already painfully aroused cock, forcing him to clench his thighs. The time he'd spent in the club had answered at least one question. He was definitely interested in letting Daddy push him past his current limits.

Horny and distracted, it took a second to register what Daddy was doing. Adam's eyes widened as he clutched at his chest.

He shuddered, recalling the one time he'd flicked channels and come across a programme of a woman giving birth. He hadn't been quick enough to change the channel, and he'd seen the large chair they'd used. The centrepiece was divided into two, so the woman could rest her legs on the split base. This allowed the midwife to effortlessly get between the woman's legs to help deliver the baby.

The large leather chair they'd just been sitting on was dismantled and transformed in much the same way. The leather base moved and split down the middle and would allow for the same level of access the midwife had required. Only he knew damn well what Daddy would be accessing as he moved the final pieces into place.

Adam trembled.

Why was a seat like that in Nathan's office? Adam then mentally slapped his forehead, when it dawned on him exactly why there was a chair like that in the room.

Daddy's efficiency gave him a moment of doubt until he derailed all Adams thoughts with a wicked grin. He gulped, his gaze moving back to the chair. His colourful imagination was already seeing himself spread out for Daddy's pleasure. Adam clasped his thighs tighter together. His hand roamed to his straining erection, working to free it from its leather confines.

"What do you think you're doing, boy?"

Adam jumped, hand dropping from his half-open zip. His gaze

met Daddy's. "Emm, I… emm… was helping." He flushed scarlet, realising how foolish he sounded.

"Is that so?" Daddy's dark brows rose. "Then continue. Daddy will just stand here and watch to make sure… you don't help too much."

The sexy drawl made Adam's thrumming cock take notice. It leaked over the leather jock he hoped Daddy was going to love. He took a deep breath, willing his trembling fingers to work as he fumbled to finish opening the zip of his trousers.

He huffed in exasperation. The leather was no longer his friend; it stuck to his sweaty skin. This was not how he saw this happening. *Sexy, yeah, right.* He probably looked like he was having a seizure, trying to wriggle out of them. Sticky and sweating, he heaved a sigh of relief the moment he managed to get the trousers down his legs. Unwilling to think about how he was going to get them back on, he threw them in the corner of the room.

"Now what do we have here?" Daddy growled.

His head shot up. The stain of desire on Daddy's strong cheekbones made Adam stand up tall. He held Daddy's gaze, spreading his arms out a little. Deciding to show off a little, he did a small twirl.

A rabid snarl made his heart rate accelerate. When he saw the feral glint in Daddy's dark eyes, he barely managed to stay still and not step back.

"Come here." The demand brooked no argument.

Adam swayed his hips provocatively, wanting to entice Daddy into breaking the iron control he liked to maintain. He stepped to within a couple of inches, his feet sinking in the carpet underfoot as he tilted his head back, keeping eye contact. His tongue slid over his full lower lip, making it slick and shiny. Putting his hands on his hips, he gave Daddy a sexy sneer. "Yes, Daddy."

Empowered with the knowledge Carl loved him, Adam couldn't resist yanking his chain. The excitement and wonderment of those three words overshadowed all his old insecurities. No one could tell him he wasn't ten feet tall or fucking invincible. He wanted to revel in these new feelings for as long as possible.

"You wouldn't be trying to goad Daddy would you, my gorgeous boy, hmm?"

A shiver rippled down Adam's spine at the sexy promise on Daddy's face.

"What? Me, Daddy? Why no," Adam said innocently, fluttering his eyelashes.

One minute he was standing, the next he was in the chair. His chest seized at the mere seconds it took for his legs to be bound by the restraints. His arms were wrapped around the back of the chair and handcuffed to a metal rod he'd no clue was there.

Completely incapacitated, he wheezed in panting gasps, leery of the way Daddy stood over him with an evil smirk on his face. Air backed up in his lungs as Daddy moved and undid the buttons at the sides of his crop top. The leather parted and was pulled over his head.

Adam glanced down, and his eyes bugged out. The word debauched sprang to mind. Black leather straps secured him to the chair, with his legs spread wide. The dark leather stood out starkly against his golden thighs. His solid erection poked out the top of the tiny pink leather jock, pre-cum leaking over the leather, darkening it and showing how excited he really was. Not that his freight train breathing, heaving chest and trembling limbs weren't already enough of a giveaway.

Sucking in some much-needed oxygen, Adam prayed to whatever God was listening he wouldn't come before Daddy touched him. The months of orgasm denial were a distant memory. The excitement, combined with Daddy's declaration of love, had him teetering on the edge, and he was sure one caress to any part of his body would be enough to send him flying over it.

Daddy walked to the large desk and faced him. Adam strained to see what was in the drawer Daddy opened. The sexy sneer gracing Daddy's face set Adam's teeth on edge.

"You know what this is, boy, don't you?" Daddy chuckled devilishly.

Adam's eyes were glued to Daddy as he opened his hand to reveal a penis wand. He couldn't speak. His tongue was glued to the roof of his mouth, so he simply nodded instead. The large bottle of lube that followed was used to coat the thin wand, making Adam's thighs strain to close. His cock twitched, his mind and body debating whether they were going to like having his cock stuffed full.

The threat Daddy had issued weeks earlier came to mind, and Adam groaned. As if Daddy read his mind, he explained what he was going to do.

"I made a promise to you, didn't I, to fill your pretty little hole? Only Daddy broke his promise. But don't worry. I'm going to make up for it now."

Adam released a snort of disbelief. "Oh yes, Daddy, this is all about me," he quipped.

"Now you wouldn't be cheeky, would you boy?"

The low growl set Adam's body quaking. Goosebumps erupted all over his naked skin. Chewing his lip between his teeth, he worked to stop the mewl escaping at the naked desire in Daddy's molten eyes. It seared through his body and reached his battered soul, bathing it in warmth and love.

He lowered his gaze, offering his submission. "No, Daddy," he acquiesced. His tongue felt thick and clumsy in his mouth.

Large hands came into view. The jockstrap was lowered. Daddy manoeuvred the leather to trap his balls in a tight grasp as it freed his erection. His cock slapped excitedly against his stomach, smearing pre-cum on his skin. Adam moaned. What was going to happen next? His thighs twitched at the endless possibilities.

"What is your safe word?" Daddy asked.

His voice sounded as if his vocal cords had been rubbed down with sandpaper. The sexy rasp did a number on him. "T... T-shirt," Adam stuttered.

"Good boy. Now, remember if this gets too intense, don't be afraid to safe word for Daddy."

With no further instruction, Daddy came over to the chair.

Adam strained against the seat. The slippery wand teased his slit before the tip was pushed inside. His eyes scrunched shut. The sensation caused Adam to hold his breath. His arse clenched against the seat when Daddy's warm, slick fingers stroked his cock.

He whimpered, and his cock bucked while Daddy slowly inched the wand further into his body. On a rush, his lungs emptied. He locked his legs to the chair, frightened to move an inch. His eyes rolled into the back of his head at the fullness and pressure inside his cock. A relieved sigh left Adam's lips when Daddy clipped the wand to the head of his penis to hold it in place.

Okay, I've got this.

A howl rent the air. Adam's eyes fired open, and he rocked forward at the intense, painful burn at the tip of his cock. Daddy's teeth nipped again, making his eyes water and slam shut again. His hips juddered against the chair, but it was impossible to evade. The dark chuckle warned of more to come.

"Arrghhh, fuckkkk," Adam screeched.

His blurry eyes stared down at the sharp-toothed nipple clamps adorning both his nipples. They caused his tiny hoops to stand proud from his chest. He shook his head. "Please noooooo, don't pull them," he begged, to no avail.

His head thudded back against the headrest of the chair. His cock bobbed frantically, and his legs and arms shook. Sensations fired from the tips of his nipples, right through his chest, down his abs to his groin. Daddy tugged on the tiny hoops, elongating the tips of his nipples till they were twice the length and swelled painfully.

Adam squirmed, cussed, and shouted. Tears dripped down his cheeks and chin onto his collarbones. He sniffed noisily when Daddy finally stopped torturing his tender and abused nipples. Wilting into the leather seat, Adam's chest heaved from the brush of warm air stroking over his tender buds.

A moan fell from his lips. His hands scrabbled at the back of the chair. The clang of metal grew louder as Daddy brandished an anal wand. His blurry eyes counted the number of beads. Adam gulped at the size of the last one, easily bigger than a golf ball. His channel clenched, and he had the safe word on the tip of his tongue. *Be brave, be brave. I can do this.* He kept up the litany.

That was right up until Daddy eased down between his spread thighs, focusing on where the anal beads were headed for. The moment the cold, slippery rubber touched his overheated skin, his mind shut down.

The feel of the first bead sliding in was enough to have him cant his hips, the burn delicious after feeling so empty. He whimpered as the next bead popped past his rim, stretching him. He didn't get a chance to breathe out before the next two eased in. He wheezed and gasped in a much-needed breath. His thighs trembled at the stretch. Adam lowered his gaze, and his heart stuttered.

Daddy's hand was wrapped around the remaining three beads. "Daddy... I"—his head shook—"can't."

"You know what you have to do to make Daddy stop." That was the only warning he got. The wand was pulled back and thrust in deeper. The next two beads slid home. Waves of pleasure clouded his mind. His channel convulsed, and his rippling stomach clenched. His cock bobbed, making the wand rub against his nerve endings. "Arggghhh... Fucccccckkkkk."

Vision turning white, Adam clung on to the metal bar holding the handcuffs. He strained to keep present. His mind had other ideas and floated off into heaven. He could hear the cries, but they sounded far away when the last bead sunk home. Body bowing, muscles locking tight, cock throbbing, Adam bucked in desperation. Pain morphed into a pleasurable beast that attacked his body, leaving him helpless to the onslaught. His hips thrust violently against the chair, and spurt after spurt of hot cum erupted from his cock. Sticky warmth was the last thing he felt as his head flopped back against the chair, and he sank into delightful oblivion.

Chapter Twenty-Eight

Carl

CARL LISTENED TO PAULO HIS NEW TRAINEE CHEF WITH HALF AN EAR as he explained what was going into the soup he was making. Paulo worked diligently, and Carl refused to sigh when he looked at him expectantly. With what had happened last night going through his head on constant replay, Paulo was lucky Carl had the wherewithal to nod.

Like that's new! he grunted, rolling his eyes when the sound made Paulo jerk.

The guy was proper jittery, no matter what Carl did. Paulo was more nervous than an eighteenth-century virgin on her wedding night. "Paulo, do you mind me asking what has you so fucking nervous? It's not like you're cooking for the Pope or anything," Carl asked with a grin lighting his face, aiming for light-heartedness.

The pinched smile he received in return told him he was failing miserably to lighten things between them. Paulo had been working with him in the kitchen for just over a month. In all that time, he continued to act like a frightened rabbit. Fear and lack of balls in a kitchen, where head chefs could be brutal, never worked.

Thoughts about how Paulo might not make it, Carl kept to himself.

A pink hue crept under Paulo's tanned cheeks when Carl glanced over and caught Paulo staring at him with something akin to hero worship in his gaze. Was Paulo suffering from a little hero worship? Was that why he acted scared? Carl's mind wandered back to the first few months he'd worked with Massimo Bottura. Those months had been the worst of his life. He sniggered, looking back at how he'd been a bungling idiot most of the time, stuttering and dropping stuff all over the place when Massimo spoke. He'd inspired and terrified him in equal measures.

The deep-seated joy and the calm aura Massimo exuded when he was creating magic in the kitchen inspired Carl to work hard. He vividly recalled the first experience of tasting Massimo's risotto alla pescatora, and his mouth watered. It had been a religious experience for him. He'd been hooked after that, craving Massimo's culinary genius, wanting nothing more than to be the same.

Paulo muttered, "Che cazzo è."

Carl quickly translated the Italian and roared with laughter, though he was perplexed as to why Paulo was muttering "What the fuck." Carl wiped his eyes and glanced around. The whole kitchen had come to a standstill.

"Get back to work. Nothing to see here," he said, grinning at the staff. He looked back at Paulo and slapped his shoulder playfully. "I think you and I are gonna get on just fine."

The door swishing open from the dining room captured Carl's attention. Twisting his head towards the door, he switched his attention to the man standing in the entranceway. His heart clutched as Adam hailed Scott, who stood at the serving counter waiting for Billy to finish plating a meal.

Then Adam glanced at him, offering a saucy wink. His body went on full alert and had him wishing the kitchen were empty. He shifted and willed his cock to behave.

The slight hitch in his boy's breathing was the only outward sign that he wasn't as calm as he was trying to portray. Carl adjusted himself before he stepped around the counter and walked over to Adam.

They hadn't spoken last night after they'd left the club because

Adam had been too out of it. Adam's orgasm had rendered him unconscious, and when he'd roused, he'd been too tired to do more than snuggle. When they got back to Carl's, they'd gone straight to bed, and this morning, they'd woken up late and had to rush to get to work on time. The drive was fraught with rush hour traffic and had been a complete nightmare, requiring all his attention. Then Seb had immediately collared Adam, needing to discuss some problem they were having with a sister restaurant booking system.

How long have you waited for Adam? *Years. So get a fucking grip.* Carl rubbed at his neck. The large tight knots in his shoulders were killing him.

How was he supposed to behave around his boy at work? *Fuck.* Did his boy want their work colleagues to even know they were a couple? Would Adam be happy with Carl touching him or kissing him in public?

He fidgeted, waiting for Adam to acknowledge him, while shoving the endless bombardment of unanswered questions to the back of his mind. His boy's sea-green eyes flickered toward him, and the urge to drown himself in their depth was too much to resist.

Carl crowded Adam. *Fuck the answers.* Cupping Adam's cheeks, he gently caressed the smooth skin. He lowered his head and gently kissed the mouth that opened in surprise. He swallowed the dreamy little "O" and soft sigh that followed. He kept the kiss light, even when he ached to deepen it and take what he wanted. The taste of his boy's sweetness lingered on his tongue before he eased back.

Their gaze locked, and everything faded away. The noisy kitchen, the scents of frying meat and spices, all disappeared at seeing the love shining up at him. He swallowed past the need that gripped him by the throat, and made him want to confess how he felt. He dropped his hands when they went to tighten and draw his boy back to him. Not quite convinced he had enough control to keep touching and not ravish Adam right in front of the staff, he took a step back.

Only when his brain came back online did he notice the complete silence and utter stillness around them. He swept his gaze around the room, seeing several stunned expressions and a couple he couldn't decipher. His brow furrowed at Paulo's and Lenny's odd expressions. Before he had time to think about that, a resounding cheer distracted him, making him grin.

"Shush, you lot. Or we'll have the boss reaming our arses for being too noisy again," Carl shouted good-naturedly over the kitchen din. The noise would surely bring Seb from the dining room to see what the commotion was about.

The chorus of "yes chef" had him glance at Adam. He stilled, his throat clogging as he'd gone to swallow. His hands gripped Adam's in a deathly tight hold. "No. Don't you dare. Please, no tears," Carl begged.

The watery gleam shining in Adam's eyes increased. Panicked, Carl yanked his boy behind him, heading straight for the locker room, shouting at Billy, "Gimme five." Carl shoved the door open and pulled Adam behind him. The door slammed shut on several interested stares.

Carl dragged Adam to the bench and sat, pulling him into his lap. Adam's wet cheeks glistened in the overhead lights and made Carl feel like shit. "Oh, you have to stop that. No tears. You're killing me. Why the hell are you crying?" More than a little disgusted by how whiny he sounded, Carl heaved a defeated sigh.

"You kissed me in front of everyone," Adam said like it made complete sense.

At a loss to understand how a kiss could result in tears, Carl's ire rose. "Is this some sort of revenge for last night?" he said accusingly.

Adam's wet chuckle and headshake only increased his confusion.

"Well then, why the bloody tears?" he asked, mystified.

"Because, you silly fool, you laid claim to me so beautifully without caring what anyone thought. You didn't care that anyone could see. See that I love you. See that you-"

With a snarl, Carl slammed his mouth over Adam's, not letting him finish. Adam straddled him, and Carl circled his arms around his boy's waist. He groaned as Adam thrust his hips, grinding their cocks together. The heady mix of arousal, his boy's sweet lips, and the declaration of love left him defenceless. He rode the waves of his emotions, wanting nothing more than to express how he was feeling.

His mind swam with possibilities. The image of Adam at Christmas surged into his consciousness, along with it what he wanted to do. Carl eased back, not giving in to the driving need to take charge.

"Noooo. Why do you do that? Kiss me like I'm your most favourite three-course meal and then stop before we get a chance to taste the dessert," Adam whined.

"A three-course meal." Carl snorted, his eyes dancing with humour. Only his Sugar Lips would compare them to a meal. He shook his head, remembering why he'd stopped. He opened his mouth but shut it just as quickly when the door behind them opened, revealing a very pissed-off Seb.

A growl of frustration rumbled out of him as he eyed the unhappy face in the doorway. Seb's appraisal of him and Adam before his face turned stern gave Carl a hint of what was coming.

"You do realise we have a full restaurant and another sitting to get through, don't you?" Seb asked.

While he frantically tried to come up with something to say Carl shrugged.

Then Seb pointed at both of them, his eyes drilling holes in them. "For God's sake, put Adam down and get back to work. If I catch either of you so much as looking at each other with a heated stare, I'll kick your backsides to Timbuctoo. Got it?"

Stood by the door, Seb held it open, his foot tapping.

Carl refused to hunch, even when he felt like a naughty five-year-old caught with his hand in the cookie jar. He lifted Adam and set him down on the ground. The cheeky grin and blush coating his cheeks had Carl reconsider for a second, but then he caught Seb's scowl. He bit his tongue to stop himself from bitching about the lost opportunity. He watched Adam skip out of the room without a backward glance.

Carl got up and followed at a slower pace, his cock still not getting the message that the fun was over.

When Seb laid his hand on his arm, Carl stopped mid-step.

"What the fuck are you playing at, Carl?"

Not quite meeting Seb's gaze while he scrambled to come up with an answer to appease him, Carl's cheeks heated.

"Listen, Carl, I get it. I've had a couple of moments myself where I've forgotten I'm at work. But fuck, Carl, pull it together. We have new staff that require your guidance, and I'm sure that does not include how to seduce your boyfriend at work."

Chastised, Carl offered a nod of understanding. He would have been the first one to call anyone out for being unprofessional. How did he justify what he'd been doing? *Love.*

Emotions riding through him like a bunch of wild horses, he raked his fingers through his hair. His gaze searched Seb's. Would Seb understand the need riding him?

His heart was already several steps in front of his brain. "Do you have a minute to talk about something?" he asked.

Seb huffed out a sigh, but he stepped back into the room and closed the door behind him. "What is it now?" he asked, sounding exasperated.

Carl swallowed the laughter and explained himself to a wordless Seb.

"Okay...are you sure?" asked Seb hesitantly when Carl finished two minutes later. The alarm on Seb's face made Carl take stock.

Is this the right thing to do? *Yes, yes, yes. Ten times yes.*

Carl grinned at Seb. "Absolutely. I'm one hundred per cent sure this is the right thing to do for me. For us," he said with utter conviction. His heart fluttered in his chest, dancing with excitement at the prospect of what was to come. He patted Seb on the shoulder and sauntered past, merrily whistling to himself as he walked back into the kitchen.

"Accidenti," he declared to the kitchen at large. "Damn" was right.

Carl sweated, his back drenched under his chef's top. The hissing and bubbling pots kept him from doing something about it. The sounds that came from the cooker were the only noise in the normally raucous kitchen. The quiet solace was a change of pace, and he found it soothing as he prepared the meal he'd been planning for the last two weeks.

With the craziness of the restaurants, his work schedule, and Adam's busy life, they'd barely managed more than a few hours together. This Sunday hadn't come around fast enough for Carl. His frustration had led him to have a lengthy discussion with Seb the previous week. The lack of cohesive planning around scheduled days off had been the main topic of conversation. Seb had grudgingly agreed to change their schedules, with a promise from Carl that their relationship wouldn't interfere with the business. The agreement had been easy. He just hoped he could keep to it.

His pulse skipped a beat. His hand lowered to the small box tucked in his pocket, and he sucked in a steamy breath. *You got this. He loves you.* "Fucking A, he does." He chuckled to himself at the nerves he could plainly hear in his voice.

He wiped his hands on the kitchen towel, pretending not to notice how they shook. He checked the time for the umpteenth time and lowered the heat under the bubbling pots. Leaving them to simmer, he went to recheck the small dining room.

He walked through the door, his critical eye finding everything as it should be.

The scent of roses drew his gaze to the petals scattered on the table. He had Richie to thank for that tidbit. His boy was a bit of a romantic. So, taking Richie's advice, he'd bought several bunches of pale lemon roses and matched them to the dinner plates and tablecloth. The romantic and dreamy quality of the setup gave his stomach butterflies.

He picked up the crystal flutes, checking they sparkled, before checking the silver cutlery for water stains. Passing his inspection, he went to the cupboard used to store the wine coolers. He took out a plain sliver cooler and placed it in the stand next to the table.

After one final check of the room, he went back to the kitchen to retrieve the champagne. Once he was happy with everything, he hustled to the locker room for a quick shower.

Ten minutes later, he dried himself with shaky hands, admiring the simple black tailored shirt and trousers that hung on a hanger off his locker door handle. Brushing his hair back off his face, Carl took a breath and dressed. He picked up the cologne Adam had bought him for Christmas, and squirted a couple of sprays into his palm. After placing the bottle down, Carl rubbed his palms together before applying the scent to his face. The fragrance, one of Adam's favourites, wafted around him, and he hummed in satisfaction.

His stomach clenched at the sound of his phone buzzing. He picked it up off the bench and read the SOS text. His mouth dried, and his tongue stuck to the roof of his mouth. He clumsily shoved the phone into his trouser pocket and ignored his reflection in the mirror in front of him. The last thing he needed was to see the nerves dancing all over his face.

Don't fuck this up.

Chapter Twenty-Nine

Adam

ADAM GAVE RICHIE A SEARCHING LOOK, HIS EYES WIDENING IN disbelief. "You can't be serious? Why would I want to go into work today and collect a file you left on Seb's desk?" he asked for the third time when Richie was no closer to giving him a straight answer.

His neck prickled, and his belly flopped when he saw the nervous twitch at the corner of Richie's mouth.

"Because I'm your best friend and you love me." Richie fluttered his eyelashes, offering a bashful smile.

"But why can't it wait till tomorrow? Or better yet. You go and collect it. It's not like you don't have a car. The other option is to ask Seb. I'm sure he'd go and get it for you. Where is he anyway? He's usually closer than your shadow," Adam said.

"Ha fucking ha, ha. He's out, grabbing a few things we needed. And if you didn't notice, he took my car. Daddy's is in the garage for a service."

Richie averted his head and sorted through the paperwork on his desk. Adam narrowed his eyes. "You're acting weird. You never work when we have plans. Are you sure you're not in cahoots with Carl? He's been acting strange as well…" Adam paused at the flush riding Richie's face. The twitching at the side of Richie's mouth increased, a sure sign he was hiding something.

An odd sense that he was missing something filled him. Adam fidgeted. The last couple of weeks it seemed everyone was either hiding in corners and whispering or acting all over the top with him. For the life of him, he couldn't figure out what was wrong.

The loving way Carl behaved towards him was wonderful and exciting. *So what's bugging me?*

Carl had been preoccupied and zoned out every now and again. Adam's questioning to see if there was a problem was brushed off. Though it hurt to be shut out, he had tried to be understanding. He had. *How could Daddy forget I was even in the room with him?*

Adam ground his teeth together as he recalled Carl's insistence on honesty since the night at the club. Was it supposed to only work in one person's favour? He gave a disgruntled sigh, his gaze fixed on Richie.

With all his attention back on Richie, Adam tried to figure out why he was insisting they should forgo their afternoon plans. Cocktails, nibbles, and some fun versus driving to work to collect a fucking file, of all things.

I'm definitely missing something vital. What the hell is it?

"Spill," he said. "You aren't telling me something."

Richie sagged, holding up his hands. "Okay I give in." He hesitated. "Carl wanted to cook you a nice romantic lunch at the restaurant."

Adam danced on the spot. He forgot his worries, and a smile broke across his face. "A romantic lunch, oh my God." Adam stilled when he glanced down at his pressed jeans and mint-green polo shirt.

"Oh, fuck. What time is he expecting me? I need to go home and get changed. Why the hell didn't you just say this earlier?" he asked. Not giving Richie a chance to answer, he barrelled on, "I could already be halfway home. Shit, I need to go. I'll see you tomorrow, and you better pray I'm not late and ruin the meal."

Richie roared with laughter.

Adam was already heading for the door, uncaring that Richie was laughing at him. Preoccupied, he didn't see Richie pull out his phone as Adam waved him goodbye.

Out of the house, he ran to his car, his chest heaving with excitement. The fresh spring day buoyed his mood, along with the light traffic. He got back to the flat in record time and was half undressed before he hit the bottom stair. Breathless and giddy by the time he made it out of the shower, he mentally flicked through his choices. Once dried, he ran to his wardrobe, choosing a fitted pair of fawn trousers, a cream shirt, and a deep brown waistcoat with a matching dickie bow, remembering how much Carl liked the one he'd worn at Christmas. The brown loafers he pulled on finished the outfit. He took a minute to admire the ensemble while he styled his hair. A spritz of aftershave and he was heading back out the door, in a record thirty minutes. He would have high-fived himself if he wasn't in such a rush.

Back in the car and heading to the restaurant, his mind whirred. Was this the reason why Carl had been preoccupied? *You should have trusted him.* Kicking himself, Adam tried not to let his insecurities diminish or overshadow the love Carl had lavished on him. The old niggling voice that said he wasn't worthy wanted control.

The recent conversation with Richie pushed past the negative voice. The positive reinforcement about worthiness surged to the forefront. All Adam needed to do was accept his right to love and happiness, like Richie said. Richie assured him that if he accepted it, everything would change.

I'm worthy of love. I am.

At hitting slow-moving traffic he moaned. The busy road had him focus on the traffic rather than his woefully low self-esteem.

He parked up and hopped out of the car, and with trembling fingers, he pressed the car fob to lock the doors. His gaze was drawn to the delicate clouds, floating loftily on the light spring breeze. The familiar scents of petrol fumes and garbage shouldn't have settled his nerves, but they did.

The alley to the back door was empty as Adam rubbed his sweaty palms down his trouser legs. Soundlessly, he opened the back door leading into the kitchen. About to shout, he shut his mouth. What had Richie said? *A surprise. It's a surprise. I need to act surprised.*

The litany died as soon as Adam stepped into the kitchen. The sight of Carl standing not ten feet away dressed all in black dried his mouth. The pale yellow bloom in his big meaty fist stood out boldly, along with the gorgeous smile lighting his handsome face.

Adam's breath hitched. His hands fidgeted at his sides. What should he do?

Carl lifted his hand and held the flower out towards him, answering the silent question. Adam was sure he'd be embarrassed later by how fast he'd snatched the bloom from Carl, but at the moment he couldn't care less. Burying his nose in the flower, he inhaled the sweet-smelling scent.

He lifted bashful eyes to the man waiting silently in front of him. "I love it, Daddy."

"Richie snitched on me, didn't he?" Carl sounded resigned.

Adam's lips twitched and spread into a smile. "Yep. You'll need to pick a better ally next time."

"Cocky. I like that, Sugar Lips." Daddy sniggered. "You're already thinking about next time, and we haven't even started yet. What's to say you even like what I've planned?"

The arched brow and dark promise in Daddy's eyes set Adam's arousal from simmering to boiling point in half a second flat. He clutched at the stem of the rose, willing his pounding heart to slow down so he could catch a breath. He already felt fit to burst, and as Daddy pointed out, they hadn't even made it to the dining room.

"You better lead the way, Daddy, before I combust from excitement over here," he said with an impatient tone. He didn't want to rush, not really. He wanted to glory in the moment, but his cock definitely had other ideas, and it wanted them to get this show on the road. He refused to sigh at the battle between his head, heart, and cock. Uncertain at this point which would win out, he took the hand Carl held out.

As if sensing the war raging inside of him, Carl gave a wicked smile as he took hold of his hand. He sucked in a breath and let Carl guide him into the main dining room, but it quickly became apparent that it wasn't their final destination. His brow rose, but before he could ask, he cottoned on to where they were going, and he stumbled as he gasped. *Oh God.*

The small private dining room door stood open and offered him a glimpse inside. His lungs seized, his eyes blurred, and a sob stuck in his throat.

Oh my God, oh my God, don't cry. Don't fucking dare cry.

The sob didn't listen to reason and escaped before he could stop it. The flower fell unheeded to the floor as he rammed his free hand into his mouth, doing his best to stifle the sobs, clutching Daddy's fingers in a death grip.

"You did all this for me?" Adam mumbled past his fist.

His unwavering gaze never moved from the table sitting in the middle of the room. The petals, the gleaming glasses, the plates covered with silver domes that didn't stop the delicious scents from filling the room, all set his heart racing. Emotions rode him harder than a jockey rode his horse at the Grand National.

He trembled, working to keep himself from flying into a million pieces.

"Well, who else would I have done it for?" The chuckled response had his gaze shifting to Carl.

Love. It shone down on him brighter than the sun on a cloudless summer day, the warmth melting him into a pile of goo. Adam was moving before he'd even released the hand he'd been holding. He jumped at Carl, not in the least bit surprised with the ease at which Carl lifted and held on to him. The show of strength had Adam's groin tightening and showing its appreciation.

He laid kisses all over Carl's face. "Thank you, Daddy, I love you. Did I mention that recently? Because I do," Adam muttered in between kisses.

"Stop or we're never gonna eat," Carl rasped. "I didn't go to all this effort to waste the food."

Adam moaned and reluctantly stopped. He wiggled and slid down, making sure to rub his aching cock over Daddy's. He kept the snigger in, with difficulty, when Daddy gave him a threatening glare.

"Sit… or you'll find yourself with a sore backside while you're eating."

The threat rang true and did little to help Adam's trouser situation. He groaned while readjusting himself.

His pulse skipped a beat when Daddy held out his chair for him, indicating he should sit. How he managed to walk to the table was beyond him. He sat before his legs gave way, a shiver racing down his spine. *What the fuck? Daddy's on his knee.*

Why is Daddy on one knee?

The reality sideswiped Adam. Air got stuck somewhere between his throat and his lungs and made it impossible to think. That is not a ring box?

The tiny black velvet box that sat in the palm of Carl's hand said differently.

Adam blinked, hoping against hope he wasn't imagining what was happening. He found the urge to scream "Daddy is proposing" far too tempting. He sucked his lips into his mouth, just to be on the safe side. He valiantly tried to stop hyperventilating when his vision blurred, but a wetness dripping off his chin alerted him to the tears streaming down his face.

Mortified at his reaction, Adam rushed to scrub at his face. This was not how it was supposed to be. Who'd want to propose to a man with a snotty nose and red-rimmed eyes?

There you go, jumping the gun. It could be anything in that box.

"Pay attention, Sugar Lips."

The husky demand broke Adam's stupor. His blurry eyes locked with the intense black ones of Daddy.

"I knew when we met that there was something about you that

called to me. There were so many reasons why I should have stayed away from you. The work contract, the age gap, my sexual preferences, and not least of all, the fact that you don't have a submissive bone in your body.

"Yet none of that made a damn bit of difference. My heart was defenceless against the growing love you brought it. Your generosity, your humour, your joy for life, your feistiness, and fuck, all the other numerous parts that make you irresistible to a cranky old bugger…"

"You're not an old bugger, though I won't disagree with the cranky," Adam quipped, tongue in cheek.

Carl pushed a finger against his lips.

"See, you have to keep me on my toes," Carl growled, "but for once be quiet and let me finish."

Adam made a motion of zipping his now free lips, grinning foolishly at the humour dancing in Daddy's eyes.

"Fuck, you make my heart sing, boy. I have to pinch myself some days just to make sure it's real." Carl paused. He flipped open the box lid, drawing Adam's gaze.

The ball of tears Adam thought he could control got lodged in his throat and made it impossible to swallow. His hand trembled as he reached towards the stunning ring. The sparkling lights above his head caught the gleaming white band encrusted with tiny colourful stones. Instantly he was reminded of bright sunny skies just after a rainstorm, when the rainbow revealed itself in all its colourful glory.

A shiver raced through him while his hand hovered over the ring. Was this real?

Fuck, I hope so.

"Will you marry me, be my boy?"

Adam launched himself out of the chair at Carl. They landed in a heap of limbs, the thick carpet cushioning their fall, but Adam didn't care. His hand was already reaching for the ring. "Yes. Yes. Oh God, please don't let this be a dream," he begged. His mouth latched on to Carl's, not giving him time to respond.

The kiss seemed endless. The desperate need eased as the kiss deepened and reaffirmed the reality of the moment.

Adam released a grumble of protest when Carl shifted and finally released his swollen mouth.

"Stop that. You've got a lifetime of kisses coming," Carl reprimanded but without heat. "I want to see if the ring fits. And if you didn't notice, I went to a lot of effort to make this moment perfect. We're eating the lovely meal I slaved over, so stop trying to spoil it."

The evil glint in Daddy's eye as he shifted warned of a punishment if Adam wasn't careful. He swallowed his snigger, knowing fine well that it wouldn't do him any favours, considering how Daddy was now eyeing him.

Then he couldn't help himself. "Dominated but not subdued, Daddy. Remember?" he said with utter confidence.

His laughter peeled out as he landed on his back on the carpet with Daddy looming over him. "Is that so? Then let's see what Daddy can do about the dominating part."

The threat and the weight of Daddy's groin pressing down had him beg, "Bring it on, Daddy."

Epilogue

SEEING WHERE THIS WAS GOING, CARL BANGED LOUDLY ON THE TABLE when Seb's cough was ignored. Slowly the sound of voices died down. The forty staff employed in the three restaurants settled in their seats and all faced towards him and Seb.

Sitting in their favourite booth, Carl eyed the room full of men. The mixture of resignation and boredom was nothing new. Overseeing the three restaurants took time, patience, and a lot of hard work to make them run like a well-oiled machine. This was just part of that process. The bi-monthly meeting for staff was mandatory and established before he started working for Seb. Though it made good sense to get the team together to discuss issues, poor reviews, and anything else that was happening, he understood it was still a pain in the arse if you had to come in on your day off.

He rested back against the booth resignedly and waited for Seb to start.

The first item on the agenda was bound to cause a bit of hilarity after he'd announced his engagement to Adam last week, to all the staff.

"Thank you everyone, for attending," Seb started.

Carl muttered under his breath, "as if we have a choice." He shut up when Seb pinned him with a cynical glare.

"As I was saying," his eyes making a point, before looking back at the full dining room and continuing, "thank you for coming. We have several things to discuss today. The first being your contracts—"

The murmur of voices made Carl bang the table again. "Pipe down and just listen," he shouted over the noise.

"Thank you, Carl."

He grinned, nodding at Seb. "You're welcome. Crack on."

He could all but hear Seb's teeth grind together as he trust his jaw towards the room.

"Listen"—Seb held up his hand—"it's nothing drastic, but after Carl announced his engagement, as well as my own personal circumstances." Seb coughed, pausing briefly.

Choking on his laughter, Carl cleared his throat. He gave Seb an A for effort when he carried on valiantly.

"I felt it was ridiculous to have the clause about members of staff dating each other."

Sudden movement caught Carl's attention. Matt's head firing up from the table cloth he'd been staring intently at piqued Carl's curiosity, though he was taken aback by Matt's expression. The glare he gave Seb got Carl narrowing his eyes. What's his problem?

His gaze swept the room as he scratched his head. Was it too much of a coincidence to find one lowered head in the sea of people staring at Seb?

Contemplating the crown of Theo's head, he glanced back at Matt, who was staring at the table in front of him once again, his fingers playing with a fork.

Carl paid no attention to Seb as he continued to discuss the changes. The more he watched the two men, the more he got the sense there was something going on.

The weight of Adam's hand on his leg disturbed his thoughts, and he raised a brow in silent question. Adam's head tilt and subsequent jab to his ribs had him looking at Seb.

Heat flooded his face, comprehension coming a little too late. "Can you repeat that? I was lost in thought," he muttered.

"I said was there anything you wanted to add about the contract, or have we covered everything."

Not sure what he'd discussed, Carl shrugged. "As long as the guys realise I'm not gonna tolerate any kitchen dramas because of who they're fucking, then I don't give two flying shits who's boffing who."

The gasps and laughter flooding the room drowned out Seb's spluttering and Adam's raucous laughter.

"What?" Carl asked innocently, not fooling anyone.

Seb shook his head at him but carried on with the agenda after everyone settled down. Carl made an effort to listen, only adding his comments as and when he needed too.

Three hours later, he'd gone from leaning towards a possibility that there was something going on between Matt and Theo to being one hundred per cent positive that there was. He dragged Adam to one side. "Is there something I'm missing between Matt and Theo?"

Adam glanced at the two men in question.

"I've no clue. Matt is a bit of a flirt when we go out. He flirts with anything in a pair of tight trousers. Though I'm not sure I've seen him flirt with Theo, now you mention it."

"He better fucking not be flirting with you," Carl said in a harsh whisper not meant for anyone else's ears.

"Now what was that you said about no dramas? That applies to you, Da... lover," Adam reminded him, patting his arm.

"Good save there." Carl lowered his mouth to within an inch of his boy. "But if you want to call me Daddy, I don't give a fuck who it offends. You're my boy and my Sugar Lips. That ring on your finger isn't just for show. It means something to me. A symbol of *all* we have, and if people don't like it, then fucking tough."

The hitch and glittering eyes had Carl lower his mouth the last inch and lay his claim.

He pulled back breathless, the sound of cheers and catcalls of "get a room" prompting him to lift his hand and throw a V at the staff milling around. Carl winked at his crimson-cheeked Sugar Lips before swinging around to go back to the kitchen. He halted mid-stride, seeing Paulo trying to evade him.

His brow furrowed. What is his problem?

One syllable, monotone answers were all he'd been getting for the past week, and it was starting to grate on his last nerve. He didn't want to admit he's missed Paulo's constant questions. And okay, Paulo was often a nervous wreck and a little all over the place, but that was a damn sight better than what he'd been getting for the last week.

Carl stepped into Paulo's path, not letting him escape. "Paulo, you okay? Anything troubling you, you wanna talk about?" he asked, trying to recall what he knew about Paulo's life. He barely resisted the urge to curse aloud at coming up empty-handed. Nathan's eidetic memory would have come in handy right about now.

The sigh slipped past his lips without permission when the information about his cooking experience sprang to mind. Why hadn't Seb asked about Paulo's family? Did Paulo have friends in London?

The unanswered questions left a sour taste in Carl's mouth. He offered an encouraging smile to the silent man, who stood looking like he'd rather than be anywhere but near Carl. His thoughts were confirmed when Paulo turned his back on him, saying nothing and shuffling off.

"All right then, I'll take that as a no," Carl muttered under his breath.

More than a little pleased that it was Paulo's day off and he'd not have to tolerate his sulky behaviour, Carl stomped into the kitchen to prepare for the evening dinner service.

On hearing a clatter, he looked around distractedly. The sight of Lenny grappling with two large pots got him moving across the kitchen. "Fuck, Lenny. Are you trying to break your back?"

"I'm stronger than I look," Lenny panted, a cheeky grin plastered on his glowing face.

"Yeah. Yeah. Give me one of those." Not waiting for an answer, Carl snatched the top pot off Lenny. "That might be the case, but you ever heard about the lazy man's load."

"Argh, chef, you ain't callin' me lazy, are you?"

Carl observed the other man's stained red cheeks and sparkling eyes and plonked the pot back on top of the one Lenny still held. "Nope. I was just trying to be helpful. But sod ya." Carl hid a smile as Lenny struggling to hold on to the heavy pans.

"Sorry, chef," Lenny said breathlessly as he staggered off to the dishwashing room.

Carl kept his chuckle in check until he disappeared through the open doorway. He glanced at Billy as he came out of the locker room, wrapping his apron around his chef whites. He'd already pulled his jet black hair into a ponytail.

"It always surprises me how fucking strong he is," Billy murmured as he passed Carl.

Straining to hear, Carl eyed his second in command. Billy had followed him from the previous restaurant they'd both worked in. There was no question Carl wanted to carry on working with the quiet, unassuming man. In all the years they'd worked together, Carl had not once heard him raise his voice. His temperament was perfect for the kitchen, and his cooking skills were phenomenal. But so were his observational skills.

Carl's thoughts went back to Paulo. "Do you know anything about Paulo and his personal circumstances?"

"What? Why? Is there something wrong?" Billy asked distractedly, his gaze not moving from the food prep he'd started.

"Not sure. He's been a bit off with me this last week, and I have no clue why."

Billy's reply was lost under the racket coming from the locker room. Carl ran to the closed door, his heart leaping at what he would find. "Who was in the locker room with you?" Carl shouted over the ruckus.

Remembering he was talking to the world's quietest man, Carl didn't wait for a reply and burst through the door.

I fucking knew it!

The thought, along with his brain, froze at the sight of Theo attempting to kick Matt in the balls, who had him suspended in midair.

Carl's ire rose on a wave of dread that he'd somehow misjudged Matt. The temper colouring his face and sparking in his eyes would have worked better than any paint stripper. The heat was ferocious and got Carl stepping forward when Theo was dropped to the ground with a thud. His feet clattered against the tiled floor as Matt drew back and tucked his fisted hands into his pocket.

"What the hell is going on here? And what did I just say about having to deal with other people's shit, no more than three hours ago, hey?" Carl said.

Matt said nothing, his face a stoic mask.

Theo growled at them both, stomping towards Carl. "Ask the arsehole over there. All I did was talk about our ability to date other work colleagues, and he lost the fucking plot," Theo fumed. His face was a similar colour as Matt's as he sailed out of the room.

Carl watched Theo leave before eyeing Matt. The utter dejectedness clued Carl in to precisely what the problem was with Theo talking about dating someone else. "You need to tell him how you feel—"

Matt held up his hand, silencing him. "Don't fucking start with me. If it wasn't for your fucking contract clause, I wouldn't be in this mess. I have a boyfriend, for fucksake."

Sympathy washed over Carl on hearing the edge of desperation underpinning the accusation. Carl understood how restrictive the contract had been. Maybe not so much for him, but definitely for Seb, who'd spent a long time using it as a barrier, as had Adam.

He sighed. "Listen, if you want Theo, and judging by the anger you were directing at him, I'd say that was a given, you might want to reconsider if your boyfriend has the same appeal as Theo. If he doesn't, then do both of yourselves a favour and end it. It's not fair on either of you."

The contemplative expression Matt wore had Carl slap him on the back. "Life is too fucking short for regrets, man."

A small nod was the only acknowledgement Carl got. Not sure what else he could say, Carl left Matt alone to his own thoughts. A sudden urge to go find Adam had Carl walk straight through the kitchen and out into the dining room. Billy said nothing as he passed, but Carl didn't miss the look of speculation on his face.

Noisy clatter had Carl glance up as he walked into the dining room. Scott and Sawyer were busy clearing the tables of all the glasses and plates staff had used. He gave them a brief nod and walked to where he knew he'd find Adam.

The carpet muffled the sound of his steps, so when he walked around the partition wall into the reception area, Adam didn't look up.

Warmth rushed up his chest, and a giant smile lit his face.

Adam was sitting at the front desk, huddled over his computer, squinting at the screen. The pinstriped jacket that matched his trousers hung on the back of his chair. His blond highlights gleamed against the sun pouring in through the windows.

The urge to touch snaked its way through him, wrapping around his control. Carl shifted.

As if sensing him, Adam lifted his gaze from the screen. His furrowed brow smoothed out, and love filled his sea-green eyes until they sparkled like emeralds. The breath seized in Carl's lungs. His heart swelled with the love that, if he was honest, had planted itself inside him the moment Adam had challenged him during the interview. How fucked would he be if Adam ever came to the same realisation?

He took the last couple of steps to his boy, reaching for him. He wrapped his arms around Adam and tugged him off the seat. Without words, Adam snuggled into his arms, laying his head against his heart.

Who'd been dominated, and who'd been subdued? It didn't matter, because what they had together worked for them.

And wasn't that just fucking perfect.

The End

Other Books by the Author

Puzzle Pieces: La Trattoria Di Amore Series (Book One)

Why was he so drawn to a man when he dated women? A man who kept his true self hidden. A man who wanted to be his Daddy.

Richie Bellinger learnt just how cruel life could be: a family in crisis; he is left alone to deal with the unthinkable. His life in complete turmoil; he is drowning.

Until Sebastian became the one thing he needed.

Sebastian's need to be a *Daddy* shows Richie he can choose a different life that makes him complete in ways he'd never imagined.

Sebastian's ability to push past Richie's defences has him opening to something he's never considered, loving a man.

Sebastian showing his flaws gives Richie the power to embrace a new life.

But Richie understands life can come and bite you on the ass when you least expect it. A cheating girlfriend, a death, a discovery, a best friend, and a need to be out for Sebastian all work against Richie. Can he work past all the barriers to find happiness in the most unlikely place?

Puzzle Pieces is the first book in the La Trattoria Di Amore series and can be read as a standalone.

It is an MM romance with Daddy Kink, out for you, light BDSM play, an age gap, and a Daddy who needs to understand it's alright to let go of the past. This book has a HEA.

Where it all Began: Manx Cat Guardians Origins (Book 1)

Why did he crave something that would condemn him to a life of purgatory? A man who was born to be king. How could a lowly servant be the one thing he wanted more than his crown?

King Óláfr the Black was a Norseman and was no stranger to suffering: pain was nothing he'd not experienced time and time again at the hands of those who pertained to love him. It hardened his heart to what could be.

Until fate stepped in, in the form of a Guardian Cat, Maximillian.

Maximillian's need to connect the two soulmates gave Óláfr his first and only taste of love.

Maximillian's ability to go against the laws of his kind gave Óláfr an unthinkable decision.

Maximillian shows Óláfr that fate will not be messed with, not without consequences.

But Óláfr knows he's being watched, his people thirsting for blood. A priest, a fire, a blood eagle, and a promise of redemption. Can two souls searching for love find each other again?

Where it all Began (Manx Cat Guardian Origins) the prequel to Manx Cat Guardian Series, these books are not standalones, and this book links directly to Searching for a Soul to Love. They should be read in order to gain the background.

It is an MM historical romance, with soulmate connections, slow burn, angst, and an ancient paranormal cat that likes to interfere. This book has a cliffhanger with no HEA until book 4.

Trigger Warning: There are some scenes of violence.

Seeing Beyond the Scars: Manx Cat Guardians (Book 2)

Why did his new neighbour make him want to change and leave his protective shell? A man not frightened to show the world who he was. Would Martin stay or run when faced with Brad's past and his scars?

Brad Cummings lived a quiet controlled life: the world he created was not through choice but from necessity. A traumatic past left him unable to see past his scars.

Until fate steps in with Martin.

Martin's need to show him how beautiful he is both inside and out leads Brad to finally understand the true meaning of love.

Martin's ability to have fun allows Brad to stop existing and start to live for the first time in his life.

Martin shows him that not all families are the same: a family can be more than a blood connection.

But Brad has learnt the hard way, being himself is not always a good thing. A mischievous cat, a prying neighbour, a sexual awakening, and a father intent on harm, turn Brad's ordered life upside down. Can he trust an instant connection and believe in soulmates?

Seeing Beyond the Scars is the second book in the Manx Cat Guardian Series, these books are not standalones and need to be read in order to gain the background.

It is an MM romance, with hurt comfort, steamy instant connection, light aspects of BDSM play, and an ancient paranormal cat that like to interfere. This book has a HEA.

Trigger Warning: There are aspects of child abuse and some scenes of violence.

Destiny Collides Past and Present: Manx Cat Guardians (Book 3)

Why did his new housemate make him want to break the promise he made to himself? A man who has learnt to face his own demons. Could Stuart help Joe face his and survive to meet their destiny?

Joe King travels to the Isle of Man to stay with his best friend: in need of a place to mentally and physically recharge. A wrong choice blinds Joe to the possibilities of destiny.

Until fate steps in with Stuart.

Stuart's need to care for him shows Joe that the right person can heal all wounds.

Stuart's ability to fight for what he wants gives Joe the courage to take a leap of faith and trust again.

Stuart shows Joe that he will go to any lengths to protect their love.

But Joe has learnt over many months of running there are some things you can't escape. A mischievous cat, a protective best friend, a shooting, a kidnapping and an ex-boyfriend who won't let go, turn Joe's world into chaos. Can he trust in those around him to bring his destiny back to him?

Destiny Collides, Past and Present is the third book in the Manx Cat Guardian Series, these books are not standalones and need to be read in order to gain the background. It is an MM romance, with hurt comfort, soulmate connection, steamy scenes, and ancient paranormal cats that like to interfere. This book has a HEA.

Trigger Warning: There are some scenes of violence.

Searching for a Soul to Love: Manx Cat Guardians (Book 4)

Why did one touch from a man he didn't know leave him reeling with a sense of knowing? A man—or was he a warrior?—who carries a heavy responsibility. Could Aaden share the burden with Greg so they could finally right a wrong?

Greg Kelly was stuck in a rut: in a relationship with a man who treated him like a booty call. A realisation with profound consequences left him floundering.

Until fate steps in with Aaden.

Aaden's need to right the wrongs of the past release him to find a new beginning he never knew he wanted.

Aaden's ability to see past the peculiar is what his soul has been searching for.

Aaden shows him that truth and honour are what make him a man to keep for eternity.

But Greg learns that even when things are meant to be, fate can interfere. A boyfriend, a kidnapping, a hidden soul and a sexual connection casts Greg into a world of make believe. Can he trust in what Aaden feels for him and allow two lost souls to reunite?

Searching for a Soul to Love is the fourth book in the Manx Cat Guardian Series, these books are not standalones, and this book links directly to Where it all Began. They should be read in order to gain the background. *It is an MM romance, with soulmate connections, slow burn, steamy scenes, and ancient paranormal cats that like to interfere. This book has a HEA.*

Trigger Warning: There are some scenes of violence.

The 12 Disasters of Christmas: Manx Cat Guardians (Book 5)

How did Brad find himself planning a Christmas Eve party? A party, he didn't want in his home. Can his budding relationship with Martin survive?

Brad has never had a memorable Christmas: the family he was born to made sure of that. With his first Christmas with Martin looming, Brad's plans are blown out of the water.

Until Joe, Greg and Nick step in.

Nick's need to offer friendship without the boundaries of his past opens Brad's eyes to all kinds of possibilities.

Greg's ability to love unconditionally allows Brad to experience what life is like with true friends.

Joe shows Brad that sometimes a little kink can be the spice of life.

But Brad has never taken again for granted. A witch, a car accident, a disappearing cat, a secret, a lie, an artful dodger, all work against Brad, Joe, Greg and Nick. Can they work as a team and give Brad the Christmas he dreamed of?

The 12 Disasters of Christmas is the fifth book in the Manx Cat Guardian Series, these books are not standalones, and need to be read in order to gain the background. It is an MM romance, with soulmate connections, voyeurism, hot steamy scenes, and ancient paranormal cats and a very naughty witch that likes to interfere. This book has an underlying secondary story that is left on a cliff hanger.

Laws of Attraction: Manx Cat Guardians (Book 6)

Why did he have to want the one man he couldn't have? A man that was honourable to the core. Was it possible to turn years of a love hate relationship into just love?

Nick Riley learnt from a young age there was more than the eye could see and the heart could grieve: the reality of this is suddenly thrust upon him. A visit to his brother leaves him struggling to face what he thought was in the past.

Until fate steps in with Brody.

Brody's need to make amends for something he didn't do frees Nick to claim what was rightfully his.

Brody's ability to listen without judgement breaks through Nick's protective shell to reveal his tender heart for the first time.

Brody shows him that lace and silk can be the way to a man's heart.

But Nick had learnt that all may not be as it seems. A spell, a lie, a witch, a king, a boyfriend, and a misconception all work against Nick. Can he find his way through the labyrinth to the truth?

Laws of Attraction is the sixth book in the Manx Cat Guardian Series, these books are not standalones, and need be read in order to gain the background. It is an MM romance, with a love hate relationship, soulmate connection, slow burn, steamy scenes, along with a man who loves silks and satins. There are ancient paranormal cats and a very naughty witch that likes to interfere. This book has an underlying secondary story that is left on a cliff hanger.

This book has a HEA.

About the Author

Hi all,

My name is Jayne and I live in the Isle of Man. A tiny place in the Irish sea. It's an island steeped in folklore and history and just begs to have stories written about it, and one of my true inspirations.

I also have another career as a nurse manager of a hospital, out of hours. I've been happily married for over 25 years to a wonderfully complicated man, and I have a wonderful daughter with two very young grandbabies. I am also an identical twin, so if you see me, check, as it may not be me.

I have written contemporary and historical gay romance with a paranormal twist, and now daddy kink with BDSM and some spanking. My head is so full of ideas; I never know where it will take me next. But saying that, there will be a book seven in the Manx Cat Guardian series which will also be a daddy kink book (eye roll) even when I'd decided there wasn't going to be any more in that series. There will be a more books in this series. I have plans to start another series called The Playroom which is a spin off from Carl's connection to the BDSM club.

I hope you have enjoyed this book, and if you are in need of more, then you can find all my other books, on Amazon and in KU.

If you're interested in keeping up to date with what I'm planning then why don't you follow and join me on the following links.

You can find me and follow me on:

You can find me on:

Facebook—JP Sayle author page, Jayne Paton or JP Sayle

Facebook Group—JP Manx Minxs

Twitter—JPSayle69

Tumblr—jaysayle

Instagram—jaynepaton

Amazon—JP Sayle

Goodreads

Bookbub

jpsayle.com

If you would like to give me any feedback or just have any questions, go ahead and friend me on Facebook, and I would be happy to answer anything. Well, almost anything. I hope you enjoyed this second Daddy Kink book. If you would also like to leave a review, then I would love to read your thoughts.

Thank you for taking the time to be part of my dream.

46685019R00162

Printed in Poland
by Amazon Fulfillment
Poland Sp. z o.o., Wrocław